DUCHED

Duched (The Duched Series #1)
By Xavier Neal

©Xavier Neal 2016

Cover by Dana Leah

All Rights Reserved

License Note

No part of this book may be reproduced, scanned, or distributed in any printed or electronic form without authorization from the author. Any distribution without express consent is illegal and punishable in a court of law.

This book is a work of fiction. Names, characters, places, and incidents are either the product of the author's imagination or are used fictitiously, and any resemblance to actual persons, living or dead, events, or locales is entirely coincidental.

Subscribe to my newsletter!

https://bit.ly/NLSignUpFreebie

Table of Contents

Dedication

Warning

Playlist Selects

Chapter 1

Chapter 2

Chapter 3

Chapter 4

Chapter 5

Chapter 6

Chapter 7

Chapter 8

Chapter 9

Chapter 10

Chapter 11

Chapter 12

Chapter 13

Chapter 14

Chapter 15

Chapter 16

Chapter 17

Chapter 18

Chapter 19

Chapter 20

Chapter 21

Other Works

Thank You

Dedication:
To The Universe...Thanks for letting me feel like royalty in my own way.

WARNING:

This novel contains graphic language, sexual content, and adult situations. Some readers may find content triggering or disagree with it entirely.

This novel also breaks the 4th wall and "talks" directly to you as a reader. These are "private" conversations they are having with you "individually". (Think looking directly into the camera, talking to the audience style.) They are in bold print and italicized to indicate the breakage. This particular style can take some adjusting to, so please proceed at your own risk.

Thank you.

Playlist Selects

Here are five songs from "Duched Series" playlist!

Feel free to follow the playlist on Spotify to find more songs I felt related to the book.

1. Suit & Tie (Ft. Jay-Z) – (R&B)

2. Let Love In – The Goo Goo Dolls (Alternative Rock)

3. First Love Song – Luke Bryan (Country)

4. Drip – Marc E. Bassy (R&B)

5. The One – Backstreet Boys (Pop)

More songs: https://bit.ly/DuchedSeriesPlaylist

CHAPTER ONE

Kellan

"It was just a game of strip poker. It is not as if I *married* a stripper."

That I could understand my older brother flipping out about.

"You couldn't have just closed the curtains?" He huffs. "The damn curtains, Kellan!"

"I *could have*, but then how would they have taken such a fantastic shot of the lucky ace tattoo on my ass?"

You want to see it, don't you? You want to be flashed or see me completely naked? Naked. Always choose naked.

His wife giggles from behind the magazine she's pretending to read.

"Really, Soph?" His annoyed expression falls to her. "You do realize laughing does *not* help this situation."

"What situation?" Sophia snips on another snicker, dropping the object back into her lap. "Kellan was simply...*being* Kellan."

"You're defending him?"

"No," she says slowly and looks up to lock eyes with him. "I'm just saying he has a point. It's not as if he *married* a stripper or did something *worse* like burn down a church in the middle of Sunday service."

I extend my legs across the red cushioning of the love seat. "Are you saying if I burn down a church *not* on a Sunday *that's* acceptable?"

Sophia rolls her eyes.

Did you not feel as if that was valid information to know? Oh, relax. I would never burn down a church. I prefer my media attention to center around my clothing or lack thereof.

"Your brother was simply having a little fun."

"Something I swear *you* used to be," I tease.

They say blondes have more fun. Truth is…we really do. Between my hair, my bright blue eyes, and my toned muscles from a timeless love affair with lacrosse, let's just say the fun never stops coming my direction with open legs. Or mouths. Rarely hands. I prefer the other options first anyway.

"Right, Soph? He used to be fun, didn't he? He wasn't always…scowling?"

She giggles again, and my older brother oscillates his glare between us.

For the most part – looks-wise – we're practically identical, except for the fact that expression on his face has been more prevalent lately. I blame the pressures of being the *royal couple. Our entire country, Doctenn, – along with several others – is waiting and watching for their next move. Speculating. Scrutinizing. Spreading lies about Soph having surgery to tighten her tummy to keep my brother happy. People gossip about his wife's choice in winter wear and exercise routines. His decision for them to attend or not attend someone's 'grand' birthday party. When, oh when, will they* finally *bear another heir to the throne that isn't anything more than just a title in a long list of other titles? A throne built on mutually assured prosperity that's discussed over brandy regardless of what time of the day it may be. I assume if I cared more about what they thought or gave a damn about what is expected of me, I might frown a little more than I do, which is practically never. Kristopher used to smile quite often too before his love life was all the media wanted to talk about between my father's impeccable ability to soothe strained relationships from our family's past, and my inability to keep the royal jewels in my pants from being shined. Or at least he used to smile…more. According to him, I came out of the womb smiling and have yet to truly stop except for our mother's untimely death.*

"Kristopher *is* fun. He's just wearing his responsible, big brother face," she brushes away as she turns the page in her magazine.

"Responsible, big brother face or king in training face? Because I swear that's the same face father makes minutes before he begins his loving yelling, or 'shouting' as the rest of the world calls it."

"Has it ever occurred to you he has merit to his shouting?" he defensively counters.

I shake my head with a smirk. "None of my behaviors are *new*."

"*Precisely*." His hands wrap around the back of the red couch in our palace library where his wife is sitting. "You may dread the title of Duke and the social responsibilities we carry as Princes, but you have to grow up sometime, Kellan. For Christ's sake, you're almost thirty! It's time you start behaving as such."

Dread the titles. Dread the social politics. Dread the long list of should dos and never dos. The only thing I don't dread is the royal jets I use as my private taxi service to fly around the world on every whim I have. Beats the hell out of drowning in an ocean of archaic expectations.

There's a small pause that's followed by Sophia humming, "Perhaps you're right, Kellan. It *is* his king in training face."

I immediately chortle. "*Thank you.*"

Our joined laughter unsurprisingly gets drowned out by another grunt of annoyance from Kristopher. "Do not agree with him right now, Sophia."

"Why?" She glances up. "Because you said so? Because as a lady of the court I should hold my tongue?"

Her mocking causes me to smile wide.

I'll admit. It's a guilty pleasure to watch her push back at my brother. It's the reason he married her. She refused to bend to his every whim and carry his opinions as her own. Just makes me laugh in moments like this he seems to forget that.

"Need I remind you we're not in the 1500s anymore and that you can't behead me for having a different opinion than yours?"

Playfully, I add, "If you beheaded her, who would suck your cock?"

Her sarcastic look falls to me, yet she retorts, "Because that was a problem for the beloved Prince Kristopher before me? If I recall correctly, his reputation for being an insufferable ass hound was *worse* than yours."

"I'm in the room." Kristopher joins the conversation on a pout. "And I may have enjoyed my fair share of the opposite sex-"

"In the courtyard," Soph begins to list, "in the pool, on top of your father's-"

"*But*," he clears his throat, "I knew I had to grow up, eventually. Change. Become a more respectable adult and proper pillar for this country."

"By marrying the woman with the Jessica Rabbit tattoo on her lower back?"

Sophia and I laugh while my brother's hands go flying in the air.

Hey, it's a pretty sexy tattoo. She's lying on her side in that red dress in a very provocative pose. That little beauty is the reason why she's not allowed to wear bikinis in bodies of water outside their separate home on the property. I know Soph **looks** *like a polite, refined, and down-right proper lady, with her elegant asymmetrical dark brown hair cut and natural make up, but if that were the case my brother would've never married her. He gives me hell for being the wild one yet fails to remember once upon a time he could almost give me a run for my money. Almost.*

"All I'm saying, Kellan, is maybe it's time to dial back the behavior? Remember that you represent a royal bloodline, hell, an entire *country* at times? Maybe…be less selfish in the choices you make?"

"Are these suggestions or instructions?"

"*Kellan.*"

As usual, his chastising begins to bore me, and I toss my head back to stare at the ceiling. "*Fine.* I will remember to close the goddamn curtains if it prevents you from giving me another lecture on the repercussions of such an innocent behavior."

"Innocent?!" His shriek makes me laugh again.

Oh, it's alright that you did it, too. He sounds as if he's sucked back too much helium when it gets that high.

"Kellan, when do you leave for the states?" Sophia's change of topic pulls my attention back down.

"Why? Tired of me making your husband's blood pressure rise?"

She gives me a slight shrug. "If it's not you doing it, it's me."

"You? I'm assuming this is bedroom related?"

Her jaw drops when he cuts her off immediately. "Do not answer that."

He plays a prude, but one of these days reminds me to tell you about the phone calls our parents received during our time at boarding school for the inappropriate study system we developed. It involved upper-class females and maple syrup.

"When *do* you leave?" my brother sighs, running his fingers through his freshly cut hair.

"In the morning," I announce at the same time I pull my vibrating cell phone out of my navy-blue pants pocket.

"And you're going just for a week this time?" Soph questions.

"Roughly. The charity run is on Saturday. I'll return here Sunday."

Kristopher finally takes a seat beside his wife. "And what are you running for this time? The fight against childhood diabetes? The fight against childhood illiteracy? The fight against childhood petlessness."

That last one is not a thing.

"The Collin Murphy Foundation. They are a research foundation that helps fight childhood cancer. Their main base is here in Fayeweather, but they partner with a slightly smaller sister branch in the states."

He slowly recalls, "Oh…This is the one you do every year."

"Indeed." I hum my answer as I open the text message from an unknown number. To my pleasant surprise, it's a fair-skinned female with her long, blonde hair pulled to one side of her face and lips painted bright red to match the pushup bra she's sporting.

The caption underneath reads:

Wanna make me a princess?

Ah. This is one of the strip poker losers. Then again, are there ever really *any losers in that game? Who doesn't love to see people naked?*

The grin on my face causes my brother to grunt, "Please, tell me that's not a dirty photo." When I glance up and expand my smile, he rolls his eyes. "Fine. Please, tell me you can at least *remember* the name of the woman in the photo."

Marilyn? Mindy? Melody? Melissa? I'm getting a rather strong M feeling. Doesn't really matter, though. I'm not gonna call her. Not just *because she's trolling to wear a crown-like so many of the women I meet, but because it was just a wild weekend at the Walngnaski Ski Resort. Think Vegas in the snow. What happens in Walngnaski stays there…except for whatever the paparazzi parasites manage to document. I.E. my ass through the glass window. In my defense, that was the craziest thing I did all weekend unless you consider challenging some American senator's son to a drinking contest crazy.*

Kristopher sighs and shakes his head. "And you wonder why I worry…"

I don't wonder. Nor do I actually care. *As far as I'm concerned, I'm just having a little fun. And there's nothing wrong with having a little or in my case an awful lot of fun. What else am I supposed to do to pass the time in my seemingly superficial reality? Play cards with my dead grandmother's bridge club and pretend it's making a difference? No. Unlike my brother, who has buckled under the pressures of being a Kenningston, I refuse to let my last name rule my entire life. Not now. Not ever.*

CHAPTER TWO

Brie

I hate the youth of America. I really do.

"And then Becky told Kimmy who told Julie who told Michael, that I was the one who said his girlfriend looked like a troll in that selfie. And I did. But she shouldn't have told her! Becky swore she wouldn't!" The thin fourteen-year-old squeaks to the girl beside her as they move forward in the check-out line. "Becky is lucky I don't post Snapchat about what she did with Julie's boyfriend while she was away with her family snowboarding."

"ID," I interrupt, which causes her to glare at me.

Oh, yes. Because I'm *slowing down* her *day*.

She rolls her eyes and reaches into her designer bag. Unable to immediately grab it, she drops her purse, and it accidentally lands on the edge of her tray. Like the world's worst catapult, it launches a horrific combination of ingredients straight at my face. Caesar salad dressing and raspberry applesauce trickle down my glasses while I wipe away spinach leaves from my cheeks.

I fucking hate my job.

The laughter of the teens in line erupts at the same time strips of lemon herb chicken comically drop from my hairnet.

Yes. As a fucking lunch lady, I actually have to wear a hairnet. Health department requirements. Don't think this is what they originally had in mind for the reason it needed to be a necessity.

"Um, *hello*," the bratty brunette whines.

I open my eyes to see her displeased expression.

She's upset? Did I just shower her with food in a room full of adolescents who can't wait to post about this on Instagram or Snapchat or Look At Me As I Go? Not exactly how I want my face across the internet…Not that I ever really want my face across the internet.

"I need a napkin," she huffs. "It's on *my shoe*."

My eyes glance over the shoes that probably cost half – if not my entire – paycheck. Before I'm even given a chance to possibly lose my outwardly calm disposition, one of the older cafeteria women, Bernice, places a hand on my shoulder. "Go get cleaned up, Brie. I'll handle it from here."

With a smile of gratitude, I whisper, "Thank you."

She hums, steps in my place, and says in a sassy voice, "You can get your own napkin on your way to get a new plate of food. Next!"

I wade through lingering groups of teens where the giggles seem to be growing, straight for the employee's restroom in the back.

You're probably wondering what exactly had to go wrong in my life to make me decide to take a job as a cafeteria worker at a private school, right? Well, that makes two of us. But you want the truth? It's the pay and flexibility. My main priorities at this point in life are finally graduating and being able to pay for it. Ollander Academy here in Highland has given me wiggle room to do just that. You see, it's not just a simple private school. No. From what I understand, you have to be on the waiting list for this place by the time you're fresh out of diapers. The tuition alone is high enough to rival what I've been scraping together to pay in my college education, and the interview process for both parents as well as students is on par with the hoops you go through trying to work for Google. While you've seen the obvious downside to such an elitist school, the upside is they pay their employees more than you'd expect, and I don't just mean the teachers. Most of us not in the classroom make what the average teacher does in the public school system. They basically hired me to be a fill-in. An extra pair of hands to help cover vacation days, sick days, and any other cafeteria grunt work they could conjure up around my class schedule. For the record? Oven cleaning? 'Bout as much fun as a routine vaginal exam. Haven't had one of those since I got an IUD put in three years ago. What? Too personal?

After using a damp paper towel to wipe myself down and glass cleaner for my glasses, I head towards the front, thankful this is the final round of lunch being served. As soon as she spots me, Bernice motions her hand for me to help in the back instead. Relief instantly washes over me.

Would you really wanna be the subject that breaks up their afternoon gossiping about who is cheating with who? I didn't think so. And yes, they're always that vicious. I've been here since August, and I'll be the first to say teenagers are mean. Both boys and girls. That's right. The guys are just as cruel verbally and physically. The worst part about the whole experience isn't even the mind-boggling way they treat each other, it's the fucked-up way they treat us. Like we're all just servants for their whims. You wouldn't believe how many of these private school teens treat the staff like we work directly for them. Like they're at home and their parents could walk in to fire us for not bending to their demands. It's disheartening to say the least. Awe. Don't worry too hard. Just a few more months of this, and I'll be free to pick a job that's less torture. Or at the very least will have the opportunity to.

The rest of my shift consists of prepping a few items for the opening breakfast crew, washing the dishes along with drying them, wiping down all the tables once the room is empty, and cleaning the floor. By the time I'm pulling into a parking space at my apartment complex, my feet are debating whether or not to just fall off in defeat. It takes a moment longer than I want to collect the items that fell out of my bag when I was forced to make an abrupt stop in rush hour traffic, but it's the digging around for my disappeared cellphone that pushes my lingering irritation over the edge.

Just as I unlock the front door, my roommate, Jovi Carter, and her boyfriend, Merrick McCoy, are coming out of her room on the opposite side of the apartment.

"There you are!" She joyfully exclaims.

She's just naturally cheerful. We first met in A Thousand Words, A Thousand Pictures, a class I swear whose sole purpose is to weed out those who only picked art as a major because they thought it was going to be easy. At that time, her joy seemed forced, but after her boyfriend moved to town, I realized she was just lovesick. She's been a bright ray of sunshine ever since she's been back in his arms.

Jovi's mocha-colored face instantly becomes concerned. "You're home late."

"And messier than normal," Merrick chuckles.

Stop staring. He's not that *attractive. I mean…I guess if you're into the whole hot, tattooed, bad boy thing with a heart of gold or whatever. Yeah, I'm full of shit. Obviously, I know how yummy he looks. He's a total hottie and madly in love with my adorable roommate. They're so cute sometimes it's sickening. And by sometimes, I really mean* most *of the time.*

After flashing him my middle finger, I sigh, "Relax. I'm fine. Margret just happened to decide today would be the perfect day for me to clean on top *and* underneath the tables."

He immediately teases, "And the white splotches on your shirt? They're not from the principal are they?"

Jovi lightly hits him in his lower stomach.

As you can see, he's got a mouth. And he's cocky. And charismatic. It's a really terrible combination. I honestly don't understand how she decides when it's time to kiss his face or slap it.

"*Dean*," I correct with a sarcastic smirk. "And no. This is what happens when teenagers get pissy and don't pay attention to what they're doing."

"So, not a food fight?" Merrick jokes again.

With a glare, I snap, "Please, tell me you're leaving."

"Yeah," he turns his black baseball cap around before adding, "but you're coming with us."

"I'm sorry, what?"

"Merrick got us *all* tickets a few weeks ago to the Treme showing at the Flatone Gallery," Jovi attempts to spring the memory free from wherever it's imprisoned in my brain. "Remember?"

He drapes his arm around her black coat-covered shoulder. "Because I'm an amazing boyfriend."

Jovi looks up at him. "Sweet."

"Fantastic."

"Thoughtful."

"Incredible."

"And humble, too," I add with another fake smirk.

It takes him a minute to realize the joke.

Okay, so not always the brightest. Just proof no one's perfect.

He drops his jaw in preparation to retort when Jovi continues, "Come on, Brie. You've been dying to see this showing as much as I have."

"But my feet are dying more," I counter in a whine. "Plus, I've got a test to study for and need to work on my final portfolio project that I haven't even started and-"

"All of which you can do *after* the showing," Jovi sweetly argues. She slips out of her boyfriend's grasp and makes her way towards me. "Look, we won't even stay long. We'll go grab a quick burger, swing by the showing, and make sure to have you home before ten o'clock."

Her big brown eyes suddenly become irresistible.

Ugh. They're made for each other. Between her pout and his charm, I swear they could take over the world.

"Please?"

"Fine," I sigh. "Let me get the smell of apples and adolescents off of me first."

Jovi squeals over her victory.

Maybe a glass of wine and spending some time staring at the former Ashwin University graduate's art pieces are exactly what I need. A blunt reminder of what I'm working so hard to one day possibly achieve. Maybe I'll be inspired to move in a new direction. See a route to take with my passion. A path I haven't seen before. Because as of right now, I'm months away from a BA in Art with absolutely no fucking clue what to do with the rest of my life. Hell, what I **want** *to do for that matter. Who knows...Maybe being at the showing will give my life the little nudge it needs. Can't blame a woman for hoping, right?*

CHAPTER THREE

Kellan

I shove my hands into the pockets of my black suit pants. "Remind me one more time, why exactly we're here. You know I hate art like this."

"Because Dana made me swear, I'd take her," Hugh huffs as he swipes two glasses of champagne from a waiter passing by.

Taking one, I question, "Is this some sort of power play? Is she withholding sex from you? Using it as a weapon in her pursuit to control your life?"

His head tilts at me. "Speaking from personal experience?"

"Of course not," I lightly chuckle. "You should know by now my dick is the ultimate weapon and it's always loaded."

He lifts his glass and mumbles behind a sip. "*Horrific*."

Hugh Delmar and I have been mates since his parents shipped him to boarding school at thirteen. Apparently, he had an early addiction to stealing his mother's prescription pills and a fascination with fondling her friends. Shipping him out of his country to ours might not directly fix the issues he so clearly had, but it would at least prevent the media from watching him self-destruct his way through puberty. While Hugh's hatred for his parents continued to grow over the feeling of abandonment – according to the therapy sessions he told me about in mocking – he managed to find solace in a new sport. His first week at school I caught him staring in confusion at the game of lacrosse and offered to explain it, after poking fun at his atrocious American accent of course. What? They are vastly inferior to ours. We all know it.

"Look," Hugh begins with a heavy sigh, "I *really* like Dana."

"You really like every woman you date. You're a serial dater."

"You say that because you're afraid of monogamy."

"I say that because you're afraid of being alone."

"Perhaps…," he quickly shakes his head, "but…I *really* like Dana."

"You said that already."

"She's different-"

"Three tits?"

"She's smart. Kind. Has a job. Doesn't live off her trust fund. And she would rather become a lesbian than ever sleep with you."

"Doubtful."

"*Direct. Quote.*" He beams. "I'd really like to see where this goes, which happens to mean doing things she enjoys. Like art showings."

"Why can't she enjoy things that are actually fun? Like white water rafting?"

"You hate white water rafting. You hate how it frizzes your hair."

He makes that sound so feminine. What? No, it isn't. There's nothing wrong with caring about your hair.

"True, but you know what I mean."

"I know you're being a pain in my ass because you're bored."

"Extremely. Art showings are the very definition of *boring*."

Yes, they are! Splotches of paint covering a piece of canvas? Oooo...Call the No One Really Gives a Damn Police and let them know one of their most-wanted figures has escaped!

"Well, Dana enjoys them, and since you showed up a day earlier than anticipated, you're going to have to deal with it."

It was either leave a day early or spend it listening to my father drone on over appropriate and acceptable public behaviors. At least this way, there's the possibility for fun. What do you mean do I mean fun or sex? They are the same thing, aren't they?

After he has another sip, he tries to reassure me, "No need to fret, Ebenezer."

He's promptly tossed an annoyed glare.

"We probably won't be here too long. She really just wants to meet Treme and purchase one of his pieces."

"To sit comfortably above your kennel?"

Hugh rolls his green eyes as he sighs, "I'm sure you can find *something* here to occupy your attention and make the headline of a bullshit blog."

"Are you trying to get rid of me?"

"Yes." Seeing Dana head in our direction, he expands his smile and commands through gritted teeth, "Now, make this portion of the evening tolerable, or I'll let Dana play cupid for the rest of your trip making life absolutely miserable for you."

"You're a bastard."

"And that's why we're friends," he mumbles before asking loudly, "Have you met Treme yet, babe?

Babe? A bit trite of a nickname for someone who claims they're head over heels.

"No," she pouts and moves into his embrace. "He's surrounded by women worshiping his every move. I can't get even get close enough to call out his name and potentially be heard."

Hugh's face seems to fall. "I'm sorry, babe. What can I do?"

He sounds genuine. How…unexpected.

"Would you like me to send Kellan that direction? Give the women something else to follow around for the evening?"

With an amused expression, I ask, "Did you just offer me up as a sacrifice?"

He gives me a quick glance. "Yes."

"You didn't even hesitate."

"You didn't exactly object."

Deeming his point fair causes me to nod and have another sip of champagne.

Even those who don't recognize exactly who I am in this country, still have no problem coming after me. Guess I look close enough like someone who should matter even without trying. Hey, I'm not egoistical. I was simply stating an observation.

"Would you?" Dana's overly thinned eyebrows shoot up. "Would you just stand in their general eye range? I'm sure it would distract enough of them for me to actually ask about the painting that I want before another buyer beats me to it."

Hugh gives me a stern expression.

He looks constipated, doesn't he?

"Fine," I sigh and have another swig. "I've been meaning to give Swiss a reason to earn his pay."

Swiss is my security detail in charge of following me around whenever I enter the states. We pay to keep his calendar free considering I have no defined schedule and my father requires all members of the royal family to travel in public with protection. I believe it's ridiculous to have that rule while I'm here. Outside of the major cities that are heavily populated by celebrities, most people rarely recognize this face as anything other than a bedmate they desire. Hell, until Kristopher married Sophia whose father is American, most of this country didn't give a shit about Doctenn's socialites. This is interesting considering the impressive mix of their language and culture has been smashed into ours for generations. However, the minute an American woman began dating an actual prince, their interest spiked, turning our royal family into a constant trending topic for this country as well as our own. Guess I should work on keeping my pants up or the curtains closed, hm? From the messages my brother has been sending me today, my little stunt is gaining me more attention than ever before. Apparently, the naked blonde who sent the photo yesterday is an American actress this country adores. Can't say I feel the same. Her cock sucking ability lacked focus and effort. Hope she gives more energy in rehearsing her lines than she does in foreplay.

Dana quickly squeals, "Thank you, Kellan! Thank you so much!"

I give her a wink and stroll off towards the left where a group of overly eager women are gathered around a thin man with intricate designs buzzed into his jet-black hair.

This should be relatively easy. Like taking a toy from a toddler.

Sauntering Treme's direction with my glass in one hand and the other in my pocket, I scan the gallery in hopes of finding someone to actually pass the time with.

As you can see my best mate's mission is to please his girlfriend for probably the next hour and as I might've mentioned before, I find art dreadfully boring. You might not feel that's necessary to repeat, but quite frankly it is. Keep your hopes up that I find someone who feels equally annoyed by the subject so that we can sneak away together. Perhaps on the balcony. It's been a while since I've made out with anyone on a balcony. Doesn't just the idea feel like something out of Romeo + Juliet? The film, of course. Not the dreadfully long play.

I prepare to pause just behind the man of the evening when a pair of long, latte-colored legs glide into my view. My eyes waste no time roaming down her backside that is presented to me. I'm immediately intrigued by the shoulder tattoo I can't quite make out from this distance and pleased with the deliciously round ass being displayed in an unusual black cocktail dress.

It is unusual, isn't it? Between the way it has one thin strap while the other is thick and how it seems to purposely hug her hips tightly yet loosely fall to the back of her knees suggests the designer was indecisive. Or perhaps, the designer made it for indecisive women. You know, women who struggle to make decisions happen to adore me. I have no problem taking control. I rather enjoy it.

Casually moving her direction, I continue my observation while nursing my half-empty beverage. The woman – who for some reason hasn't changed art displays yet – tilts her head to one side as if in contemplation.

When I arrive beside her, I paste my attention on the piece of so-called art and question, "Deciding whether it looks like a swan or duck?"

"Actually, I was wondering why this one was done with pastels while the majority of the others were done with watercolors."

"Maybe he got bored."

"Maybe this one means more to him."

Oh…Lucky. Me. She's actually into art. Figures, one way or another I would be forced to pretend that any of this shit is remotely fascinating. At least with her, it might end with the two of us mixing paints. You like what I did there? Fine. It wasn't my most clever moment but still a good one.

"And the answer is a swan," she states giving me a quick smirk before strolling away. "*Obviously*."

Her remark causes me to grin in return and follow.

Maybe she won't be as dull as I was assuming.

This time when we stop in front of a display, I ask, "What about this one? A game of Twister gone awry?"

The corner of her lip tugs upward.

She has a sense of humor. I like that…

"Should I go ahead and put my right hand on red?"

"Abstract art is an acquired taste." She turns and gives me a snarky smirk. "Like dating you, I imagine."

Huh. Not sure if I'm more impressed with her remark or the speed at which she had it ready to deliver.

"I'll have you know, everyone *loves* me. I'm like a coloring book. Easy to enjoy."

"You're more like finger paint. So simple it's irritating for anyone with a mental capacity past Kindergarten."

I drop my mouth at the same time there's a tug on my arm. "Excuse me." When I turn to view the interruption, I'm not surprised to see a woman with long blonde hair and a barely-there red dress. "Did you drop my number?"

"*See*," the brown-skinned beauty whispers seconds before the sound of her heels moving redirects my attention.

Don't agree with her.

Politely, I remove my arm from the stranger's grasp to follow the other female. "Actually, I was in the middle of a conversation with-"

"Not interested," the woman calls over her shoulder as she turns the corner.

Of course, she's interested. She's just playing hard to get. And I'm not fucking finger paint. Or paint by numbers. I heard that!

The blonde tries to stop me again, but her words don't register. I turn the corner in the same direction the dark-haired woman did yet am not instantly rewarded with her appearance. On a curious hum, I continue to examine the crowd on this side of the exhibit, which is filled with what appear to be portraits. While part of my attention is being summoned to glance at the bright paintings, the other is determined to find where the coffee-colored female went, not only to prove her wrong but to get the last word in the conversation.

Bad habit. What can I say? Whenever arguing, I happen to have a compulsive need to have the last word.

All of a sudden, an arm and arm couple steps into my pathway exposing the camouflaged minx.

I plant a pleased smirk on my face, move into the position beside her, and state, "Hiding?"

She doesn't bother looking in my direction. "Following?"

"Perhaps," I reply on a sip from my glass. "Are you a fan of Treme?"

To my surprise, she questions, "As a person or an artist?"

"Either."

"Not really."

Her answer arches my eyebrows.

"He attended the same university as me. We actually started at the same time but because he never had a problem scraping up tuition, he graduated long before me." The slight bitterness in her tone is unmistakable. "He was a talented asshole then and from what I've managed to overhear him say to the groupies at his feet tonight, he's a talented *rich* asshole now."

Curiosity gets the better of me. "If you despise him-"

"I never said that."

"You didn't have to. Only a complete idiot wouldn't have picked up on that."

She finally turns to me and snips, "Which you're trying to prove you're not?"

The fire in her toffee-shaded eyes expands my grin. "I was trying to understand why you're here if you hate him." Her lack of an answer pushes me to prod. "Here to see if maybe his work wasn't as amazing as it used to be?"

"You think it's amazing?"

"I think it's rubbish, but in all honesty, I think that way about all art in general."

Confusion coats her expression at the same time she folds her arms. "All art?"

"Well, art in *this form*. Paintings. Portraits. Sculptures. Things of that nature."

"We're talking the classics, too?"

"Yeah. I don't really get the point." I shrug my indifference. "Why pay homage and thousands of dollars to people who simply threw colors together? Then there's the fact quite often those colors don't even create an actual picture, just stains stupidly placed on a canvas."

Her jaw drops in what appears to be appalled.

Okay. It appears as if we're back to not having fun. I know you're thinking that I really should find that blonde again, but this view is much better even if the conversation is painful. Just look at her soft, full lips. The tiny mole right above them. Wonder how amazing they would look wrapped around my cock? How effortlessly they would graze my shaft while my hand grips the back of her hair to help keep her in place?

Suddenly, she snaps, "First off, stop thinking about me naked."

Taken off guard, my own mouth cracks open.

Of course, she is naked in the scenario. Why would she be clothed? How bloody vanilla are your fantasies that you would assume she'd be clothed?

"Second, the art of this medium isn't about the pictures you may or may not see. Art and I mean all art, not just paintings and sculptures, but music and literature and theater, are reflections of the soul. They're products of *passion*. They're humanity's way of whispering through a medium to ignite, or reignite, those little sparks that set your spirit on fire. Maybe the reason you don't get it is simply that you have yet to see one that speaks to you." Her speech shuts my mouth, which is when she finishes with, "Hope you find it soon because I'm done talking to you."

She turns and heads away from me once more, except this time I'm not certain if I'm following her just because of the physical attraction or an uncontrollable need to continue to argue.

It's not like I've never met a woman not interested in me. Albeit it's rare, but it happens. And it's not as if she's the first woman to snap back or push her opinion around during a conversation. I don't know exactly what it is that has me trailing after her like a lost puppy she needs to take home, but I have every intention of finding out.

Her movements stop sooner than expected.

I give the canvas covered in four blue dots a glance.

"Now, this is just crap," she mutters under her breath.

I chortle, "*Oh?* Doesn't speak to 'your soul'?"

She tosses me a sarcastic glare at the same time she bites, "Why won't you go away?"

"Because you don't want me to."

Her ring-less left-hand lands on her hip.

No wedding rings. Good sign.

"And what exactly gives you that impression? Was it when I walked away the first time? When I told you I wasn't interested? Or maybe…*maybe* it was when I told you I was done speaking to you? Was that it? That was it, wasn't it?"

"You claim you want to me go away, yet you continue to engage me in conversation every opportunity presented."

By the way, she's trying not to smile, I think it's safe to assume she finds my logic valid.

Obviously, you agree.

"Look, while you've got the whole gorgeous *True Blood* actor thing going for you-"

"Thank you."

"I've…got a boyfriend, so you should just move on now."

She's not a very good liar. Oddly enough, that's a relief. Most of the women I surround myself with are professionals, like deception is an Olympic sport. At least when she says something to me, I don't feel compelled to immediately question if there is a self-serving ulterior motive. Hey, remind me to grab her name in a moment. Can't believe I've yet to do that. That's so unlike me.

I try not to smile. "You have a boyfriend?"

"That's right."

"Is he here with you?"

"Yup."

"Where?"

"He's right over there." She motions her hand behind her. "The guy by the far wall with the backward black baseball cap."

My eyes immediately cut in that direction. As soon as I spot him, I nod. "You mean the one making out with the chick who is also wearing a little black dress?" Her head spins around to check and I chuckle, "Though I must say I find yours more enjoyable. I appreciate the angled cut in front playing peek-a-boo with the idea of what's underneath."

Still facing the couple making out, she grouses, "*Seriously?* It's like they have fucking magnets in their mouths."

"*It's charming.*"

"*It's disgusting.*" On a heavy sigh, she turns back around to face me with a scowl. "Fine. I don't *really* have a boyfriend, but I have no interest in joining what I can only assume is a very long list of one-night stands."

The instant rejection isn't surprising.

Did you really expect anything else?

"Kellan!" Dana's voice calls my name with such excitement it causes my eyebrows to lower in perplexity. "Ohmygod, Kellan!" The moment I look over my shoulder, she points at the painting we're in front of. "He sold it to me! Can you believe it?!"

Disbelief drops my jaw.

She can't possibly be serious. What on Earth could this possibly "say" to her? Shall I use this in my argument with the gorgeous girl whose name I still don't know? Damn! How do I still not know it?

"Yeah, no thanks to you," Hugh huffs from behind her. "All you had to do was stand there long enough to be the bait and somehow you managed to fuck that up. If we hadn't bumped into Treme's agent while having a smoke, you would be buying that painting from whoever beat her to it as an apology."

No…Probably not.

I roll my eyes at his irritation and turn back to where the reason I was distracted to begin with, should still be standing. Disappointment and aggravation fill my chest at her unapproved disappearance. Refusing to instantly give up, I let my eyes search the direction her friends were kissing to see that they'd vanished as well.

Of course, she's gone. She's used every out offered just as she's used every invitation presented. She is exactly like her attire. Though, after having had a real conversation with her, I believe my original assumption was wrong. She's not indecisive. Quite the opposite. She – like her dress that I wish would've ended up on my hotel room floor tonight – is the embodiment of a conflicting urge to remain greatly guarded and wildly wicked. I'll confess. The idea of a woman willing to be naughty just for me *has an unexpected appeal. Hm. I like the unexpected. It's where the real fun truly begins…*

CHAPTER FOUR

Brie

The vibrating next to my ear causes me to groan.

Damn it. Did I really fall asleep studying at the kitchen table again?

On another low grunt, I struggle to sit up in the wooden chair just as the vibrating stops. I grab my phone and swipe to open the new message waiting for me.

Dad: Can't go tonight. Sorry to cancel last minute. Needed at the store. Marissa called in. Love you.

A heavy sigh of irritation escapes me.

It's not like he works at a top-secret facility that can't function without him. He works for a grocery store chain that has at least four other managers they could call when one decides they don't feel like showing up. But who do they always call first because they know he won't say no? That's right. **My. Dad.** *Ugh. This sucks. I'm not even pissed about the fact I'll basically be throwing money away by us not going. I'm pissed I'm not gonna get to spend time with him.* **Again.** *Between our hectic schedules,* *it's something that's crossing the very thin line into impossible, unlike my mother who rarely ever seems booked. She's often a little* too *available if you catch my drift. A benefit of being a paid hair magician I suppose. Her hours are hers to do with and reschedule as she pleases. Her client bends to her will because the woman is. Just. That. Good.*

A light knocking on the front door drags my attention away from the disappointing text.

Who the hell could that be? Jovi would've texted if she left her keys and Merrick...well, as much as I hate to say this out loud, that asshole has his own key. I swear sometimes it's like he already lives here.

The knocking persists, and I stare at the door from across the room wondering how long it will continue before they give up.

Not a huge fan of answering the door. Period. Truthfully, the only person who tends to knock at this time is our bitchy downstairs neighbor who thinks she has an elephant parade living above her.

The knocking suddenly gets louder and sharper, almost impatient. Curiosity yanks me onto my feet and towards the demanding presence waiting on the other side. I attempt to flatten my thick, wavy hair that had been doubling as a pillow and wipe away any possible drool that proves you can't really learn the answers to a test through osmosis.

Believe me. After almost ten years of cramming for tests, if it hasn't worked by now, it's never going to.

I unlock the door and crack it open to see someone I have no reason to.

What the hell? Are you seeing this?

The blonde model from the art show flashes me the same arrogant grin he was flaunting last night.

What? No. I don't know his name and don't technically know that he's really a model but come on. Teeth that white? Eyes that bright? Face that flawless? Build that…bicepy? He's either a goddamn model or the gene pool lottery winner of the millennium.

"Latte?"

Without hesitation, I shut the door and lock it again.

"Not a morning person?"

"No. I'm not a *stalking* person."

"I'm not stalking you."

"The fact you're on my front doorstep would be a valid argument for the opposite." Leaning my body slightly against the door, I snip, "And I don't know about whatever country you cruised over from but stalking in the United States is very much *illegal*."

I refuse to admit how sexy his accent is. Wait. Shit. I just did, huh? Nope. Never happened. You're dreaming. Maybe I'm dreaming? Maybe I'm having a long lucid nightmare?

"It's illegal in Doctenn as well," he casually informs. "Fairly certain stalking is illegal in all countries."

"Yet here you are."

A long moment of silence falls, but I'm not remotely convinced he's given up.

Come on. What kinda guy would go through all this effort into finding you then give up the minute you told him to?

I lift myself onto the tips of my toes to peer through the peephole.

Like a know it all, he raises one of the cups in front of it and repeats, "Latte?"

"You mean the coffee you poisoned so you could rape and molest me?"

"Doesn't rape cover molesting?"

Glaring at him through the tiny hole, I grunt, "Semantics? Really? You're a complete stranger on my doorstep, stalking me, and offering me a drugged beverage, yet you have the balls to stand there and try to argue *sexual semantics*?"

The blonde chortles and shakes his head. "Not a complete stranger. We met last night."

"You stalked me then, too."

"My name is Kellan. Kellan Kenningston." After the statement, he lifts the cup he had been offering me, has a sip, and smiles. "Not drugged." As if he can see his victory, he asks, "Now, do you mind inviting me in to finish this conversation? It's a bit frigid outside."

I lower myself back to my feet and reluctantly open the door.

*You better be prepared to tell the cops everything that happened here if this goes bad. I mean **everything**. Make sure to emphasize how he harassed me and not how hot he is. Priorities. Know your priorities.*

"My roommate's dad is a cop," I inform immediately. "And not just like a run-of-the-mill cop, either. He's a Police Commissioner. So, if you hurt me, she'll make sure he hunts you down and gives you a cellmate who will appreciate your gorgeous mouth in a way you probably won't enjoy."

Kellan steps inside past me. "I think your mouth is gorgeous, too."

That...That backfired a little. It's not what I meant! I mean yeah, he's got an incredible pair of lips. Lips that could probably pay my body the devotion it hasn't received in a very long time, especially if they start at my inner thigh and slowly travel towards my...

"Now, who's thinking about who naked?"

Of course, he would be naked while his mouth is exploring me there! Otherwise, that would just be a waste of a fantasy! Wait. Why am I fantasizing about a stranger? A very hot, very British stranger? Not British. Doctenn. They're like cousins or close enough, right?

He expands his smirk as he offers me the cup once more. "Latte?"

"How did you find me?" I take the beverage. "I didn't even give you my name."

"For the right price, there are very few things that cannot be found or covered up, Brie."

"How very double o annoying of you to say." Bracing my back against the door for a second time, I have the tiniest taste of the drink. "Why are you here?" Another sip is swiftly had. "What do you want?"

Kellan braces his muscular frame along the backside of the couch. "Go out with me."

"No."

"I'm only in town until next Sunday."

"That sounds like nine days too long."

"I'd love to spend at least one of those these nights with you."

"You're looking for a *fling*," I disgustingly declare.

"When's the last time you've been *flung*?"

Not important.

Sensing his assumption is probably correct, he continues in an unexpected kind voice, "One date. That's all I'm asking you for."

"Let me get this straight. You cashed in one of your Bond like favors to hunt down my name and address just to ask me out for a date?"

"Yes." His grin grows arrogant. "It's quite romantic."

"It's quite creepy," I counter and move in his direction. "And a lie. You could've easily gotten my phone number and asked *that way*. Less invasive."

"What can I say?" His body migrates towards mine. "I'm harder to deny in person."

Only because of his goddamn eyes and smile twinkle like some weird Pixar animation trick.

"Not that hard." I wink.

"Is that a no?"

"That's a *hell no*," the reply is followed with me moving backward towards my bedroom. "Now, thank you for the coffee-"

"Latte."

"-but I have class I'll be late for if I keep wasting my time arguing with you."

Kellan nods slowly as if he doesn't believe he's been completely defeated.

Which he has. 110% defeated. I'm not going out with some smokin' accented stranger who brought me coffee even if it's the most romance I've had in my life over the past two years.

"Can I walk you there?"

From the doorway of my room, I give him a puzzled look. "It's a ten-minute drive on a good day. No way am I *walking* to campus."

"To your car then?"

"You're a little needy for someone so pretty."

The smirk I hate to admit I enjoy seeing appears again. "*Persistent.*"

"Back to stalking territory," I tease before adding, "and I'm locking my door, so don't even think about trying to open it to confirm whether or not my measurements are accurate in your fantasies."

Lord knows I'm wondering if his are.

Quickly, I slip out of my pajama bottoms and into a pair of jeans. While the first part of my wardrobe change is always the easiest – regardless of the time of year –, the inevitable hunt for my favorite sweatshirt and paint-stained chucks often has me jogging to class to prevent being late during the winter.

It's what I practically hibernate in all season.

Once I've completely changed, brushed my teeth, and managed to put all my hair into a frizzy high ponytail, I swipe the beverage from my dresser and exit to the living room to where Kellan is patiently waiting.

"Not as impressive as the little number you had on last night, but nonetheless sexy in a bang me in my dorm room sort of way."

His comment receives an eye roll as I make my way to the kitchen table to repack my bag. "Keep dreaming, James Fraud."

"You said you started at Ashwin the same year as Treme?"

"I never said Ashwin."

"It's the only university within ten minutes of here."

Damn it. Why do I keep letting information slip to him?

"Are you at least close to graduating?"

After shutting the book that I fell asleep on, I reply, "Beginning of June is when I should walk across the stage."

"You're in your last semester."

"Yeah." I shove it in my notebook, close the shoulder bag, and grab my phone. "But don't worry. I won't bore you with details of my degree."

Kellan smirks again while watching me swipe my keys off the counter. "Maybe the topic would be less boring if it were coming out of a prettier subject. *Like you*."

"Doubtful." I open the front door and usher him out. Once I've locked up, the two of us begin down the stairs when I notice a large, tan man with a buzzed haircut lurking just around the corner. "Friend of yours?"

"Not by choice."

"Meaning?"

"As per the royal pain in the arse known as my father, a security detail is required at all times. Distance, however, is debatable."

I stop my body on the bottom stair and turn to face Kellan. "Why? Are you…like…famous or something?"

The security guard chuckles under his breath.

Oh shit. Is he?! Not that it would've made a difference to my date answer. Between us though, it would be a little exciting to be able to say I turned down a celebrity. He's probably an actor or an **actual** ***supermodel.***

"Or something," he mutters prior to swiftly changing the subject. "Which way to your car?"

I tilt my head to the side. "What's or something?"

There's no effort made to answer.

"Do you not wanna tell me?"

"You won't believe me."

"Try me."

His hesitation is followed by a deep sigh, "I'm a prince."

"A prince."

"And a Duke."

"Because Disney was just handing out titles that day?"

Kellan fights the urge to chuckle. "I'm serious. I'm Prince of Doctenn and Duke of Rockbridge. Not the only prince of Doctenn – I have an older brother being groomed to represent the crown – but I am the only Duke of Rockbridge. All of it is really just useless bureaucratic titles at this point. A fancy way of saying whose bloodline lasted longer and rose higher than whose."

Great. I let a delusional sociopath in for coffee this morning. See. This is exactly what happens when I don't get enough sleep.

"Sure." I shrug and turn back around to finish my route to my car. "You don't wanna give me the real reason then fine. It's none of my business." When I arrive at my vehicle, I open the door and state, "Thanks again for the coffee."

"*Latte.*"

"God, you're one of *those* people," I mumble under my breath.

58

Thinks Monet was overrated but won't hesitate to call his barista an artist. Ridiculous.

"Have a nice day, Kellan."

I shut the door after he gives me one final wave from where he's waiting on the sidewalk. I place my coffee in the receipt-filled cupholder, toss my bag in the seat beside me, stick the key in the ignition, and turn. An unusual clicking sound escapes, yet nothing happens.

This can't be good.

I repeat the action again except this time I watch the dashboard for signs of life. Signs of hope. Disbelief pushes me back against the seat as I stare on in horror.

How the hell could this morning get any worse?

There's a light tapping at my window.

And that's why you should never ask that question.

I look in his direction with a displeased expression.

"Problem?"

"Pretty sure my battery is dead." Immediate suspicion causes me to question slowly, "Did you kill my battery, so I would have to get a ride from you?"

The sarcastic expression on his face says it all.

Hey! It could happen. He did show up with coffee out of nowhere! What? Of course, I turned my lights off last night. Oh…Oh…the light I turned on to look for my cellphone. I'm pretty sure I turned it off. Like twenty percent sure.

"Do you need a ride?"

I let my shoulders drop in embarrassment. "Yes."

"I'd love to give you one," Kellan says sweetly before letting his smile turn villainous, "in exchange for a date tonight."

A combination of shock and frustration flood my face. "Extortion? You really think the way to a woman's heart is *extortion*?"

"I honestly don't know the way to a woman's heart." He leans his free arm against the roof of my car. "I always end up taking a detour down south."

Disgusted and irked, I open the car door, pleased when it knocks into his body in what appears to be a painful way.

Prince of Prickery. Is that a real country now?

After collecting my things, I exit my car and defiantly state, "*I'll walk.*"

"You'll miss your test."

Fuck. He's right. And I know he's right. And he knows he's right, which makes this entire situation even worse. Remind me what I did again to piss off the universe this morning?

"How'd you know I have a test?"

"Saw your textbook open and your notes while I was waiting for you to change."

"Nosy."

Kellan joyfully winks.

"That wasn't a compliment."

"Come on, Brie," his smile stretches from ear to ear. "One date. That's all I'm asking for."

"Why?" I adjust my shoulder bag. "You've probably got a *literal* line of women who want to sleep with you. Why are you bothering me?"

"I'm not *bothering* you."

"You are *so* bothering me!"

"I-"

"What's really going on here? Is this that whole challenges are more fun to you thing? Is there some sort of wager involved? Just tell me who it is I need to lie to, and we can end this now with you appearing to be victorious."

He lightly laughs, and the sound is unexpectedly intoxicating.

Not. Cool.

"No bets."

"I don't believe you."

"It's the truth. You're just fun to be around-"

"You mean to argue with."

"Isn't that what I said?" I twitch a glare, which is when he adds with another grin, "*See*. I like you."

"You don't know me."

"Then let me."

Don't swoon over him! He's not a real prince!

Knowing that time is ticking for me to get to class, I shrug. "Fine. One date. And I get to pick where and when."

He surrenders his free hand. "Name it."

"Get me to class first."

"Swiss," he yells at the man who has been waiting. "Go ahead and start the vehicle, please. We'll be headed to Ashwin University."

The man nods at the instructions while we make our way in his direction.

"Swiss? Like the cheese?"

Kellan shakes his head. "Like the army knife."

"That's a little more threatening than the dairy product."

"Let's hope so," he chuckles. "Can't imagine my father would be happy paying his retainer if he couldn't do more than go well with roast beef."

"His retainer? Do you use him often?"

"Every time I step foot in the states."

"And you're from Doctenn? Which is where again?"

"It's an island country in the Atlantic. Bit to the right of the UK. We're more of a mashup of them and you, Americans. Everything from cultural to language. It's a running joke that we're the best of both worlds."

"I thought jokes were supposed to be funny."

He opens the SUV door for me, smile just as prevalent as always. "Clever."

Inside the vehicle, I slide to the other side and buckle my seat belt. Kellan on the other hand doesn't bother with mimicking my safety action. His phone seems more important.

Great date material. Can't even spend the ten minutes in the car with me without pulling out extra entertainment. He seems like a real catch. Was my sarcasm strong enough or should I increase it?

All of a sudden, he extends the phone in my direction. "Proof that I'm not the psychopath you think I am."

"Sociopath."

Kellan cocks a grin. "Semantics again."

I reach for the device, surprised to see the numerous articles waiting to be read from the Google search he did on himself. Stunned, I scroll through the images, shocked at the numerous labels assuring he is indeed some line of royalty but not surprised by the countless photos with women whose names I highly doubt he can recall.

This explains the pretty playboy arrogance and insistence on having whatever he can get his manicured fingers wrapped around. Uh…no joke. His nails are manicured. And cleaner than mine. I can't believe I'm seriously gonna go out with a guy who probably spends more time in the mirror than I do. What? Yeah. It's much easier to focus on that than the outlandish truth about the man in the SUV next to me being an actual, real-life prince.

With a crooked smirk, I snidely remark, "Your brother's hotter."

Kellan snatches his phone from my hands. "*He's married.*"

"The good ones always are."

He begins to scowl prompting mirth to flood my gaze. At the sight, he immediately looks away in a poor attempt to hide his embarrassment. The crimson color coating his cheeks causes minor guilt to cultivate.

Didn't know it was a touchy topic. Just thought it was typical sibling rivalry bullshit.

There's a long, sullen lull before I question, "So, besides stalking art students and making fun of paintings, what do you do for a living?"

The change in topic dissipates the red color with his natural golden one. "I find various ways to occupy my time."

"From the looks of those photos, I would guess you spend most of your time slut hunting."

Swiss tries to hide his laugh but fails.

Rather than scolding him, Kellan states to me, "I don't have to hunt for women like that."

"Just women like me? The ones who tell you no?"

"Don't hunt for them either."

"So, just me?"

He leans over and quietly reassures, "*Just. You.*"

To be flattered or freaked out…that is the question.

"Outside of enjoying my thriving social life, I actively avoid as many royal engagements as possible, run a non-profit organization, and volunteer my time to supporting various charities centered around children."

My bottom lip drops in surprise.

"See." He lifts his eyebrows at me with a playful smile. "I'm full of surprises."

"And hot air," I sneer in an attempt to mask my growing interest.

Kellan wets his perfect lips, yet the rest of his body retreats towards the window. "Our date. When and where?"

"We're not to campus yet."

"Almost," he instantly informs. "On a good day, ten minutes. *On a great day,* seven."

The retort receives a glare, which I assume he enjoys by the smug smirk I'm flashed.

Why does it seem to be every punch we exchange is entertaining? That he's thriving on the fact I'm not just rolling over for him? This is totally "the challenge is the only thrill" concept in full effect. Only way to kill it would be to throw myself at him like every other woman.

Kellan's blue eyes pierce mine with question.

Okay, but where would the fun in that be? Yeah, I kinda want him to go away, but I also want him to realize he's barking up the wrong tree. I'm too wrong for him and not because he's too perfect in comparison to me.

"You can meet me at my apartment at 6:30 tonight," I state at the same time Swiss stops the SUV. "Obviously, you'll need to have him drive."

"Attire?"

A fun scheme to prove this is a terrible idea pops into my mind. "Dress to impress." Instantly, a suspicious look appears, which causes me to quickly end the conversation. "Thanks for the ride. Gotta go."

On my way out, he asks, "Do you need a ride after class?"

"No, *Dad*, I'll catch a ride from one of the other kids." My smile meets his seconds before I shut the door. After one final wave, I fix my shoulder bag and hustle into the ocean of students.

About halfway to the Lancaster building, my eyes spot the two people who could have helped prevent the situation I stumbled into this morning. I swiftly snake through the crowd and bump brashly into Merrick.

His attention drops from his girlfriend to me. "And where the hell were you two this morning?"

"I was studying."

With a sarcastic expression, I ask, "First thing in the morning?"

"No better time to study anatomy." Merrick's comment is followed by a chuckle that receives him a swat from Jovi whose face is beginning to change colors.

"Yeah, well, while you were finally learning where the clitoris is, I was stuck with a car that wouldn't start."

"Aw, I'm sorry," Jovi rushes to apologize. "I'm glad you found a way here! We totally would've given you a ride if-"

"I know where the clit is," Merrick interrupts loudly. "I've never missed it! Hell, in fact I-"

"If you finish that sentence, you won't be seeing or studying it again anytime soon," my roommate threatens as we enter the building.

The two of us giggle while he pouts.

I was totally kidding about the clit thing. What can I say? Guess I'm still a little wound up from poking the prince all morning.

Stopping outside our lecture room, Merrick tugs her closer to him and sighs, "Just a few more months, and then I can spend every morning with a chemistry lesson."

I give him a questionable look. "Switching subjects to avoid trouble?"

He gives me a proud nod.

"Well, can we avoid that topic, too? I'm not quite ready to face the fact in five months I'm going to be jobless *and* homeless," I deeply sigh.

"You're not going to be homeless. We're not going to kick you out," Jovi insists. "And we don't even know if Merrick is going to move in with us or me with him or exactly how any of that's going to work."

"But it *is* going to work," he states, firmly. "This not living together bullshit has reached its end. Thank fuck."

Rather than continue the conversation or mock him for his being so in love with his girlfriend that to be away from her is some Shakespearean tragedy, I spin on my heels and say, "Grabbing our seats. See you later, Merrick."

"Later, Brie."

I take a few steps down and slide into the first seat.

They're adorable. I'll admit that. They have this whole timeless love affair romance you read about in a New York Times Bestseller or a really hopeful indie writer's big breakout. It's so perfect it almost seems too good to be true, but that's not the worst part. It's having it flashed in your face. Having a constant reminder of how you've spent the last few years of your life so caught up in trying to graduate that there's a good chance you bypassed all the roads that could've led you to have more than a degree to keep you warm at night. A degree in a subject you love yet one that may never love you back. A subject that may never earn its keep for all the money you've thrown at it. Hm…on that depressing note, wish me luck. Art History with an emphasis on the Renaissance Era sounds easier than it actually is. Let's wish for an A on this test so that I can actually **enjoy** *flunking Prince Kellan out of his date tonight.*

CHAPTER FIVE

Kellan

I adjust the collar on my navy-blue suit jacket once more. "A date, Kris. It's the thing you used to take your wife on before sitting in front of the tele with a bottle of wine did the trick."

"Fuck off," he huffs. "We still go out."

Perhaps they do. I'm not typically around to actually know their day-to-day schedule. I'm not usually around longer than I ever have to be.

"Who's the unfortunate victim this evening? Actress? Model? Prime Minister's great-niece?"

"The states don't have a Prime Minister, idiot."

"Oh, I'm the idiot? When we were in school you could barely name five states in America let alone remember they had a President and not a Prime Minister."

What can I say? Geography became my favorite subject the minute I was allowed off the island unsupervised.

"By the way, my comment was a joke-"

"Not a good one."

"However, the way you redirected the conversation has struck me curiosity."

My lips momentarily press together to prevent further speaking.

"That's not the way you typically handle that question."

Instead of denying his accusation, I slide my wallet into my pocket, grab my watch to put on, and motion my head for Swiss to know it's time to get going.

"*In fact-*"

"Why are you still talking?"

"-you normally can't wait to brag about who you're going to be shagging," he continues on as if he's actually deducing something.

Which you and I both know he's not. There's nothing there to sort out. She's just not one of the types he's listed, and it's more

amusing for me to picture his brain running on a squeaky hamster wheel than to let him rest easy. Ha. Of course, I'm an asshole. I'm the younger brother. It's what we do.

"What's wrong with her? Does she have an extra nipple or gold teeth? Perhaps six toes she hides poorly in her high heels?"

His descriptions scrunch my face. "Now I *know* it's past your bedtime. You're starting to sound insane."

"Yet you didn't deny any of those."

"Why are you still up?" I fasten my watch while walking. "It's after midnight. Don't you and the old ball and chain usually have a romp, some tea, and then turn in promptly at ten?"

Kristopher grouses louder than I'm sure anticipates, "Can't believe I actually look forward to those nights."

The elevator doors close with us inside at the same time I ask, "You're serious? You *enjoy* that?"

"I know it's hard to wrap your head around, Kellan, since pint induced comas are your favorite-"

"Sometimes *vodka-*"

"-but *yes*. I enjoy nights where the only things I have to truly care about are getting my beautiful wife off and having her favorite type of tea to make afterward."

Sensing what's bothering him, I give Swiss a quick glance and question, "Do we need to talk alone?"

"No," he lets out a heavy sigh. "No. It's fine. It'll *be* fine. It always is, more or less. However, I will say, Father has denied your proposal once more for sharing at this season's annual brunch."

Four times a year several socially privileged countries get together to compare tiaras and diamond cuff links or at least I'm assuming since I've never actually been invited to attend one by our father. He swears it would be a social embarrassment that we would never recover from as a country. Yes. He is just as overly dramatic as Kristopher. Where do you think he inherited it from? Believe it or not, generally speaking, it's always been the women who are the calm, levelheaded ones in this family. Correction. Somewhat levelheaded. Soph did demand we stop serving figs at every breakfast by covering them in hot sauce when she thought no one was watching. Anyway, these gatherings are held and multiple financial, as well as social opportunities, are presented right alongside the garlic roasted red potatoes. We're talking investment chances for personal gain. New companies developing. Old companies that'll be up for buying and revamping. Charities and other programs that warrant attention, attention that if just the right amount of people give enough of it to, could tremendously make a huge fucking difference. Like my non-profit for example.

I clamp my jaw shut as I walk out of the elevator with Swiss on my heels.

"Don't pout, Kellan," my brother promptly insists. "I pushed for it this time. I really did. He just-"

"Went with *your* proposal instead?"

His silence is all the admission necessary.

And this is where actual sibling rivalry is an issue. You see if it's what the oldest prince wants versus the younger, the oldest wins. The oldest has more to lose or gain. The oldest actually matters. Why else do you think it's so easy for me to get away whenever I've had enough of the palace walls? Fuck whoever I want with little to no scolding?

"He's…He's having Soph and I attend this year," Kristopher's explanation begins right when my bodyguard and I reach the SUV. "He believes now is an ideal time to introduce us to the customs and begin the transition of trusting the next Kenningston generation."

The information isn't surprising nor is it comforting.

"Perhaps for the summer-"

"Don't bother," I mumble under my breath while climbing into the vehicle.

"Kellan-"

"I should go."

Swiss wastes no time starting the engine and easing us into the surprisingly empty street.

"Kellan-"

"I actually do need to go, Kristopher." My eyes cut out the window to the various mixture of people strolling by. I let my attention roam over a couple sitting outside at the corner coffee shop, and the instant the winter wind kicks up, he immediately tugs her in closer to keep her warm. To *provide* for her. The simple yet powerful action successfully springs a smile to my face.

My father used to do that to my mother all the time when I was little. All he ever wanted was to protect her. Kris used to tell me stories of how horrible he was when she was pregnant with me. The way he had to be the one to tend to her needs. How all that mattered to him was her happiness. Not the crown. Not his social expectations. Not even the disapproval of his father for putting mum's health needs above his own. Eventually, the overwhelming need to care for her, transferred to us. At least until she died. Then he managed to return to the Kenningston tradition of being a shitty parent.

After a long stretch of silence, Kristopher quietly states, "You never mentioned who you were going out with tonight."

His voice takes me slightly off-guard since I thought I had already hung up. "What?"

"Your date. Who is she?"

"An art student."

There's an odd shuffling noise before he snaps, "What?!"

His surprise returns my haughty smirk.

At least I know I'll always matter to my big brother. Better than nothing.

"Did you…Did you make a bet on this woman?"

"Why do people keep assuming that?"

"Because why else would you go with an *art student*? You literally had a Hollywood starlet in your bed a week ago."

"Had her on her knees, too, but I don't hear you mentioning that."

There's a low groan from the other end of the phone.

I chuckle just as the sight of her apartment complex comes into view. "Sleep well, big brother. I have a date to please."

"Stay out of the papers, Kellan."

"No promises."

After ending the call, I lean closer to the window in an attempt to get a better look at the figure who appears to be waiting outside of her building. With one hand still on the wheel, Swiss begins to reach for his weapon and commands, "Sir, be prepared to-"

All of a sudden, the person begins to frantically wave, and I can't help but smile.

Swiss quickly arrives at the same conclusion I have, parks alongside the curb, and unlocks the doors. Before he has a chance to offer, I give him a small pat on the shoulder to let him know I can handle opening her door.

You're damn right I'm a gentleman.

The moment the door is open, I immediately drink in the face and figure I've been thinking about constantly.

Hey, it's difficult not to. She's absolutely beautiful. Even in jeans and a sweater she manages to enslave my attention. It doesn't matter that they're faded with paint stains and a couple of

holes. Do you see how they hug her hips? Expose the curves down below? How the hell could anyone resist wanting to peel those off? Then there's the fitted tight black top. The way it's clinging to her ample chest that she doesn't want just anyone exploring with their eyes or hands. That's definitely a change of pace from the women I typically come across. However, nothing beats the playful smile plastered on her face. Looking at that? Well, it feels like I'm home. Oh, God. This is exactly why I should never talk to Kristopher directly prior to a date. He's making me soft.

I fold my arms defensively across my chest. "I'm feeling a tad bit overdressed."

Brie simply smiles. "You're on time. I'm impressed."

With a shrug, I state, "You strike me as the type of woman who would have considered one minute over, one minute too late."

"Smart man."

"A compliment? That's new."

"Rest assured. I won't make a habit of it."

We exchange taunting smirks and stifled snickers.

"Why are you waiting outside?" I wave a hand towards the vehicle for her to get in. "It's not very warm out."

Brie slides her body past mine at the same time she says, "Rather get pneumonia than have my roommate and her boyfriend meet you."

I shut the door once we're both settled inside. "You're embarrassed to be seen with me?"

"Yes."

"That's a first."

"Don't worry," she softly starts, hand stretching over to give my leg a gentle pat, "I'm sure there'll be a second."

The comment causes Swiss to chuckle as well as me.

Why an art student? Because she's more fun than any of the other women I've gone out with and we've only been on this date for two minutes.

My bodyguard glances over his shoulder. "Where are we headed to, miss?"

"The Tervin Event Center. Do you know where that is?"

He nods, turns back around, and puts the car in drive.

"How'd you do on your test?" I ask receiving a surprised look in return. When she doesn't answer or explain why the expression, I add another question. "Did I say something wrong already?"

"Just…kinda shocked you remembered."

"Why wouldn't I?"

"I don't know…Maybe because you probably have more important things to think about like running a country or something?"

"Titles and bullshit, remember?"

"I just assumed you were being over-simplistic."

"I wasn't," I sigh, anxious to switch subject matters. "Besides, that test was the only reason you allowed me to save you in your moment of crisis."

Her gag makes me snicker. "Pretty sure you *caused* my random moment of crisis."

Honestly didnit. Luck was just on my side. Probably pre-paying me back for my father denying my proposal. Again.

"No. Just benefited."

"Just blackmailed," she bites back.

After another small laugh, I ask again, "The test? How'd you do?"

"Wondering if you're on a date with someone who only does well because of a different kind of brain?"

The sexual implication has my mind turning in that direction despite the fact I know she's still just trolling for a fight. "Do you? Are you *head* of the class?"

Her jaw drops. "How dare you-"

"Defend myself?" I angle my body so that my back is braced against the window, and we're face-to-face. "Don't get me wrong, Brie. I appreciate anyone who can deliver a gut check as well as they take one, but you're aiming for the boys – unprovoked might I add – and that's not quite fair."

She presses her lips firmly together to suppress a response.

"I know you think I'm a royal asshole-"

"So far so true-"

"But there's a little more to me than that." Seeing her shoulders drop in retreat, I add, "Keep the punches coming, love, but at least make the fight just."

Her heavily guarded nature makes every triumph I have so much more worth it. Half the fun is in the arguing and the other is in proving her wrong. Then again, I like being proven wrong as well. Unlike the others I've dabbled with, she's engaging a part of me that doesn't get much attention outside of my brother and Sophia's verbal lashes.

And Sophia can cut words with the best of them.

A small lull passes before she states, "I think I passed."

Unexpected success swells my chest. "What was it on?"

"Boring art crap," she snips. "Paraphrasing for you. You know, since all art is dreadful."

The mocking of my accent grabs a chuckle from me. "Was that your best accent? What'd you do? Spend the afternoon watching Chris Hemsworth films only to realize too late he's Aussie and nowhere near Doctenn?"

Brie's expression oscillates between frustration and fluster. "My accent wasn't that bad!"

"It was *horrific*."

"It wasn't!"

"It was almost as if you had a pup's chew toy wedged in your mouth and were trying to talk around it."

She immediately leans over and pegs me in the arm.

"Ou!"

"Be thankful it was *above* the belt."

It didn't actually hurt, but I am surprised she hit me. Can't say I've had a female take a swing at me since my last year in lacrosse with my own lacrosse stick at that. Long story there. Short lesson? Don't shag flatmates – during the same week – without their permission.

"You struck royalty."

"I struck *you*."

"I technically *am* royalty."

"You're more like *diet* royalty. It doesn't count," her retort gets us both laughing again.

After another shake of the head, I inquire, "What was the test over?"

"Art History of the Renaissance Era. This was just a basic name to philosophies test."

"You're right. That would bore me." When she scowls once more, I lightly chuckle in response. "To be fair, I'm not a fan of *any* sort of history. Art or otherwise."

"Shocking," Brie mocks. "What do you like then? Besides sports."

"How did you-"

"Lucky frat boy, mindless jock kinda guess," she sneers.

"I enjoy music. Occasionally, the theatre."

"How about on a more intellectual level?"

"Environmental effects on adolescents."

Her mouth becomes agape yet again.

I do enjoy having her make that face and not only because I enjoy the idea of sliding my cock between her lips.

Pleased with myself, I glance out the window just as we pull into the line at the event center. My eyes read and reread the sign repeatedly. Certain we're in the wrong area or at least on the wrong night, I turn to allow our eyes to meet. "Monster Truck Mayhem? We're going to monster truck show?"

She battles the urge to smile. "Problem?"

I glance down at my attire and state, "You said, dress to impress."

"Yes. But I never specified *who* your attire would need to impress." Her expression becomes victorious. "Next time I advise you to get *all* the information before making wardrobe choices."

Swiss pulls up to the parking lot attendant who immediately asks for payment. Brie makes a motion to reach in her pocket when I cease her movements. "I've got it." After handing Swiss cash from my own wallet, I state to her, "This game isn't over." Shedding my suit jacket, I drape it over the seat between us. "And since you don't play fair, neither shall I."

"Was that a threat?"

"It was a warning."

"Semantics again."

She's thrown a narrowed-eyed gaze that causes her eyes to flash a mesh of intrigue and excitement. Her attention drops to where I'm adjusting the sleeves of my white button-down shirt and does a terrible job at not drinking in my every move.

For fucks sake, do not remind me how* ridiculous *I look at this moment. I do wish I had different shoes above all else. These wing tips will be absolutely ruined.* Ruined. *If you'll excuse me, I have revenge to be plotting on this beautiful, brilliant albeit diabolical woman.

"I've only got two tickets." Her announcement shifts Swiss in his seat. "There might be more tickets available but-"

"It's fine," I end the conversation before it can get the direction it was headed. "Swiss can wait in the vehicle. This isn't exactly a high threat situation. Other than the fact I'm wearing a St. Valmonte suit at a monster truck show, I highly doubt anyone will give me a second glance."

My bodyguard's mouth cracks open to argue yet sees the stern expression on my face in his rearview and closes it.

Swiss, while terrifying – you can see his physical appearance – happens to be remarkably understanding. He's mastered the art of reading a situation and declaring if my request for space is acceptable or to be ignored. Most of the time, we agree on how to handle my public presence. He rarely pulls the "your father decrees" card. God, I wish I could burn that ace in the deck.

"I'll have my phone. If I need anything, I'll call."

"Don't worry, Army Man." Brie leans forward towards him. "I won't let him wander into the middle of the arena to get run over or anything. Even if a big part of me *does* want that."

He resists the urge to laugh but gives into the one to smile.

Not sure I enjoy them being on a team against me.

Swiss drops the two of us as close to the entrance of the event center as possible.

The moment we're headed towards the doors, Brie asks, "Does it bother you to constantly have a babysitter? I mean you clearly need one-"

"*Clearly.*"

"-but does it ever irritate you? Does it ever annoy the hell out of you that you can't just walk around the grocery store without an extra pair of eyes on you?"

Her odd phrasing kicks up the corner of my lip. "You get used to it."

"Ah. But that was not the question. *See.* You really are a terrible listener."

"I'm a fantastic listener. How else would I know the difference in your breathing when you're flustered with me versus when you're fantasizing about me."

Brie pins me with a disgusted look.

"You do get used to it. And honestly, it hardly even registers anymore. I've had security details since I was in diapers, so, no it doesn't bother me. They're sort of like family after a while, and as you can see, you develop a relationship that allows an amount of respectable space when the time is needed. Believe me, having Swiss around is much better than Vincent, the guard I've been ditching since I was fifteen. He's *rarely* as understanding."

"God, I can't imagine constantly having a ghost over my shoulder."

"It's one thing to become accustomed to it and completely another when you don't know anything else."

Guards and details are mundane accessories at this point in my existence. From daily activities in the outside world to dating, they've never really registered as an issue. With that said, the women I've spent the majority of my time around also have their own eyes and ears lurking at the wayside. Brie's not the first, but she is one of the few who aren't under a watchful stare. Yes, I'm sure in some subconscious part of my brain I enjoy that fact.

At the doors, Brie presents them with her phone where she has the tickets waiting to be scanned. Afterward, the oversized woman gives my attire a long, strange gaze yet keeps her opinion to herself and motions for us to move along.

Once we're inside, I question, "Which way?"

"We're gonna head to the left, but first I'm going to get something to eat. I'm starving." She glances over her shoulder at me. "And you're probably going to want to pick up some earbuds. Shit gets pretty loud."

"You don't need any?"

She smugly smiles. "I came prepared."

The urge for payback aggressively increases. "I'm going to go snag a pair. I'll meet you in line?"

She nods and migrates towards the closest concession stand. Quicker than I expect, I manage to purchase a pair of earplugs and maneuver my way back into the line where Brie seems to be unable to decide what she wants by the expression on her face.

"So, what are we having for our first date?" I ask, shoving the objects into my pocket.

"*Only date*," she mumbles her correction prior to letting her eyes gravitate to mine. "You like nachos?"

I give the list of toppings a read. "Over processed liquid cheese, beans from a can, and questionable beef. What's not to like?" When the queue begins to move, allowing us to order, I add, "It's all fine. Just no jalapeños."

Our eyes meet again. "You allergic?"

"No."

Brie turns back to the woman waiting and states, "One order of Monster nachos, monster-size with *extra* jalapenos."

How did I miss that coming?

"One monster order of popcorn. And two glasses of water." She leans over and drops her voice to an exaggerated whisper. "As you can see, someone is clearly trying to watch their figure."

The head motion in my direction makes the workers behind the counter laugh alongside the couple behind us.

"Twenty-two dollars even," the woman announces, which is when Brie looks at me.

Promptly, I question, "You don't expect me to pay, do you? Did Mistress Lacey forget to mention that all accommodations during my service are to be paid for by the client renting my time?"

Brie's eyes enlarge as it seems she's rendered speechless.

"Escorts don't pay for their own meals," I pretend to be in shock. Suddenly, I say to those that are listening, "Was it not obvious? I mean why else would someone wear something *like this* to an event? Miscommunication between her and my employer." The eavesdroppers nod their understanding, and I let my eyes meet Brie's enraged ones. "*Obviously.*"

Her bafflement remains, yet the cashier speaks again. "Ma'am. That'll be twenty-two dollars."

Brie glares at me one final time, turns towards the woman, pulls out cash from her pocket, and offers it. After returning her change, the workers behind the counter hands us our refreshments. Laughs clearly trying to be contained under their breaths.

The moment we're no longer in line, she mutters in an irked tone, *"Un-fucking believable."*

"Says the woman who tricked me into wearing a four-thousand-dollar suit to a bloody truck show."

"A little different than convincing total strangers I paid for you!"

Seeing the frustration on her face forces a smile back onto mine. "Told you it would not be fair."

Brie abruptly stops, looks up at me, and growls, "This isn't over, Duke Douchebag."

"Would not dream of it, Vanessa van Gogh Duch Yourself."

The sassy expression I crave reappears. "Not sure what's more ludicrous, the fact you think for even a moment I would ever wanna be duchess, or the fact you could turn a famous artist into an *almost* clever insult." Brie hums to herself and starts walking again. "Come on. We're right around the corner."

I adjust my grip on the popcorn and follow cheerfully behind her.

You didn't seriously think she was that upset over what I did, did you? Ha. I haven't even known this girl that long yet knew

that was nowhere near the line of too far. Rest easily; I wouldn't go there. The enjoyment is not found in hurting her. Come on. A little faith here. I'm not a **monster.**

During our climb up three levels of stairs for the top row, we're bumped into by out-of-control kids trying to drive their toy trucks, over-enthusiastic fans who are already slightly inebriated, and displeased ushers having to constantly redirect people to their actual seats as opposed to the ones they wished were theirs.

They are just very large vehicles. People can't truly be this excited, can they?

Brie drops herself down into the end seat, and I sit in the one beside her.

Unable to resist teasing, I sigh with false concern, "Should I have bought gum? You know, to help keep our ears from popping at such high altitudes?"

She gives me a phony smirk. "Keep it up and your dry-cleaning bill will be almost as ridiculously priced as the suit itself."

I reach for a chip, shaking the jalapenos free. "So, who were these tickets originally for?"

"My dad," Brie answers, a bit of sadness in her tone. "They were a Christmas present from me. Actually, they were his *only* Christmas present from me. It's not like I have a shit ton of extra cash laying around, so I saved and grabbed the best ones I could. I know they don't feel like much, but they weren't cheap."

After swallowing my bite, I investigate, "Why couldn't he come?"

"Had to work. Someone called in, and he had to cover."

"And what is it he does for a living?"

"Grocery store manager. Nothing glamorous like being king of a country, but people still need him. Too much sometimes."

The snide comment isn't missed, but I don't take the bait to fight back.

Told you. Not about hurting her. It's about humoring.

"You two close?" I question finally receiving her attention on me.

"You could say that." Her smile softens. "Two daughters and one takes after his beer and cheeseburger loving ways while the other takes after our mother with her love of Sushi and spritzers."

"Glad you're the 'All American' girl."

She snickers before she asks, "Why? You're not into the other type?"

"I'm into you."

My comment causes a small flush to her face.

Rather than continue the conversation in the direction she's anticipating, I reach for another chip. "You're the younger one, aren't you?"

A playful smile forms.

"I bet you were trouble growing up."

She leans forward and whispers, "Still. Am."

My eyes steal a glimpse of her wet lips and longingly whisper, "*Obviously...*"

Brie winks reaches into my lap for the popcorn and throws a handful at me. She starts laughing, and I immediately join her, tossing a handful at her in return. All of a sudden, a man takes the spot in the center of the arena while the announcer over the speakers indicates the show is about to begin.

With my eyes plastered forward once more to admire the dirt-covered area, I ask, "And what exactly am I supposed to do here?"

"Yell and scream when they do cool shit. Pretty basic. You know. Like you."

I give her another glance, which is when she winks. "Is there a particular car-"

"*Truck*."

"That you prefer we cheer harder for?"

"My dad's favorite is The Blue Devil."

"Blue Devil for my brown-eyed devil it is." The remark tugs the corners of her lips upward as she turns back around.

The host begins his opening speech, and I wiggle free my earplugs in preparation. My attention helplessly swings between the pending event and the playful woman obnoxiously flicking popcorn in my direction. The behavior is childish, yet I can't stop myself from responding to it. Tossing pieces into the bun high on her head. Smearing cheese on her glasses for smearing some on my pants. Turning the jalapeños into hockey pucks inside the nacho container. By the time the show is actually starting, we're covered in what should've been dinner and laughing so hard my side hurts.

This is exactly the opposite of growing up like Kristopher wants. But where's the real harm in food fighting and laughing with someone who is enjoying the moment just as much as you are? Why do "adult dates" have to consist of meals with hefty price tags and conversations about politics that neither of you really care about? Shouldn't life be enjoyed as long as no one is getting harmed?

For the next eighty minutes, Brie and I are on the edge of our seats, hollering at mind-blowing heights reached, high fiving over the total destruction of vehicles, and swatting each other's hands out of the way during attempts made to grab more food. Between the special effects to enhance the show and crowd participation to make us all feel like we're a part of the event, too, it barely registers how quickly time has flown. As the evening's final song plays and people begin to move towards the exits, it strikes me like a sharp stab in the side, just how much I don't want this to end.

Not yet.

Brie stands, dusts off the remaining popcorn, and cheerfully squeaks, "That was awesome!"

Her enthusiasm is enthralling. "I couldn't agree more! When the one that looked like a dinosaur-"

"Dinomite."

Don't look at me like that. I didn't name the damn thing.

"Yes. That one. That particular moment it looked like he was going to end up backward then didn't-"

"Ohmygod, right!" She shakes her hands in excitement. "That was so scary!"

"I absolutely agree."

Brie offers me another smile before stating, "We should get out of here. Parking lot's gonna be a bitch to get through."

"Right…," I reluctantly reply.

Our stares momentarily lock, and to my surprise, the longing in her eyes matches mine.

Perhaps she doesn't want this night to end, either?

"I'll send Swiss a message once we're outside and some of the crowd has begun to fade. Make his job less difficult to reach us." Hopeful, I add, "That is if you don't mind waiting."

Brie slips her hands into her back pockets. "I don't mind. It's really not as 'frigid' out there as you think."

Her poor attempt at an accent scrunches my face. "You have got to stop that. It's like nails on a chalkboard."

She gives me the finger.

"Not on the first date." I join her in a standing position. "Not even if you beg."

"Who would," she scoffs and spins around on her heels to start for the stairs.

"You'd be surprised."

"I wouldn't." Unexpectedly, Brie stops and turns to me. "And you're full of shit. You would totally sleep with a chick on the first date."

"Never said I wouldn't."

"You just did!"

"No…" I insist, physically catching up to her. "I implied I wouldn't with *you*."

Watching the internal debate over the notion of it being a compliment or insult merely makes me smile wider.

It's obvious which it is.

Brie starts to speak but immediately decides against it. Instead, she turns back around and continues our descent towards the rest of the crowd filtering out of the venue. While the process to get to our seats was difficult, the one to get out of the building itself is twice as hard. Between the over-hyped and over-exhausted, the crowd seems easily unstable. During our attempt to make it to the outside door, someone shoves past Brie, knocking her body into mine. Instinctively, my hand tugs her closer into my protection. I swallow the urge to smile at the action. With her tightly at my side, I slip us smoothly through the gaps, eventually guiding us to freedom.

Outside, I lead us to one of the nearby picnic tables where we park ourselves with our butts on the table and feet on the bench.

"That was a nightmare," Brie huffs in exasperation.

"It's just the end of the night. People are tired. Cranky. Ready to get home so that they are able to have some rest before work in the morning."

She groans at the word.

"What do you do for work?"

Brie hesitates to answer. "I'm a lunch lady at a private school."

She's…kidding. Is this a weird American joke that I don't understand?

Her eyes meet mine. "Seriously."

I press my fist to my mouth to block the chuckle.

"Oh…Shut up," she bites. "Not all of us are just paid to be pretty and social. Some of us actually have to work for what they have."

Now the defensive one, I counter, "I work for what I have, too. Make no mistake about that. Handouts may come with my name, but that doesn't mean I take them."

Silence falls between the two of us as our attention shifts elsewhere.

Well. That went poorly.

I give the back of my neck a small rub and attempt to make amends. "For the record, you're the hottest lunch lady I've ever met."

Brie lets out a small giggle. "I'm probably the *only* lunch lady you've ever met."

"No. I grew up in boarding school. I've met and learned to love my fair share of lunch ladies."

The word seems to part her lips in surprise.

Not that I was indicating I am in love with her. I'm obviously not in love with her. I can't be in love with someone after a single date. I mean I – Well, I – You see I – Hm. How do my conversations keep taking wrong turns tonight? With you, but more importantly, **with Brie.** *Is this a normal date problem to have because I've never had it before now. Before her.*

"Do you wear a hairnet?" I tease, thankful when her demeanor changes again. "Tell me, this. Is it pink?"

"Did they spit in your mashed potatoes and call it gravy? Because I would."

A laugh escapes and I retort, "No. They adored me. I'm quite charming."

"Yeah, you keep saying that."

"Because it's true."

Brie attempts to argue with a straight face. "To the rest of the world maybe…"

My eyebrows lift in curiosity. "But not to you?"

Her bottom lip momentarily slips between her teeth. She hums softly and turns away, her sweet refusal to answer endearing.

"I'm in town for until next Sunday-"

"So you've mentioned," she interjects, her attention pasted on the honking vehicles that are poorly moving around the parking lot.

"And I want to see you again." This time her stare moves to mine. "Have dinner with me tomorrow night?"

"Why…? Are you plotting some weird payback thing for the unconventional plans I made tonight?"

"Actually no," I promptly deny. "Tonight was honestly more fun than I've had in a really long time."

Sounds like a line, but I swear it isn't. Sex and gambling are definitely entertaining, but not quite like this. This was effortless. The smiles were genuine and not liquor coerced. Our conversations and laughs were innocent, not an attempt at manipulation to get something out of one another. It was all rather refreshing.

"You should get out more," she teases on another laugh.

"Probably." One more snicker slips between us. "So, what do you think? Dinner tomorrow night?"

Brie battles what I assume is the desire to say yes.

I'll admit. It's part of the turn on. I've never met a woman quite so determined to tell me no all the time. To crave the creation of a challenge for the sake of capability. Yes. I like a challenge as much as the next asshole with a list of names to cross off, but this is different. This is so much more than some chick who is pretending not to be interested. She has me actually convinced at times she's not. At others? It's impossible to deny. This woman makes me mad, and I crave it.

Suddenly, she shouts, "No! You can't keep borrowing my makeup and then not returning it! I don't care how hot the guy is! If he really loves you for you, he'll love you without it."

Okay…I don't crave that.

Eyes from the dispersing crowd direct themselves in our direction. Some sets are disapproving others are comedically surprised.

With a heavy sigh, I look back at Brie just as she smiles brightly. "We can do dinner tomorrow night."

"Oh, you can't pay for a date, but I'm clearly gay?"

"*Clearly.*" She playfully winks. "I mean…have you seen your suit?"

Her infectious smile makes me shake my head. "You can sleep easy tonight. I'll make sure to find my own mascara to wear for tomorrow's date."

"Good," she giggles again. "Should I wear mine, too?"

"If you want." I shrug. "Won't tell you what to wear, just advise you that it won't be a pint and cheeseburgers."

Brie smiles seconds before my cellphone begins to vibrate with a call from Swiss.

I answer only to immediately receive an ear full for not letting him know we were out sooner. His tantrum, however, falls on deaf ears. My eyes linger in Brie's, thankful she agreed to see me again.

I've only got nine days until I fly out. Eight, now that this one is over. I plan to occupy as much of my time with her as she'll let me. Doubt she'll make it easy, which will just make it more fun. My brother should worry less about my face in the papers and more about the art student effortlessly conquering my thoughts.

CHAPTER SIX

I place the curling iron down on the counter and give my reflection one final look.

"Pretty good," my mother says proudly.

Right? Not the greatest when it comes to the whole wavy hair, shape your face look, but I think I nailed it this time.

"Now, who is the guy that's worth all this trouble?"

I drop my focus back to the cellphone screen where we are video chatting.

"He's not worth any trouble."

He's not! This…This whole thing is merely my way of showcasing to him what he wants but can't have.

"He has to be."

"No, he doesn't."

"Yes, he does, Brie. I can't remember the last time you went on a date or really can't remember the last time you *cared enough* to do more with your hair than a simple updo for one."

Blow back of having a hair genie for a mother. Constantly criticized for my love of the basic ponytail and easy bun. By the way, both are always in style!

I quickly devise a way to avoid further interrogation on the subject. Calling out to no one, I question. "What's that?" After a small pause, I look back into the camera with a sympathetic look. "Sorry, mom. Gotta go. Jovi needs help bringing in the groceries."

"She does not," my mother sighs. "You're as bad as your father about faking distractions." She offers me a sweet smile on an amused headshake. "Whoever he is, I hope you enjoy yourself."

"Thanks, Mom."

"See you tomorrow for dinner?"

"Yeah."

"Good. You can tell me *allllll* about him then." She winks and ends the call before I can argue.

No need to inform me that I got traits from both of my parents. I'm aware.

I prepare to drop my cellphone back onto my bathroom counter when I notice an unread text.

Prince One-Night Stand: Change of plans. Sending a car to pick you up.

Me: Attire the same?

Prince One-Night Stand: Clothing is always OPTIONAL.

I roll my eyes at the text.

Problem is at times I want it to be optional. How pathetic am I?! Almost everything out of his mouth is coated in arrogance or makes him sound like the pompous asshole we both know he is. For some reason though, I can't resist not only the urge to knock him down a few pegs but getting to know the man he is once he's there. The one I imagine the rest of the world doesn't know exists. The one I doubt would interest them if they did. And before you start down that path, no. I don't have the whole let the bad boy change for me complex most women phase through at some point in their lives. I just enjoy us going tit for tat. Most of my conversations with the attractive members of the opposite sex are spent walking on eggshells in an attempt to get asked out at all, or

– once I've got the date – to prevent them from shutting down completely when they realize I'm not putting out on the first night. Like it's a crime to not want to have some random stranger poking around down there, doing his best to prove he's got talent? Or that he's got stamina. Or whatever skill the last girl who dumped him said he didn't have. Ha. Do men think women carry baggage? Nothing is worse than a guy trying to outperform his past self because someone he slept with faked an orgasm.

My phone vibrates again with another message.

Prince One-Night Stand: How hard did you roll your pretty brown eyes?

Compliments shouldn't go hand and hand with his impressive ability to annoy me.

Me: Hard enough to reconsider this dinner.

Prince One-Night Stand: Liar.

I begin typing a reply when he beats me to it.

Prince One Nightstand: At least I'm HOPING you are.

Don't swoon when he says shit like that! This is why I have a problem staying away from him. He's like a mosquito bite that I can't resist itching no matter how hard I try. A bug bite with a sexy as sin accent. Ugh.

Prince One-Night Stand: See you soon.

I drop the phone back on the counter and retreat to my roommate's room. I stumble out in the living room and am immediately startled when I see her and her boyfriend relaxing on the couch with a show about classic cars.

Merrick grunts, "That's barely fucking vintage."

Jovi turns the page in the book she's reading completely careless of his ramblings.

I stroll further into the space and sigh, "Merrick, you do know the people on the television can't hear you, right? When they talk, they're not talking directly to you."

He doesn't bother looking away. "That's a good thing because if they did, I'd tell them to take that piece of shit and-"

Jovi nudges him in the side at the same time she looks at me. "Ohmygod...Your hair looks *amazing*."

I strike a pretend proud pose. "Thanks."

"Can you do mine?"

"Nope. This took me sacrificing a goat and two pairs of Chucks to accomplish."

"Like a *real* goat?" Merrick nervously questions.

The two of us giggle at him as much as my snarky joke.

He continues to gawk on in curiosity, yet she questions, "Going somewhere important?"

If you must know Dr. Judgey, I was not being a bad friend by not telling her sooner. Just didn't think Kellan was worth mentioning since this is a one-time thing. No. No. Not a one-night stand. Not a one-night slumber party. Not even a one-night rub under the table. I'm not the type of woman who is okay just being a drive-thru stop and bone if you get what I'm painting here.

"I...have a date."

Suddenly, Merrick's expression shifts to surprise while Jovi slams her book shut. She very slowly, very carefully investigates, "A what?"

"A date."

"With another person?" Merrick chimes in.

I give him a sharp glare.

"Forgive him," his girlfriend quietly insists. "He's just in shock. Like me."

"Why are you two in shock?"

"You don't date," they speak in unison like a well-rehearsed sitcom.

They do that more often than people in real life should. It's one of their many disgustingly adorable traits.

Folding my arms across my chest, I argue, "I do, too."

"No, you don't," my best friend immediately argues.

"Yes, I do."

"In the years we've been friends, I've known you to go on three dates." Jovi pins me with a stern look then repeats. "*Three.*"

Uncomfortable with the acknowledgment of my lack of love life, I snip. "You kept count?"

"Preschoolers can count that high," Merrick backs her.

"Well, that explains your ability to follow the conversation."

He prepares to snip back when she lifts a hand to stop him. "It's fine that you don't date, Brie. I always assumed between studying, working, and hanging out with us, you just…didn't have the time."

The truth in her statement causes me to shift my weight.

That's a huge part of it. Dating doesn't exactly fit in when you're working two part-time jobs just to make sure you can afford rent, groceries, and tuition. Still. Hearing my lack of social life isn't erasing any of the woes related to my pending graduation. I don't even have anything in that department to look forward to when they finally stop billing me to learn.

"So, who is he?" She gleefully questions.

"He is…a passing moment," I declare in an uncertain voice.

It's not because I'm stupid enough to believe he's not. It's because the truth is all men who stroll into my existence in that aspect are. Guess I'm really no better than Kellan in that nature. At least they don't all make it into my bed like I know they do his.

"A passing moment," she repeats in a skeptical tone.

"Yes. Now, do you mind if I borrow one of your dresses? I'm pretty sure I can squeeze into one."

She gives me a sarcastic stare. "Squeeze into one? We're practically the same size."

Sweet little thing, I know. My hips are wider, and my boobs are bigger, but occasionally, we can successfully share clothes. Particularly, if they stretch.

Instead of starting a new argument, I state, "I'll take that as a yes."

Jovi nods, and I head for her bedroom at the same Merrick grumps, "Seriously, Brie. Who is this guy?"

Hearing his big brother's tone makes me smile.

He may be younger than me, but he has no problem letting his inner protective older brother quality shine bright.

Once I'm in her room, I make my way over to her closest, not answering his question.

"Does he go to the university?" Merrick's voice gets louder.

"Is he a professor?" Jovi follows.

"Why would she date a professor?" He suspiciously asks. "That's against policy."

"This from the ultimate rule bender."

"Breaker."

"How is that better?"

It's not. Just funnier.

"It means I'm better."

There's a small pause before she says, "Cocky."

"Confident."

I let their flirting fade from my ears as I thumb through her clothes until I spot the dress, I've had my eye on since she first bought it.

I couldn't afford it. Glad at least one of us could bring this baby home.

With the delicate article in my hands, I walk back to her bedroom door, shut it, and begin to change out of my lounge clothes into it.

"Are either of us right?" Jovi asks frustration now in her voice.

I wiggle into the long sleeve, black lace dress. "No."

"Ha!" Merrick triumphantly shouts.

There's a low murmured comeback too quiet to decipher.

Probably a sex threat.

After ditching my bra for not cooperating with the plunging neckline, I crack the door and call to Jovi. "Can you come zip me, please?"

She gives her boyfriend one final scold and rushes over.

The moment it's zipped, I give everything an additional adjustment, equally impressive and thankful it fits like a dream.

Jovi steps back and smiles brightly. "I really like that dress on you. The way the cream color on the body of the dress compliments your skin is insane. You look gorgeous! Like you're glowing. You know what? You should add a pair of gold earrings."

"Good call." I swoop up my clothes into my arms. "Black shoes, though?"

She nods while moving out of my way.

Merrick instantly croaks. "That's *your dress*, baby?"

"Yeah."

His eyes flash an emotion I'm all too familiar with prior to him giving me a hard look. "Keep it." Jovi squeaks behind me, but he repeats, "Keep it. No one should ever see my girl in something like that."

As the two of us approach his direction, she whispers, "They've seen me in less."

"Don't remind me," he grouses and yanks her into his lap.

"Jealous."

"Protective."

"Overly."

The sound of their argument stops, yet I continue towards my room, desperate to get away from the foreplay in motion.

*When's the last time I had foreplay in my life? Does arguing count as foreplay? Because by that measurement, Kellan and I should be rounding third base any second now. I wonder if Sir Notch in My Bedpost is even remotely as good as he thinks he is. I know I have no right to even ponder over that but come on. He is **extremely** attractive, plus he has this wolfish stare when his eyes caress my curves, which has me wishing like hell the man whore reputation I assume he has from the Google search he flashed me yesterday, is over-exaggerated. I know it's not. Hell, he hasn't even tried to deny it once. Guess that's why wishing for the opposite is pointless.*

After rummaging around my bathroom drawers for earrings, I give my reflection one last look.

Not too bad for the art student who's spent the last ten years so focused on trying to graduate so she basically has no life. Well...Here's to hoping dinner does a good job of helping me forget that little fact for a few hours.

The ride in an upscale town car to The Frost Luxury Hotel is smooth and soothing. While the drive isn't long, it manages to give me enough time to collect my composure and convince myself to just enjoy the evening. The date. The brief moment of possible romance waiting to be appreciated.

Inside the hotel, I'm immediately greeted by a woman who insists I follow her to meet Kellan. The two of us take a private elevator hidden towards the back. On our way up, she explains a little history about the hotel, how they frequently cater to those who desire discretion, and how her service is only provided for those staying in the penthouse suite.

Doubt she's actively trying to make me feel like the hooker reserved for the billionaire, but that's what's happening. The last thing this night needed was me feeling like an updated version of Juliet Roberts in Pretty Woman.

We arrive outside a set of double doors where Swiss is on duty.

"Army Man," I warmly greet.

"Miss Brie," he says with a nod before cracking the door open to grant me access inside.

I slide past him and step foot into a jaw-dropping surprise. The dimmed room is filled with lit candles from wall to wall. Most are along the edges on the floor, but there is a pair on the round table that appears to be set for two. My eyes admire the other little touches of intended romance, like the chilling bottle of what I assume is champagne in the ice bucket. The sprinkled rose petals on the ground. The white curtains pulled back to expose the gorgeous view of the city at night.

Okay…now, I'm feeling a lot less like Julia Roberts and a little too real-life pretty, pretty princess for my own good.

Soft jazz music saunters through my ears only seconds before a sharp, clean, enticing smell floods my system. Kellan nervously whispers over my shoulder, "You like it?"

I fight the instinct to melt from the sound of his voice.

Thank God I'm not wearing underwear. They wouldn't stand a chance.

"Is this why you didn't pick me up?" I ask as he moves into my line of vision. "You were too busy trying to burn down a hotel to impress me?"

Kellan lightly chuckles, slides a hand in his black suit pants pocket, and says, "Are you impressed?"

Don't answer for me!

"Depends," I start slowly, giving his eyes a minute to finish worshiping me. "How many other women do you go through this much effort for?"

He doesn't hesitate. "None."

"Bullshit."

His eyes hold mine so harshly it's almost hard to breathe. "I don't have to *try* with others, Brie. They simply trip or slip into my sheets and that's that."

I sarcastically sneer, "*Aw, how romantic.*"

"It doesn't have to be," he defensively declares. "You judge me for merely enjoying the given situations. But it's a two-person process. I make no false claims or promises to those who wander into my bed. No delusions of grandeur. No implications that it is anything more than the moment we're sharing. Expectations conjured up on their own is not my doing. I'm an adult who appreciates sex between consenting adults. There's no harm in that."

He has a fair point. It just so happens I am not *that type*.

Rather than admit he's right, I question, "So, all this is just a huge effort to get me into the sack?"

A look of sadness graces his expression. "Is that the only thing you can imagine I'm interested in?"

"Convince me otherwise," I state sharply.

Kellan's eyes dip down the front of my dress before the corners of his lips pull upward. "With pleasure."

Not a phrase he should say. Nope. Not with that accent. Because now all I want is to join the very list I shamed him for having.

He extends his open palm for me to take. "Shall we?" The moment my hand is in his, he compliments, "You look beautiful, by the way. I would've said something sooner, but you were busy scolding me for saving this date."

I allow him to lead us to the table. "How was it ruined?"

"Originally, I made the reservation for us at this bistro a few blocks over," he begins while helping me into my seat. "Somehow, they double booked me and someone else, so the options were to cancel or wait until eleven for dinner." Kellan sits in the seat across from mine. "Rather than risk the chance of giving you an out, I arranged this with the help of the concierge."

"Why not just pick a different restaurant?"

"I did. The five-star one attached to the hotel."

Curiosity leans me back in my seat. "Then why aren't we just eating there?"

"Seemed like a smarter idea to eliminate possible pawns in our ongoing game of who can humiliate who."

A small snicker proceeds my whispered words, "*Well played.*"

Kellan smirks proudly.

And damn that's a good look.

As he reaches for the chilling bottle, I ask, "Is there a menu for me to look at, or am I just supposed to trust your judgment?"

He uncorks it. "Would that be so terrible?"

"Yes."

"I don't think you could have possibly answered any faster."

"I could try."

Kellan smirks again.

"Seriously though, how can I trust a man who can't even eat jalapeños on his nachos?"

"I *can*. I don't *like to*. There's a difference."

"Not really hearing one." When he lifts his eyes to mine, I make a silly face that receives a chuckle. "Do you even have nachos in your country?"

"Something similar," he informs at the same time he fills my glass. "They're made with pita bread chips, mashed chickpeas, melted Swiss cheese and topped with olives."

I gag. "I think I threw up in my mouth a little bit there."

He shakes his head, fills his own glass, and returns the bottle to its container. "It's actually quite delicious, especially with a pint."

"Nothing out of your mouth sounded remotely delicious."

"Not even olives?"

"Olives are like reject jalapeños."

All of a sudden, the playful disagreement is interrupted by the concierge who is approaching with a tray full of dishes. Gracefully, she places a basket of fresh-baked bread, a plate of crostini, a bottle of olive oil, and an unusual looking brown dip between us.

You wanna know what the hell that brown crap is, too, don't you?

The woman sets plates down directly in front of us prompting Kellan to kindly ask, "Melinda, did you remember to bring the menu as well?"

"I did." She offers me the one-page menu being cradled by a thick holder. "And the special for the evening is Spicy Mussels with Shrimp Marinara." Once the object is in my possession, she politely inquires, "May I get you two anything else at this time?"

Kellan places his cellphone down on the table and gives her a nod of dismissal. "No, but thank you. I'll send you a message when we're ready to order."

"Enjoy."

After she's cleared the room, I quickly point to the unfamiliar food on the table. "What the hell is that?"

"Truffle and porcini mushroom dip with artichoke chunks and feta cheese."

The casualness of his answer causes me to shake my head. "You can't say that like it's everyday shit."

He cocks a smirk. "To me it is."

"Did you forget the whole beer and burgers talk yesterday? I thought you said you were a good listener."

"I am, but where would the fun be if I didn't push your comfort levels as you've pushed mine."

Don't agree with him again!

Kellan smiles even wider than before. "You like that I push back, don't you?"

"You like that I push to begin with."

"Yes," he admits while reaching for a piece of bread. "Now, you're not allergic to anything, are you?" Seeing the glimmer of an idea begin to stir in my mind, he points a stern finger. "Don't lie to get out of trying it, either."

"Not allergic to anything," I sigh and sneer at the dip for a second time. "Do I really have to try that shit?"

"Yes." Kellan uses his fork to place a little on the soft bread. "One bite."

My disgusted expression doesn't change.

"Don't be a pussy," he scolds and offers me the piece.

"Did you really just-"

"I did," he interrupts. "And I'll continue to call you that all night until you try it."

No. No way. That looks like mud water with dying frogs in it.

"One bite and you can ask me one question you want of any kind, and I'll answer completely honest. No clever retorts. No circumventing."

The offer sways my decision. "Do I have to ask it now?"

"It can be used as a get out of jail free card. It'll never expire and can be used at any time."

"Even in a crowded room full of people."

"Even then."

I give the brown dip an additional glance before shaking my head. "Nope. Stakes are still too high. I love my tastebuds too much."

Kellan has the bite he's been presented to prove it's at the very least not harmful.

Not that I was worried it was. He's not exactly a stranger on my doorstep with coffee anymore.

"One bite and you can ask me the one question, *and* I'll have the chef prepare you the best bacon cheeseburger you've ever had in your life."

Temptation finally surpasses the point of no return. "*One. Bite.*"

"*One.*"

Kellan smears the dip on another piece of bread and extends it in my direction. Instead of wasting any more time staring at the questionable concoction, I shove the whole thing in my mouth and let the assault on my tastebuds begin. Burst after burst of bold flavors swarms together until I'm pushed back in my seat from the overwhelming rich taste.

Holy hell. I think I just had a foodgasm.

"Delectable, isn't it?"

I nod while savoring the flavors floating on my tongue.

"I've got fantastic taste." His eyes give me a long, lingering stare. "*Obviously.*"

Side stepping his compliment, I reach for another piece of bread. "Can you cook?"

"No." He sips his champagne. "It's never been important to learn."

"Meaning?"

"When I'm in Fayeweather, if I'm not staying at the palace or our family's country home on the outskirts, then I'm crashing at our high-rise penthouse in the city, all of which have cooks. Other than that, I live in and out of hotels, dining out almost every night."

Between bites, I manage to ask, "You don't have your own place? Anywhere?"

Kellan shakes his head. "No. I never stay in the same place long enough to need one. It's one of the benefits of being able to work from anywhere that provides an internet connection."

Unsure how I feel about that, I finish the bite, grab another hunk of bread, and openly confess, "I can't cook, either."

"No?"

"Nope. My roommate does most of the cooking since it's her boyfriend who eats most of our food, and I usually have dinner with my parents on Sundays, so I'm pretty much covered. Before living with Jovi, I grew a huge appreciation for microwavable meals."

Kellan has another drink. "Can't say I've ever had one."

"Lucky you."

He flashes me an amused grin.

"You know, for a guy always eating meals on the go, you sure don't look like it."

"You can thank lacrosse for instilling a great workout regimen in me."

"Lacrosse? What is that? Like hockey in the field?"

"No…That's *field hockey*."

His jeer causes me to playfully snap. "Thought maybe it was like the whole you call it football; we call it soccer thing."

"It *is* football. You use *your feet*. Hence the name. Americans are just too stubborn to accept it."

I glare at his comment before tossing the last piece of my bread at him.

He chortles prior to brushing it off.

"*Oops.*" I teasingly sneer. "Didn't mean to get your four-thousand-dollar suit all dirty. Oh, wait. Is this one the same price, or dare I assume more?"

"More."

Surprise drops my jaw. "Seriously?!"

"Important date. Better suit."

I continue to impishly taunt, "Better suit, better shoes?"

"Yes."

"Better cologne?"

He winks. "You tell me."

I wet my lips in an attempt to prevent myself from admitting just how much I enjoy it. "Same watch, though? Did you forget to pack others?"

Suddenly, Kellan's playful demeanor dissipates.

Not my best joke but definitely not a total mood killer.

He gives the accessory an adjustment while informing, "It's the only one I wear. My mother gave it to me for my birthday."

"Mama's boy?"

"I was when was she was alive, yes."

The confession shuts my mouth tightly.

Oh shit…I didn't mean to – I shouldn't have said – I…Fuck. I really messed this up.

An uncomfortable silence struggles to settle between us, yet he playfully pokes, "*Daddy's girl.*"

I can't help but smirk. "What about you? You close to your father?"

Kellan's body hardens further. "Not really. When my mother passed away, we built a mutually enjoyed emotional wall between us."

"How did she die?"

"Breast cancer."

"How long ago?"

"Almost fifteen years."

I reach for my glass. "What about your brother? Are you two close?"

"Practically identical," he finally starts to smile again. "Even if you think he's hotter."

"By like a point."

His eyes light up. "Oh, just one now?"

"Maybe like half of one," I whisper between sips. "Do you just look-alike, or is he a cocky, art-hating sports-loving asshole, too?"

Kellan lets loose a hearty chuckle, and the sound seeps through me in unexpected ways.

Is it weird to enjoy hearing someone laugh this much?

"We're different in ways that matter," he casually replies. "We were more alike before he met Sophia, his wife."

"Do you not like her?"

"I *adore* her. She drives my brother mad just because she can." The sound of his laughter continues to reverberate around the room.

No. No, it does not sound familiar.

"In fact, he asked her out *seven times* in ten days before she agreed to have coffee with him."

"Seven times?! I knew I should've held out longer!"

Kellan rolls his eyes, grin still lingering. "That long, and I wouldn't have been in town anymore."

The realization of this moment being one of our only, causes my shoulders to drop.

I know I don't have any right to be unhappy about that. We just met. We hardly even know each other.

"Dance with me." His declaration is followed by him wiping his hands on his napkin and standing up.

"You're not gonna ask?"

He extends his hand for me to take. "No."

After wiping my own, I drop it in his and allow him to whisk me away to move to the music.

I swiftly wrap my arms around his neck while his hands take their time delicately exploring my curves in their pursuit to rest on my hips. His attempt to handle me with tenderness is so surprising it pulls a sweet sigh from my lips.

One minute he's Prince of Pompous Asses and the next he's Prince Charming. I'm gonna need him to decide one or the other. Pick a paint pallet. He can't be both. I…I…I don't know how to handle both.

"What are you in town for?" I softly ask as our stares connect.

"The Collin Murphy Foundation charity run. They are a research foundation in Doctenn that helps fight Childhood Cancer.

Their main base is in Fayeweather – where I'm from –, but they partner with a slightly smaller branch here in the states. One of my old mates from boarding school is highly involved in the American division. He suggested an annual run to help raise funds in the states after hearing about the triathlon we do in Fayeweather. I've come every year to participate since it began."

"Which was?"

"This will be the fifth year."

Impressed by his commitment, I offer him a bright smile. "How long is the run?"

"5K," he casually replies. "Nothing I can't do in my sleep."

His ego's overdue appearance causes me to roll my eyes.

"Care to join me for the event? I can pull a few strings and arrange you a spot if you like."

"That would be the worst date ever." The two of us laugh, and I add, "Totally not the way I prefer to be sweaty and winded."

"I can gladly arrange other ways to accomplish both of those." When my eyes lower to a disgusted glare, he chuckles, "You should swing by the run. Cheer me on. The encouragement would be welcomed."

My face tilts sarcastically. "Because your ego really needs any more attention?"

Kellan gives me a small shrug. "Couldn't hurt."

We snicker once more and move the conversation along. He explains how the money that is raised by the run is funneled into the organization and also regales me with stories about the young visitors that wait for them at the finish line. It turns out that the children who wait for them to complete the race have all been positively affected by the institution. Kellan enthusiastically explains how his mother was a huge donor to the non-profit from the moment they started in their country and used to take him along to the hospital when she would visit the families with supplies. As he recalls delivering meals, playing board games with dying children, and playing practical jokes on the doctors just to see the patients laugh, his entire presence illuminates to the point it's impossible to look away.

How can anyone be two people at once? You've met him. He's all flashy suits and cocky comments one minute and the next, he's **this.** *He's caring and concerned with something so much larger than himself. Determined to make a difference in lives most people wouldn't give a second thought unless they were directly being affected by it. It's like having someone splash white paint on a black canvas. The contrast isn't just striking. It's beautiful.*

"Oh, dear lord," Kellan mumbles in a slightly embarrassed tone. "I'm rambling."

"It's adorable," I warmly reassure.

His blue eyes flash relief before his grasp tightens. "So adorable you want me to kiss you now."

"*Wrong.*"

You shh.

Kellan lightly laughs, licks his lips, and lowers his voice. "Give me ten seconds to change your mind."

"Seven."

Swiftly, his mouth descends mine, taking advantage of my parted lips from a word barely finished. The moment our tongues touch an immediate irrefutable hunger is ignited. His fingertips lock onto my hips while we begin a battle in uncharted territory. The need for dominance from both of us is apparent. Within seconds, every roll of our tongues is so aggressive and so avaricious it seems that the only possible way to sate our appetites is to devour more of each other. To put me on a list I swore I was too good for. To put me on a list I hate to admit I want to be added to.

Kellan's lips abruptly slip from mine, leaving me breathless. "Only needed five."

The cocky remark is rewarded with my mouth conquering his this time. A greedy groan rumbles through him that's short-lived by the sound of another vibration. Our tongues briefly connect once more, lightly tapping together, before I'm pulling away insisting he answer it.

"Could be important," I quietly push, hands sliding down his taut chest.

God, that's firm.

"More than this?" He gives me a stern expression while swiftly shaking his head. "Not a chance in hell."

I briefly bite my lip prior to letting my better judgment do the talking. "Probably not, but why don't you make sure?"

The vibrating pauses, which is when Kellan attempts to argue again, only to be cut off by the sound starting its second round.

He folds his hands with mine, and I tease, "You think I'm gonna run away while you talk on the phone?"

"Not risking it," he sighs as he moves us back towards the table.

The minute we arrive my eyes steals a glance of the face lighting up his screen.

She looks really familiar…Ohmygod wasn't she in that spy movie that just came out?!

Unfortunately, I'm not given any longer to further decipher where I know her from. The woman's face quickly disappears from him ignoring the call. At that moment, my grip on his loosens from me realizing, I've just been saved by the blonde.

That would've been a completely different T.V. show, huh?

Kellan quickly attempts damage control. "She's no one special."

"According to you they never are."

A hurt expression begins to cultivate. "Brie-"

"How long after you've screwed me until you begin to ignore *my* calls? Until I'm just another number on a long list of other numbers you let lie around for in case of pussy needing emergency?"

"Brie-"

"You say you don't lead anyone on, but what the hell do you call this shit here with me? All this wining and dining? Is this just really extended foreplay?" His mouth twitches to reply, but I lift a hand to silence him. "Never mind. I don't really want the answer to that. Look, you asked me to dinner, and I, *technically*, ate with you during this time, which means I fulfilled my end. I'd like to go home now."

Kellan runs a hand through his blond hair in frustration. "There's no convincing you to stay, is there?"

"No."

He momentarily presses his lips together clearly resisting the desire to argue with my decision. "Give me a minute, please. I'll have Swiss bring the car around."

I watch as he turns on his heels and heads for the doors in silence.

There. Problem solved. I didn't wanna be a one-night stand, and now I won't be thanks to what I'm assuming is his last one. Hey, I'm all for women who wanna get theirs, who don't mind a moment of fun or aren't looking for more. I get it. I really do. More Spice Girl Power to you. But personally? Right now, I've got enough uncertainty looming in my near future without having to add possible permanent booty call to the list, which is only a fraction better than a one-off. I know that's what he was going to try to counter with. Try to tempt me with the idea of just enjoying a fling for a few days. Have some fun. And while this has without a doubt been the most that I've had in years with someone of the opposite sex, it's not worth hating myself for in the morning. It's not worth the idea of having to accept what would be the simple truth of letting myself fall for the bullshit he worked a little harder to sell. I'm not looking to be one of Duke Kellan Kenningston's state side sometimes. Not now. Not ever.

CHAPTER SEVEN

Kellan

"Why am I seeing an online report for you breaking the heart of some American actress?" Kris huffs from the other end of the phone.

"Because you have nothing better to do than to read trash on the internet?"

The snarky comment receives another grumble. "*Kellan.*"

"What?" I snap into the phone. "I am particularly not in the mood to have this pointless discussion."

To my surprise, he asks, "Everything alright?"

No. The same actress who could barely get me off now can't seem to bugger off. It was just one bloody weekend in the mountains for Christ's Sake. No one falls head over heels in love in just one weekend. Why are you leering at me like that? What did I say? What am I missing?

"*Kellan.*"

"Quit saying my name like that. *I'm fine.*"

"You certainly sound fine."

"*I. Am.*"

"Very believable, baby brother."

"It should be since I truly am. And the woman you are referring to is the same one I played strip poker with in the mountains. It was a meaningless weekend *then*, and the only reason it has any meaning *now* is because of the wrench it has thrown in my relationship."

"Relationship?"

Realizing my mistake in the choice of words, I lean back in the conference chair I'm currently occupying. "I misspoke."

"What relationship?"

"I meant…"

What exactly did I mean? Brie and I aren't dating; bloody hell, we've only known each other for a few days, yet I can't seem to get past the tantrum she threw at the end of dinner two days ago. And not just because that was the last time, I heard from her. You know, she's not the first woman I've crossed paths with who is easily blinded by the women who have or who are aiming to keep my mattress warm, but she's the only one I've come across that creates lumps of guilt inside of me over the subject. Ever since she demanded to be taken home knots of bitterness over past actions have been constricting in the pit of my stomach. I'm torn between the idea of this being actual shame or just indigestion. Most likely just the latter, yes?

Kris finally breaks the long lull of silence. "You meant what, Kellan?"

Hearing the taunting arise from the choice of endearment shuts my eyes.

"That you've finally met your match? Finally met someone who doesn't take your past inability to keep your tool in your pants as casual as the others?"

The smug tone in his voice clenches my teeth. "You're a bloody bastard, you know that?"

"That's what big brothers are for," he mocks as he laughs. "Wait until I tell Sophia, you've fallen in-"

"I haven't fallen *anywhere, with anyone, in anything*."

"Your bed included, I bet."

No. I have yet to find the nearest bar and bury my sorrows in a pint and petite pair of legs. Truthfully? I'm still hoping for the pair of brown ones who captured my attention days ago to change their mind.

"I'm hanging up now," I declare and end the call before the conversation can further digress a direction it has no business going.

Like I said previously. No one falls in love over a weekend. Myself included.

The conference doors open, and Hugh strolls in with another brown box. Immediately, a look of irritation arises on his face. "Have you even started assembling the VIP donor packets?"

My eyes shift to the mess waiting to be put together on the floor beside me. "They don't have legs. They aren't going anywhere."

"But they *need to*," Hugh whines. "Why did you volunteer to help if you're just going to sit in that chair and pout?" The box drops down on the edge of the table drawing my attention to him again. "And why are you pouting? You've been obnoxiously intolerable for the past two days."

"You're complaining about your friend *not* bothering you," Dana questions as she enters the room with another box. "That's not…*strange* to you?"

I casually wave my hand in her direction. "What your lovely girlfriend said."

"And you're complimenting her as opposed to ridiculing me for caring about her." His palms fall flat on the table. "What the hell is wrong with you? Are you sick? Do you have the flu? Do we need to chopper you into the nearest hospital?"

And people say I have a flare for the dramatic.

"I'm fine."

"You don't sound fine."

"I need people to stop saying that because I truly *am*."

"You're lying."

"He is most definitely lying. He's not fine." When my eyes meet Dana's, her stare turns even more skeptical. "But he's not sick, either. It's something else."

"This conversation is just going in circles like Carry Go Round," I attempt to change subjects. "I'm going to get started on these bags."

Dana's expression transposes to one of confusion. "Um, what's a Carry Go Round?"

"You know the child ride that carries you around and around while you sit stationary on a fake horse."

"A carousel," Hugh explains on a small headshake. "They screw up so many words in his country."

"Your country is the one that muddles up words."

He immediately rolls his eyes at my rebuttal.

"Moving on. You needed one-hundred and fifty bags, correct?"

Hugh nods and points to the unopened folder on my right. "In there you will find a list of items each bag should contain. The personally signed thank you cards are in the box Dana just brought in."

"We appreciate the help," Dana sweetly states. "We weren't expecting Diana to go into early labor."

"It's not a problem," I politely assure.

And it's not. Stuffing tote bags for those that are running who donated over five hundred dollars will keep my attention away from the lack of response I'm receiving from a sexy art student who is convinced I'm nothing more than a panty collecting playboy. Is it wrong to have hoped after spending two nights with me, she would see something else? We didn't even kiss until the second night! Damn near a record for me! Wait. That last little bit fits better with her side of the argument rather than mine. Ignore it.

"Not a single complaint?" The suspicion in Hugh's voice forces me to turn around to open the boxes at my feet. "Is your sickness contagious?"

I roll my eyes.

Don't laugh. He's not funny. He's an idiot.

"It's a woman," Dana says slowly, voice approaching. She doesn't wait for confirmation before accusing, "He's upset over a woman."

"Is this about the chick you took to dinner on Saturday?"

"He took someone to dinner?!" His girlfriend rushes to ask. "Why didn't you tell me?!"

"I didn't think it'd matter," Hugh retorts at the same time I begin to unload the box of engraved gym towels. "He rarely has the same dinner date twice."

Why would I when the amount to choose from is abundant? Yes, I'm aware of how that also fits in with Brie's accusation. Thank you.

"What happened?" Hugh mockingly interrogates. "Did she throw wine in your face before she agreed to sleep with you? Cry in the middle of it when she realized she picked the wrong man to give her virginity to? Demand a two-thousand-dollar bottle of champagne and pâté after you failed to give her the big O?"

I swiftly spin around in the chair and point. "I've never once failed to give a woman the big O."

My best friend victoriously smirks.

Fine. That got under my skin, but it's not what you're thinking. It's not because I actually have come up short in that department. Believe me. Kris and I shared a beautiful tennis instructor who spent a copious amount of time one summer giving lessons on how to serve more than the ball.

"She didn't sleep with him at all," Dana deduces too quickly.

I promptly shift my attention to her. "I liked you better when you were picking out pathetic art pieces."

"Hey!" She squeaks. "It's a masterpiece!"

"It looks like a Smurf sneezed on a piece of cardboard."

"Forgive him," Hugh demands making his way towards me. "He gets rather grouchy when his cock hasn't been touched in a few days."

"Is that an offer?"

His eyebrows lift as he leans against the edge of the table beside me. "You've never taken rejection well-"

"I haven't had to become accustomed to it like you."

"-but I've never seen you *this level* of pissy from some random woman not wanting to sleep with you."

The truth in his statement tightens my jaw.

"Typically, you just move on. No extra thought given to the woman whose loss you believe it is. What's so special about this one? Beer flavored nipples? Double-jointed? Gymnast?"

I lean back in my chair. "How hard would your jaw drop if I told you I've already had all three of those?"

There's a small gasp out of Dana, but her boyfriend shakes his head. "You haven't."

"How do you know?"

"Because I would've heard about the beer nipple chick fucking immediately. That's not something that doesn't get shared over a drink or a late night with a bottle of tequila at a gentleman's club." After receiving a nod of agreement from me, he commands, "'Fess up, Kellan. Who is she, and why do I love her for making you miserable already?"

"You're as bad as my bloody brother."

"With all the hell and torment that you've given the two of us over the years, did you really think we wouldn't strike back the moment the opportunity presented itself? I honestly never thought the day would come when Kellan Kenningston would fall in-"

"Not. In. Anything." I state sharply.

"You so are," Dana disagrees.

"Just because Hugh was ready to wed you after one glance at those in a pushup bra," my finger casually points to her chest, "doesn't mean all men are that way."

She scoffs, folds her arms across the area, and snaps, "You know, sometimes you make it extremely difficult to like you."

"Just sometimes?" Her boyfriend good-naturedly mocks.

"I'm starting not to blame her for not answering your calls or texts."

I tilt my head in curiosity. "What makes you think-"

"Because if she were giving into every tactic, you've tried you wouldn't be taking your sweet time to stuff these bags. They'd be halfway done already because you would hate the idea of keeping your prize for a hard day's work, waiting." Dana's smile matches the one Hugh flashed moments ago.

Is that a couple's thing? Do you just begin to resemble one another after a certain period of time in looks and mannerisms? How odd.

"Who is she?" Hugh resumes his inquiry.

"She's an art student. I met her at the showing. We had a minor issue at dinner and instead of discussing it – like civilized adults – she demanded to be taken home. I've been calling and messaging ever since but…" I give my hands a slight toss in the air. "*Nothing*."

Might I add the amount in which I am doing both things is out of my nature? I called three times on Sunday, and so far, twice today. Throughout both days I've made attempts to apologize, to provoke an argument, to tempt a snide comment, really anything I could think of to rally any sort of response, yet she's given me nothing. She's turning me into the very person whose phone call I denied at dinner. However, we haven't slept together, making me more pathetic for being this desperate. You don't have to bother agreeing. I am well aware of the fact.

"I sent her three-dozen long stem roses yesterday and chocolate-covered strawberries today."

"So sweet," Dana swoons on a soft smile.

"*I know.* All of that and still not a single word."

"What was the minor issue?" Dana asks with genuine concern.

"Did you imply you had sixteen centimeters waiting for her when you could barely make fifteen?"

With a proud smirk, I smugly correct, "Try *twenty-one.*"

For those not on the metric system – thus proving once more how stubborn Americans are – it's about eight inches. Hugh being the American jerk who went to school in Doctenn often prides himself in his ability to drunkenly tell others they've got small cocks in two forms of measurement.

"Bull."

"My dick hasn't shrunk since the last time you accused me of being an inadequate length to compensate for the fact *you're* not as long as *you'd* like."

"Fuck you. I'm-"

"Excuse me," Dana interrupts moving our attention to her. "Can I suggest something before you two start breaking out rulers?"

I motion a hand for her to continue.

"Talk to her."

Wow. She really is a ditz. There's an idea I hadn't let cross my mind. Perhaps I would've if it weren't for the fact that's not even possible when someone doesn't answer your cell.

"Swing by her place and make amends *face to face*."

The thought I've tinkered with begins to tumble around once more.

"Trust me." She softly smiles. "It'll mean more than any present or half-assed, phoned in apology ever could."

Perhaps I'll give her one more day and then try that. Honestly? At this point, I'm out of bloody options. Even if she refuses to go out with me again, at the very least, I want to prove her wrong. I want her to know all of this isn't some drawn out attempt to sleep with her. I mean, of course, it wouldn't bother me if things ended up there sooner as opposed to later, but I enjoy her company in ways that pale in comparison to those I've slept with. She's the first person I can recall having as much fun out of bed, as I imagine I would in it. That must count for something…yes?

CHAPTER EIGHT

Brie

Prince One-Night Stand: Morning beautiful.

I groan at the text and push the device to the opposite end of my bedside dresser.

Every. Fucking. Morning. Same text. Relatively the same time. Does royalty not know the definition of sleeping in? This is a rare occasion in my life. My professor canceled class today meaning two extra hours of sleep before having to prepare myself to listen to teenagers whine about their flawed appearances and bias teachers. Puh-lease. They wanna learn about real biased teachers? Wait 'til they get to college where if you sit in the front row with a low-cut shirt you're given extra credit. Yeah. Not one of a community college's higher points they mentioned in the brochure. No, I haven't always gone to Ashwin. I got all the basics I could and transferred over. Cheaper and smarter.

For the next several minutes, I attempt to return to the land of sleep where Pierce Wyatt, the television star who plays a vampire cursed to save the world, was about to peel off his wet shirt and feed me grapes.

I don't know why it was grapes. Not really what I was focused on.

After failing miserably at that but successfully twisting myself in my sheets, I grab my glasses from the nightstand, wiggle on a pair of sleep shorts, and head for the kitchen where Jovi happens to be standing in front of the open fridge. I watch in silence as I approach the unusual situation.

All of a sudden, Jovi lets out a long moan, tosses her head back, and mutters, "Ohmygod…"

For the love of all that is sacred, please tell me Merrick is not on the other side of her on his knees.

"These are so good," she whispers and reaches into the fridge for something. "How are you this good? How is that possible?!"

Now just a few feet away from her, I ask, "What the hell are you eating?"

Jovi squeaks and drops the chocolate-covered fruit in the process.

Ah.

A guilty look flushes her light brown complexion. "Don't be mad at me!"

"I'm not."

"Okay, but if you are-"

"Again, I'm not. Have as many as you want. I refuse to eat 'em."

Prefer my fruits not coated in culpability.

Jovi licks the chocolate off her thumb. "What did this guy do that is so awful it's making you protest perfectly great dessert? *Gourmet dessert,* Brie. From Yasmine's Yummies. Yasmine's. Yummies. You have any idea how expensive these are?"

I don't, but I'm not surprised that they are. Kellan only likes bullshit that's expensive and flings. Actively avoiding him and all things related to him will help me prevent myself from becoming the one person I expressed repeatedly that I have no desire to be.

"Talk to me," she warmly encourages at the same time she finds the fallen strawberry to throw in the trash. "Maybe I can help."

"Or maybe I can," Merrick's voice unexpectedly joins the conversation.

"Doubtful," I mumble to myself.

He greets her with a chaste kiss and immediately questions afterward, "Why do you taste like chocolate?"

"She was eating the dessert of the man who disgusts me."

Both sets of eyes land on me in unison.

"*Disgust*?" Jovi asks, leaning her back against the counter. "Three days ago, he was just 'a moment'. Now, he *disgusts* you? What happened? Did he try to…to…do something you didn't want him to?"

Her inability to complete the sentence causes me to smile, and her boyfriend's frown to harden. "He better not fucking have." His entire body stiffens in defense. "Is this something *I* need to handle? Does he need his ass handed to him? Do I-"

"Slow down, Cujo," I playfully mock. "It was nothing like that."

Same topic. Different direction.

"Then what?" Jovi pushes.

"It's not a big deal. We're just looking for different things in life. He's looking for a one-off while I'm looking for…Well, I'm looking for…" The end of my sentence fades into uncertainty.

Okay, so, maybe I don't know **exactly** *what it is I do want, but at the very least, I know it's not him. Er…Yeah…Maybe it's him but definitely not his type. I don't wanna be one of many. I wanna be the last one. I wanna be the only one. Ugh. I've got to stop watching the Hallmark channel this long after Christmas. It can't possibly be healthy.*

Softly, she whispers, "Do *you* even know how that sentence ends?"

I don't reply.

Merrick folds his arms across his chest. "Are you sure that's what this guy is into?"

"The random ex hookup whose call he ignored during our candlelight dinner fed me those breadcrumbs."

His head slightly sways back and forth prior to arguing, "But maybe it's not like that with you."

Being equal parts annoyed and suspicious causes me to lift my eyebrows.

"Maybe you're different."

"Oh right. Because guys like that don't ever go to extreme lengths to get laid."

"They don't," Merrick rebuts without hesitation. "They don't have to."

Hate how much he sounds like Kellan right now.

"If he's the type of guy you believe he is, the kind that loves 'em easy, and has no problem jumping from chick to chick, then the fact he's putting real effort into trying to impress you says it all. The chase of the challenge will push a guy like that to come after you for a couple days, but then the need to keep his ego stroked will have him stray from your no to a definite yes. If this guy is doing shit he doesn't typically do, it's because he has no intention of treating you the way he typically would if you were anyone else. And trust me. Once a guy finds the girl worth doing shit that he never saw himself doing before, every chick from the past becomes nothing more than a haunting mistake he wishes he could erase."

His words burrow deeper than anticipated despite my best defenses. "It was only a couple of dates, Merrick. You're talking like he's in love with me."

He gives me an offhanded shrug. "How do you know he's not?"

"Did you miss the first part of that sentence where I said we went out on *two* dates?"

"Didn't even take me that long to fall in love with Jovi."

The adorable confession grabs a frustrated sigh from me.

"My point is, don't be so quick to write him off if you're into him. And you definitely are."

I attempt to argue when his girlfriend snips, "Don't bother denying it, Brie. I've never seen you *this upset* over a guy one way or another."

Because I don't get upset. We talked about this. Most guys don't even make it far enough into my life to warrant advice from the world's cutest but most meddlesome couple. Maybe they're right. Maybe they're wrong. We'll never know…because I'm **still not answering him back.**

"Shouldn't you two be making out in the back of Merrick's truck or something? Or I don't know…maybe going to this big noisy place we call college? Basically, anywhere that's not directly in front of me with judgmental, made-for-a-tv-movie eyes?"

The two of them chuckle and link hands. In an upbeat tone, Jovi questions, "You gonna meet us for dinner and drinks after work?"

Between you and me, I doubt that I'll be in any mood to watch them drunkenly suck face.

"I'll let you know once I get off if I'm up for it."

She offers me a sweet smile and nods. "Alright. We probably should head off to class before all the good parking is taken."

"By good parking, she means the back lot where we can make out between classes." Merrick waggles his eyebrows.

"Ugh. I know."

Wish I didn't. The two of them carelessly making out in the middle of the day isn't a sight anyone should have to suffer through.

Once the two of them leave, I take a long hot shower, throw on my uniform for work, and spend the spare time I have watching old reruns of FRIENDS. Just past the credits on the third episode, the alarm on my phone indicates it's time to get going. I slide the device into my sweatshirt pocket along with my wallet and grab my keys from the coffee table in front of me.

As soon as I open the front door, my eyes effortlessly lower to a glare.

Are you kidding me?!

Kellan offers a cup to me from his sitting position on our apartment stairs. "Caramel macchiato?"

I shut and lock the door behind me. "Are you capable of ordering anything that doesn't sound pretentious?"

When I turn back around, he offers me the other cup in his grasp. "Raspberry hot chocolate?" Seeing the start of a smile on my face causes his own to grow. "Can we talk?"

My back braces itself against the door. "I thought it was clear I had no interest in doing that by the way I've ignored all your calls and texts."

"Which is why I'm here in person." His beam brightens, increasing the speed of my heart. "I'm more charming this way."

That's only because you can see his eyes and smile twinkle like someone left the picture filter on.

"Five minutes," he pleads.

His bright blue eyes continue his begging until I can feel my mouth caving without my consent. "*Two*."

Kellan motions to the space next to him where I sit as requested.

He hands me the hot chocolate and confidently announces, "I like you, Brie."

"I like me, too. I'm hard not to like."

My joke receives a small chortle. "I mean it. I enjoy your company. You make me laugh. You're not afraid to give me shit. And you listen when the conversation veers towards things that truly matter to me. You don't spend time telling me the things you think I want to hear in order to get something to benefit you. In fact, the only thing you do that I don't enjoy is judging me for having a promiscuous past."

"You're not a girl. You don't get to say 'promiscuous past'."

"That's quite sexist."

"Well, so is it when a woman is shamed for having multiple sex partners and a guy is high-fived."

"Maybe she should be high-fived," he surprisingly retorts. "If she feels she's that fantastic in the sheets and feels she should be enjoyed and praised over then give her a bloody high-five. If she feels her worth is between her legs because she has nothing else to offer then by all means, make it a double."

Unsure of how to reply, I remain silent.

"Most men who behave as such – treating women like trophies of accomplishments – fall into the latter."

"What about you?"

"Contrary to your belief, it's not about how many women I've been with. It's about the fun I've had."

Gotta say…Not really feeling any better about him.

"That's why I do most of what I do. I don't understand why anyone would live in a world where they're bloody bored or fall asleep miserable at night from another mundane moment. I've grown up with death. I've seen it take people in various stages of who they are or who they were becoming, and when it struck my doorstep, the decision to live as though your days are yours was an easy one. There are so many decisions in my life that are not my own that I will be damned if the ones I'm allowed to make aren't something I enjoy. I will not apologize for simply reveling in food or sex. To be completely honest, I don't even think it bothers you that I've had multiple partners. I think what truly bothers you is the fact part of you still wants me *in spite* of that."

My mouth bobs around desperate for a retort.

He can't be right! He just can't! I don't want him. I want him to go away. I want him to stop calling and sending presents. I want him to stop showering me with undeserved attention. I want him to stop making Merrick's speech possibly true. That's the worst shit of them all!

"That's why you've given me *three minutes* instead of *two*."

"Maybe, I'm just not good at telling time." After a deep sigh, I simply shake my head. "I'm not interested in being an ignored phone call, Kellan. It's that simple."

"Well, neither am I," he sharply states. "After three days of ignored messages and calls, I realized I don't have any desire to go through that again. It was driving me bloody mad. So, I'll always answer you if you'll always answer me, regardless of where this does or does not end up. Sound fair?"

The unusual yet sweet proclamation has me fighting the instinct to smirk. "Sounds fair."

Kellan's eyes light up in relief and hope alike. "Are you off somewhere now, or do you have time to take this conversation inside?"

"Work." I twist the cup in my grasp, thankful it's keeping my hands warm.

"After?" He cautiously questions. "Maybe we could order in? Catch a film?"

"*Movie*," I poke fun at his word choice, which causes us both to snicker. "Two dates in a row behind closed doors? You ashamed to be seen in public with me?"

"Not in the mood to share." His confession is followed by him leaning over towards me. "And I have every intention of making up the lost hours I spent in punishment."

Suddenly, the isolated memory of our kiss breaks free and engulfs my thoughts. Without resistance, my mind recalls the rough movements on his tongue. The eagerness in its speed. The hunger in every stroke. The desperation in his low groans.

Heat rushes up my neck straight for my cheeks.

Kellan wets his lips in intrigue. "*You're red.*"

"It's hot," I meekly argue.

"It's in the 50s…or 10s for those of us in the rest of the world who use Celsius."

"I'm wearing a sweatshirt!"

He says nothing, yet his expression grows pleased.

"I hope you know that I'm not having sex with you just because you apologized."

"I never said you were."

"We're not having sex."

"*Not tonight.*"

Don't agree with his addition!

"I don't think I'll be in the *mood*."

His playfulness receives an eye roll and a small headshake. "You can meet me back here around five."

As we stand, he questions, "Here? You want me to finally meet your roommate?"

A sarcastic expression crosses my face. "Absolutely not. It's tequila Tuesday at one of our favorite bars. One-dollar shots, two-dollar margaritas, and three-dollar all you can eat nachos."

They understand what it means to live on a student budget.

"And why aren't we going there? Sounds like a killer deal."

"Because you didn't wanna share," I tease with a wink.

Kellan nods and flashes another grin.

Sauntering off the direction of my car, I say, "Thanks for the hot chocolate, Kellan."

His smile swells in what appears to be pride. "I'll see you after work, Brie."

I turn back around in the right direction, have a sip of the beverage, and exhale deeply afterward.

What the hell am I doing? I'm turning into the girl who cried man-slut! One minute I'm convinced he just wants to screw me and the next I'm willing to see where all this goes? What is wrong with me?! What is it about him and his mischievous smile that makes him so hard to deny? What if Merrick is actually right? What if – Wait. Did I just say that out loud? Did I just agree with Merrick McCoy of all people? What the hell? Did Kellan spike my drink? More importantly, why do I suddenly get the feeling this isn't about to be the fling he was hoping for, and I was fearing?

CHAPTER NINE

Kellan

"This is ridiculous!" I shout in bewilderment. "We can't even agree on *toppings?!*"

"Who puts tomatoes on a pizza?!"

"It's a *margherita* pizza! That's how they're bloody made!"

"It's not a real pizza! There's no meat on it! That just makes it fancy bread!" Brie turns to screech from her seat directly beside me on the couch in her apartment.

You don't have to remind me agreeing isn't quite what we do best...However, it's pizza for crying out loud! This be that damn difficult!

"Let's get two pizzas," I suggest with an exhausted sigh. "You get your favorite. I'll get mine. You can try a piece and see it's not as terrible as you're imagining."

"That's what my mother used to say about broccoli, and I still gag at the sight of it," she mumbles and completes our online order.

I watch over her shoulder, waiting for the payment screen, yet when it finally appears it disappears almost instantly. Slightly baffled, I struggle to question, "What about paying?"

"Done," Brie announces and shuts her laptop. "I order from them all the time, so my payment information is saved. Just click a button, and it charges my card."

I do my best to hide the annoyance of my defeat. "I had the intention of buying us dinner."

She hits me with a mocking pout. "Would it make you feel better to pick the movie?"

Leaning back against the couch, I state, "You don't need to pay for me."

"And you don't need to pay for me."

Sensing a nerve being pinched, I try my best to rectify the situation. "I never meant to imply I did. It's the gentlemanly thing to do."

"So is calling a girl back who you spent the weekend with in the mountains."

Her accusation furrows my eyebrows. "Were you searching social media for updates on me?"

"Would it bother you if I was?"

Without hesitation, I reply, "Yes."

"Why?"

"Because then…then you wouldn't be the woman I thought you were."

There's not much mystery to my social shenanigans. I'm not ashamed of them nor am I the one who insists on paying someone to clean up the crazy things I do to appear as though I'm just another socialite with too much time and money. However, since my mother died, I've come to typically encounter two types of women in the process of cameras snapping my photo. There are the ones who are numb to it because they have spent their entire existence in front of flashes as well and those who crave it, who hunt for it because they themselves crave that level of attention. The latter are the sorts that mainly end up in my bed and are also the reason I don't feel guilty when I don't feed their fifteen minutes of fame by enjoying another night of casual sex with them. They're also the sorts to stalk social media for sightings. Google my name aimlessly. Tell me more about me than they ever do themselves.

Brie now looks slightly baffled. "What the hell does that mean?"

"It means one of the very things I adore about you is the fact you *don't* do those things. That you haven't been following the trash mags or their sites about my whereabouts or actions or recent conquests. Women who scan the internet for updates about me are the same ones who often end up on the list you are so adamant about avoiding."

"Is that the real reason why they end up there?"

"No," I clarify quickly, "but being a fame troll doesn't give them any benefit in the pointless pursuit to stay off of it." Before the conversation can spiral the out-of-control direction I foresee, I ask, "How did you find out about the weekend in the mountains?"

She grabs the remote. "It was trending online when I checked Facebook. Well...*She* was trending. Meegan Malone."

I knew her name started with an M!

"I recognized her face as the one you ignored on our date. The pages were all reporting how she said she was 'devastated' Prince Kellan Kenningston, younger brother of Prince Kristopher Kenningston, had 'given up on their relationship so early on'."

"Relationship?! Two days at a ski resort is *not* a relationship. I swear that one is mad."

"You mean mad like crazy?" When I nod, so does she yet in a much more mocking nature. "You're right. She spent two days with you and wanted to keep seeing you. She must be bloody bonkers." The poor accent barely blankets the underlying truth in her statement. Almost instantly, Brie realizes her slip and adds, "I mean, come on now. There's no way you're *that* good in bed."

"*Better.*"

An immediate glare is received.

I smile knowing she enjoys my company more than she'll ever truly admit. "And absolutely better than your accent."

She sneers and turns her attention back to the television. "Okay, what I'm hearing is we should watch one of her movies."

"If you want to spend the evening with my commentary on how poorly she does in her films *and* in bed."

Haven't actually seen any of her films, but I assume if she's that over-the-top off camera, she's probably much more so on.

Another sarcastic glance is tossed in my direction. "What chick would want to hear about one of your ex-flings in detail?"

"None, which is why you won't be choosing one of her films."

With a small nod of agreement, she faces the screen and returns to scrolling through our choices. After a long span of denying one another's choices, we finally agree upon a raunchy comedy just minutes before the pizza arrives.

Brie offers me the pizza boxes to place on the coffee table while she grabs napkins and bottles of water from the fridge.

At the same time she drops down onto the couch, she demands, "Hand me my box, please. I don't want it anywhere near that abomination you ordered."

With a playful smirk, I move the object to the edge of the table closest to me and state, "No."

"No?"

"You want your pizza? You either have a bite of mine first or kiss me as a fee for the insult."

"*Or* I could just reach over and grab it myself."

Her free hands start to stretch that direction, and I lift one of mine to halt her. "I wouldn't do that if I were you. I'm stronger than I let on."

She rolls her eyes and makes another attempt for the box. In a swift motion, I grab both of her hands, knock her backward against the sofa, and pin them above her head. The struggle with her arms is brief, but she doesn't completely surrender. All of a sudden, her knee starts to move forcing me to pin more of my body on top of hers.

"Kicking me in the bollocks? Over pizza?"

"You're the one pinning me down!"

"You're the one who forced my hand." She starts to argue again, and I command. "Either, kiss me or get ready to try the pizza."

There's no reluctance in her mouth pressing against mine. I release my grip to better brace myself from the abrupt impact. Our lips part and her tongue lightly tease, daring mine to pursue it for another taste. On a greedy groan, I anxiously take the bait. This time when they slowly brush together, she sweetly sighs, rocks her hips upward, submitting to me. The sweet surrender shoots straight to my cock at the same moment her hands drag themselves down the front of my cream-colored sweater, lightly clawing and scraping from the skin underneath.

Do you have any idea how easy it would be to slip off these yoga shorts she's wearing? Did I mention it's obvious she's not wearing them with underwear? Yes. She 'accidentally' dropped the remote earlier, and in the process of picking it up, she gave me a picturesque view that will be taunting my dreams for days to come. I swear she's wearing these tiny shorts – or long underwear if you will – and a fitted t-shirt on purpose. Further torture for that phone call that ruined our last date I presume.

Unfortunately, rather than rip off the article like I'm hoping, Brie pushes me back, breaking the beginning of what I can only imagine would've been an incredible foreplay session. Slightly breathless, she states, "Pizza."

I simply nod and move back to my side of the furniture where I do my best to casually adjust the bulge in my jeans.

Should I be worried about what sex will be like if kissing her is this exhilarating? I swear so much blood has rushed to cock that I don't honestly know how any other part of my body is functioning.

Once I've slid her pizza box to her side of the table, I open my own and pull out a slice only to have her snake the first bite before it can reach my mouth. My eyebrows immediately lift in shock.

Brie swallows the bite with a shrug. "I'm more unpredictable than I let on."

And that's exactly why I like her.

"Do you mean *mad*? You're *madder* than you let on."

"Definitely that but not think you're going to propose after two days in the mountains level of mad."

"She did not say that..." There's no stopping my head from tilting in worry. *"Did she?"*

"I honestly don't remember. I got a notification for something else and went there." She doesn't pause for me to comment. "Pizza's gross by the way." Her attention shifts to focus on her own meal. "It's like *bread salad.*"

I chuckle, roll my eyes, and devour the remainder of the piece. Once I've finished it, I wipe my fingertips clean and use them to gently stroke Brie's back. Surprisingly, instead of pulling away or giving me a sassy reason to stop, she scoots closer. I briefly smile to myself and let my attention admire the remarkable woman who's somehow managed to give me a glimpse of what I imagine my brother has.

Before this, I never really understood why Kris would exchange spending his life with one woman when he could have an endless amount. How any one person could be more exciting than constantly exploring what so many have to offer. Of course, you don't get the full story of someone when you only spend four to six hours with them, and during that time most of it is naked and moaning. But with that established, I hadn't felt any desire to discover the secrets they weren't willing to tell. I didn't care to learn about where they came from or where they wanted to go in life. Maybe it's because in a way they all felt like carbon copies of the same bullshit. The same pathetic tale waiting for an ending I had no interest in participating in. But for some unknown reason, it has yet to feel that way with Brie. Every moment is quite the opposite. I hate not knowing everything about her almost as much as I hate her not knowing everything about me. The constant feeling of wanting more of her, not just sexually but intellectually, is maddening. If this is even half of what my brother feels about Sophia then I understand his over-zealous behavior to defend it.

I keep my touches light while I use my left hand to occasionally feed myself pizza. The moment Brie finishes, she curls her body against mine with her head resting on my chest. Instinctively, I abandon the remnants in the box and wrap both arms adoringly around her. She lets out a soft sigh, which instantly slips a smile back on my face.

How insane is it that this feels like something we've been doing for years? Like something we will naturally always be doing?

For the remainder of the film, we remain completely embraced. Though we exchange multiple, witty comments in retort to some of the dialog in the film, neither of us attempts to leave the situation or rearrange what we've silently declared as undeniably comfortable.

The credits begin to appear, and I state, "Not as amazing as Crooked Cupid 1, but not too shabby for a sequel."

Brie looks up at me with a gracious grin. "Well, we knew it wasn't going to be as great as the first one. Sequels rarely are."

"True." The two of us exchange another smile prior to me admitting, "You know, I've actually never done this before."

"Cuddled?"

"No, I've done that."

Not a complete wanker. I'll hold a woman in bed post-sex if it's desired.

"I've never actually done the film on the couch with the pizza thing."

"What?" Brie pulls away in disbelief. "Didn't you go to college or whatever your country's equivalent is? This is like a standard first apartment, first feel her up, 1-0-1."

I don't move in case she chooses to return to my arms. "Are you suggesting I feel you up?"

Her cheeks become flushed, giving me the answer that I know her lips most likely won't.

My cock begins to swell in my jeans, yet I ignore it to reply, "Yes. I did go to uni. I went to Grindalin. They have an amazing behavior science program. The school is similar to Oxford but in Grindalin, Doctenn rather than England. Think an American Ivy League school."

"Of course, you did. Because where else would the son of a *literal* king go? Community college?" She snips to herself. "Surprised you're even allowed to date someone who did."

The underlying confession causes me to reach out for her hand. "You took your basics at community college?"

"It was cheaper…And…I'm the only one paying for my education so…yeah. It's taking me a bit longer than…practically everyone else ever."

"Nothing to be ashamed of," I reassure, relieved when she folds her fingers with mine. "If anything, it's a bigger reason to be proud of all you've accomplished."

Her attempt to smile sadly falls short.

"In all seriousness, this is the first time I've sat on the couch and watched a film with pizza and a date. I've done it countless times with mates, but never someone I was planning to get naked."

She giggles as she shakes her head.

"Most women are thrilled to be swooped away to restaurants they never pictured themselves in and by the time the meal is over, the couch is not their desired destination." I wink.

Brie gags at the action before she sasses, "Guess you turn your cellphone off for *those* dinners?" The blow is followed by her snickering. "So, it's just *that* easy for you, huh? You take some poor, defenseless woman to dinner and two hours later she joins a collection of forgotten names?"

"You make me sound like some sort of deviant."

She gives me a gradual nod until my eyes enlarge, which is when she erupts into a fit of giggles again.

See what I mean. Absolutely mad.

All of a sudden, she slides over and straddles herself in my lap. The startling shift causes my shaft to stir at the same time she wraps her arms around my neck. I fight every urge to grab her by the nape of the neck and rekindle our moment from earlier. Brie lowers her voice to a seductive tone and salaciously states, "You're not about to see me naked-"

"Shame."

"But doesn't mean your first couch date should be a total bomb."

My hands slowly snake themselves just underneath the hem of her t-shirt right above her hips. "A date with you is never a bomb."

Not even when she demands to be taken home as it's just begun.

"Good answer," she whispers against my lips.

The moment she's finished speaking all restraint is shattered. Our tongues fuse together in a blinding frenzy, each twist intertwined with impure intention and insatiable need. Brie moans softly, yet the sound reverberates throughout my entire system. The barely audible indication of her submission to me in my favorite form forces me to yank her closer. She arches into my touch allowing me to deepen the kiss as well as tightly grasp the curve of her behind. Another mewl seeps free, and I can feel the deviant she playfully accused me of being augmenting into something more ferocious. More primal. Swiftly, I rotate the two of us onto our sides, keeping our bodies tangled in the process. My hand hungrily roams every curve I'm given access to. The softness of her skin in combination with the heavenly way she smells like chocolate and berries and pizza has all of my senses in a tizzy. Before I know it, my fingertips are toying with the waistband of her shorts while she's wriggling in desperation.

I drop my mouth from hers, and she immediately whimpers.

"You said feel you up." My eyes rake over her heaving chest but eventually fall to where my fingers are lingering. "How about *down* instead?"

Brie wets her lips and slowly nods her consent. She leans up to connect our lips once more, but I shake my head refusing to miss a minute of what I'm anticipating. In an unhurried motion, I remove her shorts and am exposed to a beautiful bare sight. I swallow my gluttonous groans and gently graze her clit. She whines for more almost instantaneously as she eagerly parts her legs to gift me with better access. I impetuously slip a finger inside and am rewarded with the beautiful sound of her breath hitching. Her tight pussy welcomes the invasion, yet I pull back, the desire to drag this moment out increasing exponentially with her every passing gasp. Ardently, she grasps my bicep, rocks herself into my touch, and wordlessly demands that I move the digit faster. A small smirk spreads across my lips before I cave to the request. My middle finger gradually thrusts itself inside faster, building up more momentum during each push. I mindlessly begin to grind my body against hers, mimicking the action as if it were my cock instead of my appendage. I continue to pump possessively until her cries cultivate louder and louder indicating she's on the cusp of coming.

Fuck. I'm right there with her.

Brie screws her eyes shut at the same moment her bottom lip slips between her teeth. All of a sudden, waves of whimpers begin to escape while she weakly withers beneath my touch, coating it with warm wetness. I still my fingers and let every tremor trek through me, bollocks barely holding on by a thread.

I cannot come in my jeans. I just…I just can't. That's an embarrassment even I can't live down.

The instant my date's eyes manage to flutter themselves back open, I greet her with a soft grin. "That was bloody amazing."

The start to her smile is short-lived due to the sound of the front door trying to be unlocked.

Impeccable timing.

She pushes me out of the way, promptly puts her bottoms back on, and pretends to be searching through the channels while I wipe my hands clean.

The couple I remember from the showing saunters in with the male chuckling loudly. "I don't remember your door having so many locks."

Why do I suddenly dread the idea of Brie even pretending that bloke was her boyfriend?

"We've always had two locks, Merrick," the girl sighs before glancing in our direction. Her eyes land on me and light up. "And…who are you?"

"Yeah," Merrick echoes. "Who the fuck are you?"

I offer them a kind smile. "I'm-"

"Leaving," Brie promptly interrupts.

My eyes meet hers and can't help but notice the pleading in them is almost as loud as her cries were mere seconds ago.

Is she seriously throwing me out right after **she** *got off? That's…That's a first. You know at least I offer some post orgasm pillow talk before showing them out.*

"I…am…," my voice reluctantly agrees, "but I'll see you tomorrow. Correct?"

She quickly nods and stands to her feet at the same time her roommate questions, "Why are you leaving right now? We just got here. We-"

"He's got…stuff to do," Brie poorly explains.

I grab my silenced cellphone, slip it into my pocket, and walk around to properly introduce myself. "Indeed, I do. Conference call with my brother." Knowing my lie is believable at first thought, I quickly move the conversation elsewhere, "I'm Kellan Kenningston, by the way."

The girl shakes while sweetly saying, "Jovi. Jovi Carter."

Traditionally, we kiss the hand of the ladies we're introduced to and save handshakes for the men. I made an exception. You see the hatred in her boyfriend's eyes, don't you?

"*McCoy*," her boyfriend defensively states before I've even offered my hand to shake. "Merrick McCoy, and Jovi is my girlfriend. We clear?"

"Relax. He was here making out with me you drunken Neanderthal," Brie boldly corrects.

Hearing her proclamation paints another smile on my face.

What can I say? I enjoy the pride as opposed to the shame.

"Shouldn't you be going?" She pushes me to leave once more. "Like *now*."

"Yes." Giving Jovi and Merrick another polite nod, I say, "It was a pleasure to meet you both. I look forward to seeing you at the run this weekend."

"What run?" They quickly question in unison.

"Did Brie forget to tell you?" I pretend to be shocked. After stealing a glance to see irritation and fluster building, I turn back towards her friends. "It's quite all right. I'll inform you. I'll be doing a charity run this weekend, and Brie will be in the crowd, attending to cheer me on. She's even pitched the idea of making me a sign to hold up for support. You two are more than welcome to join her for the run and festivities afterward."

There's an exasperated sigh from the sexy woman throwing me out of her apartment.

And this shall even the score for taking that particular action.

"Sounds fun!" Jovi exclaims. "I could totally make a sign, too!"

"No! No, no, no, no…" Brie begins to mutter louder and loud. "No. *No. No…*"

"Enjoy your night," I politely say to them and give her one final smirk. "Sleep well, love."

She grumbles something; however, I exit without clarifying what it is.

You know us by now. You had to know I had one more trick up my sleeve. Where would be the fun in ending the night on a "normal" note? That's not our style. Besides, I want her there, and I know the only way to insure that is by outsmarting her. No need to fret. I'll brace myself for the inevitable backlash she's going to spring on me. In an odd way…I'm actually looking forward to it.

CHAPTER TEN

Kellan

I lean against the window in the coffee shop as I continue to scroll through the array of comments left on the photo that I posted yesterday across my media pages.

It's a shot of my watch on my wrist with the caption "Can't be late for my hot date". Cheeky and a bit corny yet thousands of comments. Most are women with some variation of "wish it was me". The innocent photo also received me a spot of speculation on the entertainment program DCW, which stands for Doctenn Celebrity Watch. It's a half-hour segmented show that brings the trash gossip they post online to the tele screen. There's a room full of the people who typically do the blogging, but they are allowed to make snide or dirty remarks for the sake of laughs. Apparently, the fact I have a mystery date sparked enough low-brow jokes to warrant a scolding message and the video link from Kristopher. I wonder if he's actually upset that I'm toying with people by keeping them in the dark about where I am and who I'm with, or if it's because he's not an exception to knowing **the who** *part.*

"Order for B. Sanders," the barista announces loudly.

I quickly rise to my feet and cross to the counter. With my phone still in my grasp, I lift it, take a shot of our two cups together – her name facing away, of course – and post it across the platforms.

The caption reads:

Coffee for 2.

Pleased with my latest harmless picture, I slip the device into my suit pocket just as the brunette woman states, "You've been in here every morning for the past three days. Always two cups. You must be the world's best boyfriend."

"I'm not…," I try to laugh through my discomfort from the label. "*We're* not…" Giving my collar a small tug, I fumble out a correct. "*We're dating.*"

Not that I would be opposed to more if it were possible, but it isn't. I leave in a few days. This ends then…It'll be for the best, trust me.

"Oh," she hums hopeful. "Well, if dating her goes wrong, you know where to find me."

I offer her a polite smile and grab the beverages. "Enjoy your day, Miss."

Though the coffee shop is basically right around the corner from Brie's apartment, it's still the safest and quickest for me to drive.

*I mean to have **Swiss** drive. I don't do much driving when he's around. Lately, I've let my mind wonder what it would be like to have my own car. To live in one place and have a reason to own it. To be able to drive somewhere unaccompanied. No, I don't even have a car in Doctenn. Driving is practically a useless skill when your security details are the ones who do it for you by mandate.*

About halfway up the stairs to their apartment, Jovi appears with a warm, surprised smile.

"Good morning, Jovi."

"Morning, Kellan." Her grin tries not to expand. "Bringing Brie coffee, again?"

"I''s the only excuse I can find to see her every morning."

She lets out a small swoon.

You too? Hm. Glad you approve of my sweet gesture.

"Is she up yet?"

"No, I don't think so. Her professor canceled class again. His daughter was in a car crash, and he hasn't made it back to town, yet."

"That's awful," I sigh, reaching the top of the steps.

"Yeah," Jovi agrees with a broken look.

I make haste to change the glum topic. "No McCoy this morning? He in trouble with you for something?"

She giggles. Turns and unlocks the door for me. "No. I made him sleep at his own apartment last night, so I could work on my paper without him constantly asking am I finished yet."

"Can't blame him." Snickers from me fill the air. "I did the same thing yesterday when Brie was attempting to write her paper on the statue of David."

"I choose Pietà."

Cluelessness cloaks my expression.

"It's another marble statue by Michelangelo."

"You are meant to be best friends, aren't you?"

Jovi gives me a giggle but nods. "Enjoy your coffee date."

"Enjoy your…class?"

She waves and scampers down the steps as I head into their apartment.

__Glad Brie has someone she can share her passion for art with. That's one subject I highly doubt I will ever enjoy.__

I carefully open Brie's bedroom door, doing my best not to disturb her if she is indeed still sleeping. It turns out she is. And it's breathtaking.

She looks like a dark-skinned angel missing from those paintings I've seen her study. Her white sheet is wrapped around her while her wavy hair is spread across the pillows as if purposely displaying her flawless face.

__There are very few women I've seen in this state. Countless times, the women I've slept with refresh their makeup before I've awoken like I'm not going to notice. Truth is, I love that Brie allows me to see parts of her other women have been too embarrassed to expose. Yes, I did just stroll in here unannounced today, but she never makes a fuss about covering herself with products. In fact, she doesn't wear much of it at all unless we head somewhere that she feels "requires" it. Soph is similar in that aspect except she does have a bit of self-proclaimed lipstick addiction.__

Suddenly, Brie's body begins to roll over onto her back. She catches a glimpse of me in the progress, which results in the shrill, sharp, scared scream.

Hope you didn't need your eardrums, either.

"Good morning to you, too, love."

"Holy shit, Kellan!" She bites and searches for her glasses on her nightstand. "What the hell is wrong with you?!"

The moment they're on her face I smile at the vision I love more every time I see it.

"Were you just…watching me sleep?"

"You looked peaceful."

"And you look creepy." Still whirling around in shock, she snaps, "How the hell did you even get in here? Did you pull some strings from a CIA buddy? Get a key made?"

Sitting on the edge of her bed, closest to the en-suite bathroom, I reply, "Jovi let me in before she left for class." Her shoulders finally fall in relief. "I already told you I wasn't a stalker."

"Walking a thin line there by popping into my room to watch me sleep."

"I popped in *while* you were sleeping. Big difference."

"Not as big as you think."

With a roll of my eyes, I offer her one of the cups. "White mocha?"

"Trying out a new nickname?" She teases. "Not gonna lie. Kinda dig it." Brie takes the beverage with one hand and uses the other to adjust the falling sheet.

A curious grin grows. "Are you naked?"

"I have on underwear."

My eyes steal another glimpse of where the sheet is pressed tightly to her chest.

"Nu-huh," she insists, redirecting my eyes back to hers. "I'm not showing."

"You think you know me well enough to assume what I'm thinking?"

"You're staring at my tits. It doesn't take a doctorate to guess what thoughts are rolling around."

With a playful smirk, I lean over and lightly press our lips together for a moment. "Good morning, love."

She helplessly smiles. "Good morning, Kellan."

Casually, I place my cup of coffee on her nightstand and pull her against me for an additional kiss. At first, she attempts to keep the kiss short and curt yet my endless nipping at her bottom lip forces her to spread them for my liking. My tongue instantly punishes her for not caving sooner causing her to leak light whimpers of approval over the aggressive action. Within seconds, her coffee is on the stand beside mine and her hands are tugging at my neck to move me closer. I give into her demand as well as begin my own by pulling at the sheet. The moment it falls, my hand cups the unprotected flesh, only to have a throaty growl released.

She pulls back, lips puffy from being overpowered, and let's free a heady moan.

Every bloody morning should start this way.

Before I've had the chance to give the soft skin another stroke, her hand glides across my crotch and grips my hardened cock with intent. The husky groan that's grabbed spurs her to give my swollen member another greedy rub. After a gentle push of encouragement to lean back onto my palms, she undoes my belt, my pants, and slides her hand from my immediate sight. The feeling of her warm palm pressed against my dick causes me to eagerly help her efforts of the jailbreak. Once my cock is in a more offering position, she carefully caresses it from root to tip with sharp motions, each one is delivered with just enough delicious force to roll my eyes into the back of my head. Brie persists with her slow, agonizing pumps like every brush has only one long, luscious mission. A dab of pre-cum seeps from the slit, and she smoothly spreads it down my shaft to assist in her exploits. My breathing significantly shortens as my mind struggles to focus on the idea of holding off the orgasm building. I push myself to run through lacrosse plays instead of succumbing to the steady jerks she's endlessly providing. Thoughts of her pussy presenting my dick with the same salacious squeezing have me clamping down on the inside of my cheek to distract me from the notion of emptying my bollocks all over her swiftly moving hand. Without adequate warning, Brie's hot breath settles against the skin on my neck, setting the entire area ablaze during her journey for my earlobe. Her teeth tug at the same time her hand does, and I'm completely powerless to stop from coming. My mouth becomes rictus while my mind becomes imprisoned in a heavenly haze with every erotic rush that leaves my cock.

I don't think I've ever had a tug job feel quite like that.

Completely spent, I fall backward, and Brie begins to snicker in a way I'm unfortunately too familiar with. Once the air has migrated back to the part of my brain that allows speaking, I ask, "Why are you laughing?"

She proudly hums. "This time *you* made the mess on your suit."

The fact I'm going to now have crotch stains should irritate me, yet I open my eyes and peer up at her with a smile. "*Worth it.*"

Brie snickers again, drops a chaste kiss on my lips, and says, "I'll grab you a towel before I hop in the shower."

Unable to do more than nod, I let her vanish from my sight, a blissful smirk still burning my lips.

If this is what it's like while we're simply just dating for a week or so, I can't imagine what dating for longer would entail. Perhaps donuts and blowjobs rather than coffee and tuggies? Perhaps bagels after enjoying her *for breakfast? I know I shouldn't wonder, I know it isn't my place to, but how about we let me just this once. I doubt I'll ever experience anything like this again.*

CHAPTER ELEVEN

Brie

I slide my hands into my sweatshirt pocket. "You *really* didn't have to switch shifts to be here with me."

"I know," Jovi says, eyes glancing back and forth between me and the empty road where the runners will be. "But there's no way I could pass this up. Part of me still can't believe you're even here."

Me either.

"Then again, you've practically spent every night with him since you made up, so maybe we should get used to him being around, on a more permanent basis?" She wiggles her eyebrows causing me to roll my eyes in retaliation.

We have spent every night together since our movie make-out session. And every morning. In less than a week, we've somehow established our own little routine of sweet good morning texts followed promptly by morning coffee delivered with a heavy tongue romp or if time allows a little more. During the day when I'm in class or have a free minute at work, we exchange quick quips, but the moment I'm off, and we're together, our time is primarily spent laughing from pushing each other's buttons and allowing our playful retorts to transform into wicked foreplay that always ends with me coming. I mean **always.** *And not just one orgasm. He has a self-set goal of at least three, but my body can never handle more than four without a reprieve. Kellan on the other hand has an impeccable rebound time and always gets off at least twice. Ready to be shocked? None of it is from sex! Just our hands. Yeah. You heard me correctly, but just in case you think you didn't, I will repeat it.* **Not. From. Sex.** *Hard to believe he's still around given what we know about him, right? While he jokes, he's never actually pushed me for more or become irked because I refuse to screw him yet. Yeah…Talk about being* **completely** *wrong about someone. Okay, maybe not* **completely** *wrong, but definitely in that department. On multiple accounts. It's not normal for a guy to get a woman off that many times with his fingers, is it? I mean, it's been…some* **time** *since I've had any kind of sex life, but I don't remember it ever involving this many orgasms.*

"Well?" Jovi pushes when I don't answer. "Will we?"

A small lump swells in my throat.

We've done everything we can to avoid talking about it, but he flies back to Fayeweather tomorrow morning. While we haven't discussed what that means for the two of us, I'm not dumb enough to believe in a long-distance relationship, especially not one that takes place in two different countries. You've met Kellan. That would go against everything in his nature, not to mention I don't need that type of stress. I've gotta focus on graduating. That's…That's the most important thing right now.

"Brie."

"Probably not." I clear my throat, needing to banish the bleak emotions. "He flies home tomorrow. He was only in town for the run."

Her brown eyes widen. "Really?"

I nod and casually shrug. "It's not a big deal. I knew that from the start. Guess in a way I didn't think it would matter. Didn't exactly plan to spend this much time together. Hell, I didn't think he'd still be interested."

Jovi scoffs just as the runners come around for the first lap.

Not leading the pack, but shortly behind is Kellan happily jogging along. He slows down a bit and scans the crowd until he spots me. The moment our eyes connect, he gives me a quick wink and picks up the speed again.

Don't remind me he's even dreamier glistening in a thin layer of sweat. Ugh. Can you imagine how hot he'd look on top of me like that?

"Why the hell would you think he wouldn't still be interested?!" my roommate unexpectedly squeaks.

Knowing it's time for another confession, I let out a deep sigh and lower my voice. "Because he basically can have any woman he wants. He's royalty."

"Royalty?"

"A prince."

"A prince?"

"Well…that and *technically* a duke."

"And a duke?"

"Yeah, I don't *really* know what a duke does, though. If you ask Kellan, he'll insist he doesn't do shit that he should."

Jovi gives me a sarcastic look. "Uh-huh. What's the *real* reason, Brie?"

"*That.*"

Before she can accuse me of anything, I lift a finger for her to hold on and use my other hand to remove my cell from my back pocket. After a quick type of his name in the search engine, I lean the phone over for her to see. Jovi instantly gasps and snatches the device from my hands. With her mouth agape, she looks through the photos and social media posts, disbelief growing with every passing scroll.

"Holy shit," her voice barely whispers as I remove my cell from her loose grasp. "I knew I recognized him from somewhere! I saw the photos of him playing strip poker with Meegan Malone!"

I unconsciously sneer.

No! I'm not jealous! We've spent more time together than they did. We've seen each other naked. I'm even willing to bet that I've had more orgasms from him than she had. The only thing I'm jealous about her having experienced won't matter by the end of the night because I will know exactly what that's like as well.

"Yeah, he's got a fetish for trouble," I say at the same time he rounds the route for his second lap.

This time he lifts his hand to wave, and I give him a small one in return.

"Is that what's bothering you? The fact that he usually spends his time with actresses?"

Her question redirects my eyes back to her. "And *underwear models. Singers. Athletes. Artists.* Not to mention other members of *royalty*." Doing my best to battle back the bitterness, I snap, "Like I said earlier, he can have literally almost any woman he wants, and he's still slumming it with me. I didn't think I'd have to worry about saying goodbye because I swore, he'd already be gone from my life by now."

Especially given the fact he didn't get to sleep with me on our first or second date.

There's no immediate retort from my best friend.

The crowd cheers in waves as people they recognize jog or walk by, and the winter wind whispers more ferociously than it has all week.

"And now that he's still here," Jovi quietly deduces, "you don't know how to handle letting go. You don't know how to say goodbye because you don't *want to*."

I press my lips together.

"You're afraid he's going to forget all about you when he gets on the plane tomorrow and no matter what he says or does, you've already convinced yourself that that's what's going to happen. That's how all this is going to end. That this whole week is going to be thrown into the bucket of crazy college moments you don't believe actually happened." She bumps into me to get my attention. When I look at her, she gives me a kind expression. "But it did happen. And he's not going to forget about you as easily as you're thinking. This is the happiest I've seen you since we met, Brie. Enjoy…whatever the two of you have and remember you're actually special in comparison to all those women who were just conquests. You don't have to have a snooty title or a fancy job or strut around half-naked to grab or keep his attention. He's in love with who you are, not what you look like or how your jewels match his."

"You're proud of that jewel comment, aren't you?"

"Little bit."

I shake my head and face the runners again. "And he's not in love with me. No one falls in love that fast."

"I did."

Okay fine. No 29-year-old guy who has made a sport of sleeping with his pick of the world's finest women would. Also, no intelligent 27-year-old woman. She wouldn't either, even if he makes her laugh like never before, smile like her troubles can actually be fixed, or scream in unwavering pleasure she had only witnessed on a Showtime Original series.

Kellan effortlessly rounds his third lap, and like he can't control himself, his eyes gravitate to mine, which is when I playfully stick my tongue out at him. He chuckles, shakes his head, and returns the gesture.

"*Yup*," Jovi arrogant whispers. "Totally. In. Love."

His eyes light up so brightly while laughing that it's blinding.

"Question is…what are you gonna do about it?"

Nothing. Absolutely nothing.

The hole in the wall restaurant around the corner from Kellan's hotel has the same homey feeling that many of the other places downtown do. While the wooden décor itself isn't unique, the barrel-style tables and corners of the bar are what give it the little touch of individuality required to survive in this city. The bar itself is home to a multitude of common and uncommon beers on tap, including Kellan's favorite.

Merrick drapes an arm around the back of Jovi's chair. "So, who won?"

"Wasn't a race," Kellan replies as the waitress places a glass of beer in front of him.

"Thank goodness for that," Hugh lightheartedly states. "We would've raised a lot less money."

I know what you're thinking. He definitely looks like a young Patrick Dempsey.

"Did you raise much?" I ask, reaching for the beer being offered to me.

"*Very much.*"

"And whatever they raise from other donors at this run, I always personally match," Kellan warmly announces.

"What happens if they raise a million bucks?" Merrick questions skeptically.

"Then I'm not gambling in Vegas that spring," he jokes, receiving a small laugh from around the table. His fingers slide over the table to link with mine. "Honestly, if the foundation were to raise that sort of money, I wouldn't hesitate to match it. It's a great cause. They've helped change *thousands* of lives. I'm honored and humbled to be a part of it."

There's a small coo from the other women at the table.

"As much as I wish I could call bullshit on that, I can't," Hugh mumbles and has a sip of his beer. "Kellan's been an active member in raising funds for years."

"I became active when Hugh took a job with them."

"Which was the best decision I ever made," he states proudly. "It was in my field of interest. It kept me close to my best friend." His attention drifts to the woman at his side. "And brought me the woman I love."

She awes and leans over to kiss him.

After the chaste peck, Merrick says, "Alright, look, I'm not shitting cash or anything, but if you ever need a volunteer to paint something or help with paint related projects, I'm all yours."

"Merrick currently paints elaborate murals indoors and outdoors at a private preschool. Outside changes with the seasons, but he also handles the painting of their booths for their carnivals and that sort of thing," Jovi explains between sips.

"He's *really* good," I insure. "Like hurts my soul to say how good he is type of good."

"Oh! Oh! We were just tossing around the idea of a summer carnival!" Dana's entire face illuminates. "Maybe at one of the children's hospitals. We might need your services for that."

"Done," Merrick states at the same time he grabs his water.

Yes. Responsible drinkers. Only one of them at a time is allowed to get wasted without a third person to drive. Unfortunately, more often than not that third person winds up being me.

"I'd love to be a part of that project as well," Kellan says, his eyes moving to mine. "I'd love any reason to return here."

A hint of a smile arrives on my face, which prompts him to lift my hand to his lips for a brief kiss. The faint feeling of his mouth on my body forces my bottom lip between my teeth.

Kellan smoothly leans over and whispers in my ear, "You drive me *absolutely mad* when you make that face."

It's involuntary. Kinda just happens when I'm turned on or start to get turned on or am about to come. Hm. That's really more of a dessert topic. You know, after we've all had a few too many beers.

Hugh playfully chastises his best friend. "Good god, man, are you going to start reading her poetry next?"

"Stop it," Dana swiftly scolds. "I think it's sweet."

"I think Hugh's just jealous," Kellan sighs returning his attention to the entire table. "It's been *ages* since he's had to share my affections."

He winks, and we snicker at the banter that's beginning.

"Woe as me," Hugh mocks, lifting a hand to his forehead. "Whatever will I do without you around to remind me why beer is better than whiskey and how a St. Valmonte *suit* should never be worn without Malencino *shoes*."

"Drown in the ocean of mediocrity," Kellan arrogantly chortles.

"If it makes you feel any better Hugh, I turned one of those suits into a napkin on our first date."

His jaw drops in shock as his attention darts to me. "Really?"

"We don't have to talk about that." Kellan lovingly squeezes my hand. "In fact, we don't have to talk about our first date at all."

I arch an eyebrow. "Embarrassed?"

He gives me a mischievous expression. "*For you*."

"What do you mean for me?"

"You were the one who hired a male escort to go to a Monster Truck show."

There's a collective gasp around the table followed by one loud, "What?!"

And this is why I can't possibly be in love with him. No one in their right mind would love someone who they wanna nut punch this often.

Over the next few hours, the six of us exchange quirky embarrassing stories, laugh at date mishaps, and munch relentlessly on appetizers. Hugh and Dana put back several beers while Jovi, Kellan, and I quit after two. By the time our burgers are delivered, everyone is so comfortable around each other, it feels like we've been doing this for years. Like this is a weekly ritual.

I hate it. I hate how easily he fits into my life and vice versa. I hate how our friends get along. I hate that this can't last. Wait. No. Sh. I didn't say that last shit. Nope. Never happened.

"Try it." Kellan turns to me with his burger held out. "It's delicious."

Swallowing the bite I had in my mouth, I give his dinner a suspicious examination. "Anything unusual on it that doesn't belong there? Peppers? Sprouts? Corn sprinkles?"

He tilts his head at me in obvious curiosity. "Like candy corn sprinkles or pieces of corn sprinkled on it?"

"*Either*."

"*Neither*," Kellan insists with a smirk. "It's got mushrooms and blue cheese."

"What is with your hatred of normal food? Did it hurt you in some way? Did it bully you in the schoolyard or whatever it is you had at boarding school?"

"No, I simply just enjoy watching you squirm."

Jovi loudly giggles, and I almost glance in her direction.

"Come on, Brie. Don't be a pussy."

"You're really gonna call me that *every time* we do this, aren't you?"

"I am."

My eyes slightly narrow.

"Have a bite. You'll like it. Perhaps you'll even love it." He barely pauses before he's pushing the burger harder in my direction. "Go on. Bite."

"You're like a food rapist."

There's a brief sound of someone laughing then a choking cough. Our eyes cut over to see Merrick pounding his chest in a struggle to breathe.

Once it's clear he's all right, I point at him. "That's what you get for being an enabler."

"It was funny!"

"Funny enough to die for?"

"Stop messing with Merrick to avoid trying something new," Kellan scolds. "*Taste it*."

I frown harder.

"It's either this or a cauliflower chip."

"Something is *seriously* broken about you. What's wrong with plain old fashion fries?"

"*Chips*," Kellan corrects with a smirk.

I drop my mouth to argue when Hugh interrupts. "You might as well give up that victory now because it's not going to happen. Trust me. We spent *years* arguing about what they're called. *Years, Brie.* It was not a fun adjustment to call them that while we were in boarding school and it's – to this day – *still* not a thing I love to call them when visiting Doctenn."

My boyfriend smiles smugly again. "A bite or a chip?"

With a roll of my eyes, I cave. "Fine. I'll try your stupid snobby burger, but for the record? *They're fries*." I have a quick bite of the strange dish, surprised at the odd combination being less disgusting than I imagined.

Whatever. Still doesn't beat the All-American, bacon cheeseburger.

"Gonna die?" He teases, placing it down back on his plate.

Rather than make an immediate retort, I dip one of my fries in ketchup and smear a bit on his face. "Long live fries!"

"Yes!" Hugh lifts his fist in solidarity.

The table erupts into laughter while Kellan merely wipes away the mess. "First butter now ketchup." Mischief appears in his bright blues. "Please, tell me whip cream is at least next."

His sexual implication unexpectedly steals a breath from me.

Before our flirtation can continue, Dana questions, "Did you say butter?"

"Do you really wanna hear about their kinks?" Hugh interjects.

"Probably since you don't have any of your own," Kellan instantly counters. "Unless you count the mut shock collar you wear around your neck."

"You guys are into that lifestyle?" Jovi sincerely asks at the same time I push my plate away.

Dana giggles, which is when Hugh hits her with an inebriated grin. "Sadly not. At least not *that* aspect…"

My best friend shifts beside Merrick who tries to redirect the conversation. "Butter?"

"We melted some last night for the popcorn," I explain. "Sorry to get everyone's hopes up on that one."

"Buttered popcorn before running?" Hugh leans back as the waitress clears his dish. "You don't usually eat anything remotely bad for you before an athletic event."

"Is that why you were wheezing out there?" I tease, loving the way his forehead wrinkles.

"I was *not* wheezing."

"You were like the little runner who could. By the fourth lap, we thought you were gonna pass out from not enough oxygen."

Laughter ensues from everyone else while Kellan pushes his plate away. "Perhaps if someone hadn't decided that one in the morning was a good time to take an interest in the hit television show *Doctor Who* – once again confusing two countries – I might not have been so tired nor needed the popcorn to get me through the wee hours."

"Wait. You're not British?" Merrick's question makes me smirk.

Kellan lets out a heavy sigh and hangs his head in defeat. We laugh again during the waitress's continued collection of the dishes. The moment she reaches for his, he looks up and politely hands her his credit card. "The tab, please. To me."

"We can pay for our meal," Merrick insists, sitting up a little straighter. "It's not a big deal."

He hates letting anyone else pay for his girlfriend. Being overprotective is just his nature. Jovi says his whole family is that way. Haven't met them yet but totally believe it.

"It's quite all right," Kellan argues kindly. "It's a pleasure to treat my mates – new and old – and my…" The term almost falls from his lips, yet he swallows it instead. He takes a beat before trying again. "My date."

That was a terrible save.

"Thank you all for supporting me today and making this trip *the best one* that I've ever had."

The start of his goodbye speech slowly begins to spill into my lungs making it hard for me to breathe.

I'll be fine. You can stop giving me that look. It's enough that Jovi is. Geez, it's like having labradoodle puppy at the table.

Hugh sneaks a subtle glance at me. "Early flight?"

He's reluctant to answer. "Much earlier than I'd like."

With the entire mood of the table shifted, the waitress bringing him the bill is a welcomed deflection. He thanks her and begins to sign the receipt while Jovi expresses her gratitude again for the food. Another round of appreciation escapes everyone else, eventually resulting in the decision for us to part ways for the evening. While Hugh, Kellan, and Dana hug and briefly mention seeing each other again, I assure Jovi and Merrick that I don't need a ride home. Merrick gets ready to further push the subject but is overruled by his girlfriend with a stern look. Outside the six of us part ways with Kellan and I heading for his hotel located to the right.

"Whenever you're ready, Swiss and I will escort you home," he sweetly promises, folding his fingers with mine.

Trepidation collides into the shaky temperament I've been dealing with since I made the decision to enjoy our last night together to the fullest extent. "And if I would rather not go home?" His eyes meet mine as we stop at the corner. "Then what?"

For the first time, Kellan appears to be rendered speechless.

Ha. I was hoping that would happen.

It takes a minute, but he eventually guarantees, "Then I'll bring you your morning beverage in bed."

The light changes to allow us to cross right as I present him with a bashful smirk.

Upon entering the hotel lobby, he drops my hand and instructs, "One moment."

I watch him shuffle back to Swiss, explain something that receives several nods, and then sharply spin around to return to me. At my side, he locks our fingers once more before guiding us in the direction of the private elevators with his bodyguard nowhere in sight.

Playfully, I say, "No babysitter close by tonight?"

The doors ding open, and he quips, "Rest assured love, I know all the emergency numbers."

For some unknown reason, our ride up to the penthouse is eerily quiet.

Was the implication for sex enough? Do I have to spell it out? I'm not sure I can get much more forward without backing down. I know it shouldn't be this big of a deal to have sex, but it is to me, alright? Not just because it's been a couple of years – embarrassing shit I'll have you know – but because despite what Jovi said, I'm still slightly afraid of being inadequate in comparison to the others he's been with. Getting lost in a sea of open legs without faces. But I want to do this. I want to be with him in the only way I haven't yet. I want to experience every aspect of Kellan Kenningston before he vanishes like the walking dream come true that he is.

Kellan shuts the penthouse door and leans his back against it. His mouth remains closed; however, his eyes are coated in caution. After much internal deliberation, he declares, "I'll be fine ending our last night together the same way we've spent all the others, Brie. We don't have to end up in bed together just because I'm leaving."

I try to still my shaky voice. "I wanna ask my question now."

His eyebrows lift to the ceiling in confusion. "What?"

"The first time we had dinner together. You told me I could have one no bullshit, completely honest answer to any question I asked whenever I wanted it answered."

"I…did."

"I'm ready to ask it now."

An open palm is gestured towards me. "Ask."

"If we sleep together…will you remember my face when you leave?" I take a brave step closer to him, wanting – *needing* – to read his expression as much as hear his words. "And I don't mean for the five minutes after you drop me off in the morning or the first hour on the plane. Will you remember my face in the future as if it *really* mattered to you once upon a time?"

To my surprise, he doesn't immediately answer. From where I'm standing, he doesn't even appear to be breathing anymore.

Well, fuck. **This *is comforting. He looks like he's been asked the hardest question on Jeopardy ever known to man.***

Kellan's blue eyes take my brown hostage at the same time he takes a step forward. "*Yes*." Slowly, his hand lifts to stroke my cheek. "*Your face*." His touch leisurely locates to my lips stealing a small gasp. "*Your kiss*." The tour continues down the front of my thin, black long sleeve shirt. "*Your curves*." When his fingertips graze my nipples, I softly moan. "*Your sounds*." This time he uses his hand to press my body firmly against his. "*Your name*." With our mouths just a breath away from one another, he sweetly swears, "*I will never forget you, Brie Sanders*."

My mouth shamelessly slams against his wanting to taste every one of those words. Almost instantly, our tongues mesh, melting away any minuscule bit of apprehension still lingering. Much like any time our bodies are within close proximity to one another, a ravenous hunger wreaks havoc, mutating light touches into greedy grabs and soft moans into savage snarls. Within minutes, our tangled limbs are hitting the bed, with our clothes nothing more than a mere distant memory of the day's activities. For what feels like hours, we take turns exploring every edge, every inch of each other that we can get our eager mouths around. While he holds his own orgasms at bay, teeth repeatedly chomping down on his bottom lip, cock continuously crying pre-cum from desperation to let go, mine are granted permission to flow freely, constantly exploding with such intensity I'm beginning to doubt that I'll even make it to the next part.

As I struggle to steady my breathing once more, I watch Kellan grab a box of condoms from his suitcase and toss it on the nightstand. Carelessly, he rips open the one he kept in his hand, swiftly covers himself, and crawls back between my shaky legs.

His fingers drag themselves up the outside of my thighs like a predator admiring his newly trapped prey.

I can't think of anyone else I would rather have devour me.

Suddenly, he rolls the two of us around positioning me on top. "It's your show, love."

With my eyes connected to his, I drag myself up and wrap my hand around his covered shaft. The moment I do, I relish the delicious way his eyes roll back into his head from the simple touch. In one slow, tantalizing motion, I slip him into my wet heat, moaning through every stretch his cock is commanding.

Kellan's fingers dig into my hips at the same time he whispers, "Bloody hell, you're tight."

I don't attempt to move. "It's been a while."

A groan rumbles through him causing my muscles to clench in excitement. "Months?" Instead of facing possible humiliation, I begin to leisurely lift myself up and down, hoping the slow, salacious distraction entices him into abandoning the needless investigation. Another deep groan escapes as his eyes threaten to close from pure, incessant content. "Brie," he fights to say, "How long?" His hips thrust upward to echo the command for an answer. When I simply moan in return, he repeats the action harder. Nudges deeper. Caresses the need to come in a way I've never experienced before. Anxious to feel it again, I attempt to increase my speed, yet he stops completely and his stare bores into mine. "*How. Long?*"

Sexually flustered, I snip, "Does it really matter?"

His head tilts to the side, and the grin I've found a fondness for appears in a way I know I'm not going to like. "Do you really want to come?"

"Are you gonna hold my orgasms hostage?"

"Are you going to force me to?" His cock pleads inside of me with a twitch. "How long, Brie?"

"Years."

"How many?"

"Enough."

"*How. Many?*"

"Two!" I huff. "Happy?! Now, can we please-"

Kellan swiftly wraps a hand around the nape of my neck and tugs our mouths together. His free hand pins me in place while his dick begins to ebulliently deliver new depths of ecstasy. Every harsh heave causes my pussy to pulsate in a powerful plead for more. I attempt to pull my lips away to free my moans, but it only spurs him to kiss me harder. *Rougher.* His mouth aggressively refuses my request and swallows my moans as punishment for even bothering to attempt to break away. The intemperateness from the combination of being dominated yet worshiped, controlled but only for the sake of my appeasement, becomes too much to bear. My slick muscles swell and squeeze and shriek in satisfaction while endlessly steeping his shaft in scorching juices. There's no staving off the blinding bliss that bursts through my entire body, and my passionate screams overpower his attempt at containment.

"Ohmygod, ohmygod," my voice chants in breathless pants against the crook of his neck. "*Yes, Kellan. Yes!*"

"*Bloody hell, love.*" All of a sudden, his arms tightly engulf me, and a low rumble rips from his lips, "*Yes.*" More groans rattle the two of us against the mattress. "Just like that." His dick wildly thrashes against my soaking wet thrums just as he possessively growls, "*I'm coming.*"

His shudders merge with mine until we're both coming so hard that I swear my soul aches.

Is that a thing? Is that what sex is supposed to be like every time, and I've just been missing out? Oh shit. Wait. Have I been doing it wrong?!

Despite being winded, Kellan strives to explain, "It matters because it tells me whether to give your body what it *wants*," his face turns towards where mine is smushed near his neck, "or what it *needs*." He sweetly pushes a strand of hair behind my ear. "And now that you've had what you *need*, I will spend the rest of the night giving you what you *want*."

I start to smile at the same time he does.

Too bad it's only one night. I would love to have a lifetime of this, but, like I've learned the hard way, you rarely get exactly what you want, so it's best to enjoy the little bit of what you're given no matter how much it may hurt when it's gone. Damn it! Now, I've got that Rolling Stones song stuck in my head. Bet you will too since I mentioned it. Haha. You're welcome.

CHAPTER TWELVE

Kellan

The sound of Brie's heavy breathing swells my chest with pride.

I did that. I wore her out to the point she collapsed in a delicious defeat. Between you and I, I was directly behind her. The minute her eyes fell shut and her breathing steadied, I draped my arm around her and followed suit. While I'm not quite sure exactly how long we were completely lost in our sexual rhapsody, I do know it's too soon for the sun to be caressing the clouds. It should still be in bed as the two of us. If it's rising that means the most amazing week of my entire life has finally come to an end. And I'm not ready for that. God, I honestly don't think I'll ever really be ready for that.

My finger gingerly grazes the curve of her back, completely enraptured with the way she's displayed for me. Her body slightly stirs as if unsure whether it should wake for more or continue to peacefully slumber.

She should always wake up for more. I want her to always want more from me. For her to be as in dire need of me as I have stumbled into becoming in dire need of her.

Now palming her beautifully firm ass, I lower my tongue to the exposed portion of her neck and lasciviously lick until it elicits a cloyingly sweet sigh. Swiftly, I slide the anxious muscle between her slightly parted lips and nudge her legs apart. My hand casually slips to the exposed territory and gently glides a finger against it. Brie happily hums her approval. One pleasing push transitions into two and three and four as the muscles grow wetter with every passing caress. Strokes are selfishly delivered from two ends, greedily building up her need to have me buried deep like I spent most of the night. I wait for her to become a whimpering, withering mess before pulling back to reach over to the nightstand beside her where the condoms are located.

Yes, I am even more clever than I appear. I put a stash on each bedside table so no matter where we ended up, they were easily accessible. However, I never imagined we could possibly risk running out. Had we not fallen asleep when we did, we might have. That would have been a new one for me as well, and I wouldn't have been happier to experience it with her.

As soon as my dick is protected, I angle her leg a little higher and sharply thrust through the tender muscles. She instantly sighs my name like a forbidden prayer while her pussy squeezes its relief regarding my return. A low growl festers in the back of my throat, and I push deeper, desperate to reassure her there's isn't an inch inside or out that will ever be forgotten. That *could n*ever be forgotten. I relentlessly rock, each time pulling my cock completely back so that her scorching heat can continuously sear every inch of my shaft during my strokes. Somewhere between her carnal cries and my barbaric rumbles, Brie syncs to my slow pumps and uses one hand to spin circles around her clit. The moment the other carelessly clutches the sheet in back bowing bliss, I pin it in place, wanting nothing to distract from the intoxicating abandonment we've fallen into. The woman I can't seem to ever stop thinking about slips her bottom lip between her teeth and whimpers louder, a simple yet cock swelling tell that announces Brie's orgasm is only a few breaths away. Her body slowly begins to seize in satisfaction, taking mine with it. Everything else ceases to matter. *To exist.* Our moans unceasingly oscillate, and my eyes fall shut, enraptured by the erotic harmony echoing around the room.

Why does this no longer feel like sex? Why is it every time I touch her it feels like so much more? What is this? What's happening to me?

Mere seconds after pulling out and swiftly disposing of the used rubber, there's a knocking on the front door that I'm dreading to answer.

"Who's knocking before the sun is even up?" Brie questions with a hint of somberness in her voice.

She knows as well as I do that our sacred time together is almost over.

I hit her with a playful smirk and grab the pair of jeans I wore to dinner. Quickly, I head out of the bedroom and for the door where the knocking is growing in urgency.

When I open it, Melinda extends the two cups in her hands. "Your wake-up call, Mr. Kenningston."

A deep sigh leaves me even though I arranged this. "Why do I feel like they moved seven a.m.?"

"Time always seems to move quickly when you live with passion instead of apathy." She gives me a small smile. "Your bags will be collected in an hour, and your requested pastries will be waiting for you downstairs when you check out."

"And Swiss?"

"Already waiting in the lobby, Mr. Kenningston."

I give her a curt nod. "Thank you."

She presents me with another polite grin and dismisses herself.

By the time I return to the bedroom, Brie has already slumped back between the sheets and began to drift back in the direction she came. Rather than wake her, I lean against the frame and silently stare, anxious to chisel into my memory every detail about her that's possible.

Look at how her soft brown skin glimmers in the early morning light. The way her lips are still pouty from our kisses. Let's not forget to acknowledge her messy, wavy hair that's practically acting as another pillow for her to sleep on. And then there's the way that her body is angled. How it's curved in such a way that there's space for me to easily fit in beside her as if we were puzzle pieces rather than people. Why the hell did I ever think it would be easy to walk away from her?

"Quit leering at me like I'm a new tie in your closet," she yawns, eyes still closed. "We've talked about this. *It's creepy.*"

And her attitude is the bow that keeps everything perfectly tied together.

"Is that any way to speak to the man who not only brought you to climax but brought you salted caramel hot chocolate as well?"

One eye pops open in suspicion.

"That's right," I smirk and approach the bed. "I always deliver on my promises, love."

She rolls over to face me though I'm unsure if the glow she's radiating is from sex or the term of endearment.

Which it is. It is a common term of endearment. Why are you asking me if that's the case here? No. No, I don't have time to have that argument with you again and *pack. And I have to pack. Kris loses his mind when I just leave luggage to be auctioned off on internet sites.*

The moment the cup is in her hands, she has a long sip and hums her gratification. "Indeed, you do."

Unable to resist our playful banter, I poke, "Are you referencing my promise to deliver you a morning beverage or my promise to give you what wanted all night?"

"Did you though?"

My jaw slightly slacks.

With a victorious giggle, she has another sip and gives me a reassuring wink.

I wasn't worried whether or not I successfully pleased her. I was there. Your mouth can fake many things, but your body can't. Well. If you know what to look for that is.

"I have to start packing." I quietly declare at the same time I sit on the edge of the bed beside her.

Her shoulders drop, but she nods her understanding. "I guess I should get dressed."

"Since I don't want the room attendants seeing your luscious body in this beautiful state, I would say that's probably for the best." This time when she smiles, I lean over and press my lips possessively against hers. There's no resistance to let me mark her in what I hate to believe is our next to the last kiss.

What? No. I can't stay. I just…I can't.

While packing has become an easy routine for me that I can mindlessly accomplish, packing whilst engaged in tangled tongues and stolen strokes is a completely different matter. However, somehow, everything ends up being prepared for the bell hops by their arrival.

In the SUV, Brie's leaned against the tie on my chest, silently picking at the raspberry cream cheese Danish, doing her best to avoid the fruit portion.

I give her forehead a sweet kiss. "You do know that raspberries aren't poisonous, yes?"

"In this form, they taste like nature's old candy." She sucks the filling off her thumb. "Next time, we should do doughnuts. Oooo or doughnut holes! Or I guess if you just *insist* on being a fancy bitch, we could do crepes."

"Did you really just refer to me as a fancy bitch?"

"You know, I actually don't mind crepes. They're basically just thin pancakes you can stuff with chocolate or caramel or again – if you just *have to be* a fancy bitch – Nutella."

"That's twice now."

"Not that there's going to be a next time…" Brie begins, pulling herself out of my grasp, "but in case there is-" Her head frantically shakes from side to side as she tosses the treat back in the box, "But there won't be. Fuck, there probably can't be. That was stupid shit to say. I-" She cuts herself off and locks eyes with me. "I'm...I'm trying really hard not to make this awkward and am failing."

"*Miserably*," I tease in hopes to see a glint of the trouble I've come to adore.

Instead, she shamefully hides her face.

It was a joke! I wasn't intending to be an arsehole!

My fingers gently turn her back towards me by the chin. "*I was kidding.*"

She tries to smile.

"You're not the only one who's terrible at goodbyes," I confess as the car pulls to a stop in her apartment complex.

"What do you usually do?" She snaps harshly. "Just tell them the money is on the nightstand and then grab a shower?"

Sensing the defensive shift in her, I push aside what's left of our breakfast and slip our fingers together. "I'm gonna let the whore comment go because I know it would be easier to leave while you're cross with me rather than…" The end of the sentence abruptly fades into the unknown. I clear my throat and attempt to continue, "Most of the time, they decide to let themselves out. They thank me for the amazing time, leave their numbers if I don't already have it, and go on their way. In the rare cases where I have to initiate their departure, it moves quite similarly. I announce I have engagements to attend for the day and offer to provide them with a ride home or wherever they need to go. I don't say goodbyes, Brie. Goodbyes mean something, and those women have always been meaningless." Her grip tightens and I reassure, "Saying goodbye to you isn't something I'm prepared for. I'm honestly not even sure *how*."

All of a sudden, she reaches up and gives my cheek a small stroke. For a moment, the two of us merely stare into each other's eyes, studying their colors. Their depths. Their intensities. Afterward, she leans over and gently pushes her lips to mine. They linger for what feels like an eternity before briefly parting to give our tongues their last taste.

Brie pulls away much too soon and sighs, "Have a good flight, Kellan."

I attempt to swallow the unexpected knot in my throat.

"You can text me when you land safely if you want."

"I certainly will."

She gives me one last smile, Swiss a pat on the shoulder, and begins to exit the vehicle. I prepare to ask if she wants me to walk her to her door if she wants this goodbye to stretch out as long as I do, but the door slams shut giving me the answer.

It's probably for the best. I can't imagine any good would come from prolonging the inevitable.

My eyes follow her movements until she's completely disappeared from my sight. At that point, I weakly instruct, "To the airstrip."

Swiss puts the vehicle in drive and makes his way back towards the entrance. As we pull out onto the main road, the loitering lump in my throat expands tremendously. I shut my eyes tightly in a pointless attempt to forget that it's there.

It'll go away. It has to.

The sound of my phone vibrating unexpectedly pierces my ears, and I rush to check it. Seeing the photo of my brother's cheerful mug during an embrace with his wife only further expands the blockage of my vocal cords.

I reluctantly answer, voice slightly hoarse. "Hello."

"Don't tell me you're still sleeping," Kristopher immediately fusses. "You knew you had to fly out this morning. How bloody hungover are you?"

The side of my head hits the window. "I'm not."

Though, I wish I were. I wish right now I was so inebriated I didn't know my own name let alone hers. That would at least start to make the pain bearable.

A small lull occurs before Kris inquires, "Are you headed to the airstrip?"

Swiss pulls up to another red light.

It's impressive that he's hit every one since we left her apartment.

"Yes."

He immediately hums in relief. "Good."

"Good? As in you'll be pleased to have me back? Not enjoying the way my absence has been lowering the risk of you having a stroke at an early age?"

"It means I can share the gracious amount of attention brewing around the annual Valentine's Day Ball," Kristopher sighs. "The media is in a frenzy over concerning themselves with what Soph is to wear and which designers won't stop calling and what we'll be serving as the special treats for the couples and what unique thoughtful gifts will we give to show our gratitude for them coming." He grunts his obvious annoyance. "I'd much rather they trip over themselves trying to decipher if you're going stag or bringing along the latest piece of ass to effortlessly fall into your lap."

I helplessly groan.

Never once have I dreaded going to it. It's one of our family traditions that started generations ago. We open part of the palace to those deemed worthy by people who get paid to make that distinction – other royalty, celebrities, million and billionaires – shower them with extravagant eats – always themed –, the finest glasses of wine – at least one sample for our coveted cellar collection –, and allow them to feel a touch of what people perceive to be the royal treatment. It's a bloody joke. Most of the traditions we still have are. Sometimes I wonder what it would be like to shake the damn thing up. Have a set of guests do something unpredictable like show up in attire worthy of the Met Gala or get caught snogging someone of the same sex openly rather than behind a closed door.

"Why does everyone care what I'm wearing?" Soph grouses in the background. "I should wear a turtleneck and khakis. That'll teach them to value what I say *less than* what I fucking wear."

The sound of her voice brings me minor solace yet uncorks a thought I had steadily been avoiding. "Is that Soph?"

"Of course, it is. My other wife wouldn't dare make such a big deal out of the annual ball."

"Your other wife also looks like a speckled frog when she's naked," she quickly quips.

"May I speak with her?"

"Why?"

"Before your blood pressure spikes, you can rest assured it's not to discuss your measurements of any kind."

Yes, even in agony, I'm still quite a bastard little brother.

There's a small shuffling sound prior to her sweet voice cooing, "His measurements will be cut in *twain* if he brings up the subject of this damn dance again."

I can't help but pour gasoline on the fire. "*Ball*."

"What do you want, Kellan?"

A deep sigh mindlessly shifts from me. "Can we actually speak in private?"

"Out of the room," she instantly fusses at my brother.

An exchange of some sort occurs but my attention is lost outside the window as the university Brie attends completely fades from view.

"Gone," Soph sings with what I imagine is an excited smirk.

"Soph..." I slowly begin, searching for the correct words to convey everything while confessing nothing. "Would it be wrong to stay?"

"Stay where?"

"Here."

"In the states?"

"Yes."

"Well, that depends."

"On?"

"If it has anything to do with the woman you had Clarence search for last week."

Did you...Did you tell her?!

Before I can prod for further information, she informs, "He mentioned it the next morning on his way to see your father. He could barely keep it in. You know, it's not every day Prince Kellan calls for a favor from the in-house security team."

Another groan escapes.

Great. Just what I needed. Rumors that'll get my father involved in my life. Swear the staff gossips more than the tabs sometimes.

"Don't worry," Soph says, dropping her volume. "I told him not to mention it to anyone, your brother included. Although…Kris does *hate* the elusiveness you've created around the subject. It's very unlike you to give subtle clues, but never an actual answer. His frustration over the subject is quite hilarious to watch."

I villainously smirk.

"However, no need to fret. Her identity is still a mystery to everyone besides me and Clarence." The pause is brief. "At least it is until you don't get on that jet to come home…"

I press my lips together and shut my eyes. "Am I mad for wanting to stay?"

"You're mad for wanting to *leave*."

You don't have to be so snotty as you agree with her.

"Kellan, you don't flee from the first woman you've ever loved-"

"I never said-"

"It doesn't have to be said to be true or felt." Her quick assessment of the situation shuts my mouth once more. "The fact of the matter is, if you weren't in love with this woman, you wouldn't be contemplating between staying or leaving. You wouldn't have spent the past week bragging about spending time with her yet never letting the world know who she is. And you damn sure wouldn't be talking to me in hopes of soothing your fears."

Did I mention my brother's wife is sassy and brilliant? I think I have, but in case I haven't, here is your reminder that she is.

My voice weakly argues, "What if it's a mistake?"

"It's not."

"But what if it is?"

"How could it possibly be one?! This is the first time in your entire life you felt like *staying still* instead of *running*. How is exploring that not a good idea? How is experiencing the one thing you've yet to truly experience a mistake?" Her words burrow themselves deep into the bones of my rigid body. "You have to make this decision all on your own, Kellan. But you should know, either way, whether I see you in a few hours or you send home an empty jet, we love you. Despite any stunt you pull, for better or for worse, we always will." All of a sudden, there are additional voices in the background that prompt her to sigh, "I have to go. Apparently, your father has requested I speak with a new stylist."

I stifle my chuckle. "Best of luck."

"In this family? I'll always need it."

The call ends just as we arrive at the light before the airstrip.

"To the right?" Swiss asks, glancing in the review mirror.

With the private strip that direction and the possibility of gaining something, I had no clue even existed to the left, my back slams against the seat uncertain of what to do next.

I guess the important question I should ask is which way will leave me feeling like my days are worth living.

CHAPTER THIRTEEN

"Missed you at dinner," my dad says into the phone between smacks.

I place my sketchpad down on my bed. "Sorry again that I couldn't make it."

He hums through the sucking of his teeth. "School first. We understand."

That was **mainly** *the case. After I cried myself into a minor exhaustion coma, I woke up and started working on the final piece of my portfolio. I've been deliberating over what it should be for months, but when I woke up, I knew exactly what I wanted to do. I immediately grabbed my sketchpad and have been working on drafts ever since.*

"Dad…"

"Yeah?"

"Why are you munching on Freddie's Fried Chicken?"

He lightly chuckles. "How'd you know?"

"You make a very specific sound when you're slinging back that kinda chicken."

"It's just *so good*."

"What happened to dinner? Mom decide not to cook?"

"No, your sister decided we should try something new, so they concocted this Mediterranean Quinoa salad with this berry vinaigrette and teeny tiny pieces of shrimp." He grunts and starts smacking again. "Swear to Freddie himself that I'll cancel the Food Network if she keeps this shit up."

I helplessly smile.

Obvious where I get my food habits from now, huh? Right down to how I compromise.

"You know sometimes, Dad, it's okay to try new things. Sometimes you even end up liking them."

Or in my case loving... Hm? What? No. I don't want to talk about Kellan.

"This is not one of those times," he firmly declares before letting out an unhappy groan. "Oh, shit. That's your mother calling. She's probably wondering where I am."

My face drops into my open palm. "What?! She doesn't know where you are?"

"Told her I needed to pick up a friend."

"You lied."

"I don't consider it a lie."

"Fried chicken is not your friend!"

"Damn sure it isn't my enemy, either!"

I shake my head in spite of the fact he can't see.

"I should probably answer that."

"You should *definitely* answer that."

"Call me later this week? When you have some free time?"

"Of course."

"Maybe we can squeeze in a quick burger or another bucket of this chicken. We both know it's worth every nickel and dime."

A faint giggle seeps from me. "I love you."

"I love you, too."

Strangely enough just seconds after I end the call, there's a knock on my door.

The first all day.

Believe it or not, Jovi hasn't come to check on me before this moment, which is totally out of character for her. She did have to work this morning and was gone before I got home, but I expected her to barge right in the minute she stepped through the door. Hm. Maybe she did, and I was too knocked out to notice.

"Come in."

Jovi opens the door and casually leans against its frame. "You okay? You've been shut in here all afternoon."

I force a polite smile to my face. "I'm fine."

*Okay, so, I'm **not** fine right now, but I will be. Eventually. If I can fall into...whatever it is I was dumb enough to fall into this past week quickly, then that means I should be able to fall out just as fast. Denial? Most likely. But could you just let me live here for a bit? It's easier than thinking about how much my chest literally aches when I think about him.*

"Fine?" Jovi repeats with skepticism.

"A little tired." My confession causes her to back down. "Didn't sleep much last night."

Excitement fills her eyes. "Please, tell me it's because of the reason I'm thinking and not because you decided to binge-watch something else together."

I let my grin grow wild. "Definitely didn't watch anything but each other last night."

Her mouth cracks open.

"And again, this morning."

Jovi's hands fly over her mouth as she giggles profusely.

Doesn't matter how old women get. We all get a little mawkish when romance is involved.

"Why are you squealing?" Merrick's voice questions from the other room.

She gives me an "oops" look prompting me to call out, "Because I said I would leave my room to be around the two of you despite my own desire for solitude."

Jovi mouths "thank you" as I gather my sketchpad and pencils.

Entering the living room, I'm startled by the sight of textbooks surrounding Merrick from his space on the floor closer to Jovi's bedroom. My head immediately tilts in bemusement. "Are you trying to build a fort out of textbooks?"

He hits me with a scowl. "*That* would actually be fun for me."

"I don't doubt it," I sigh, flopping down on the edge of the couch closest to my room.

"He's studying," Jovi answers over my shoulder. "And he's going to keep studying, or he's going to go to *his* apartment and study. Either way, he will be studying something tonight, and it's not my anatomy."

The sour expression deepens.

Doubt he ever saw his cheap comment coming back to bite him like that.

She slides onto the other end of the couch. "What about you? What are you working on?"

I drag the coffee table closer and drop my sketch pad on top of it. "Early sketches for the final piece of my portfolio."

A small grin creeps on her face. "Oh yeah? Finally found some inspiration?"

Rather than admit anything, I turn the question around. "What about yours? Have you started on it?"

"Been working on it since August," she replies confidently.

"Painting?"

"That's his skill set." Her head tips Merrick's direction. "Not so much mine I've discovered. I mean, people say I've got an eye for spotting talent of that medium, but I actually prefer photography. My final piece is the blending of three photos. One from where I used to live or my 'old life' and one from here or my 'new life' and a piece that connects them."

Jovi's face drifts over her shoulder where her boyfriend is sitting up with a sense of pride.

Another smile spreads on my face, and I drop my stare to my sketchpad.

Art doesn't always imitate life. Sometimes it's just trying to cement it. That's why the best pieces of art are often the ones that contain a memory or a story that deeply speaks to the artist. Doesn't matter if it's music or writing or photography. If it moved or spoke to the creator, it's going to move or speak to the audience. Guess it makes sense that Kellan would be the subject of my final piece.

The knock at the door immediately grabs everyone's attention.

"I got it," Merrick insists, standing up. "It's the pizza we ordered."

"You hungry?" Jovi asks me after he drops a quick kiss on her cheek.

I shake my head and return to attempting to perfect the eye shaping I've been working on for the past hour.

Haven't eaten anything since that pathetic excuse for a breakfast treat. Who on earth puts fruit on their Danish like that? Fruit is a side *at breakfast. Not a topping.*

"You're not the pizza guy," he grunts, causing us both to turn around.

"Sadly not," Kellan states as he enters our apartment.

My jaw can't seem to stop itself from becoming unhinged.

Is he...Is he actually standing in our apartment? Are you sure we're not hallucinating? Can multiple people have the same exact hallucination at the exact same time? You know...without the assistance of drugs or alcohol?

In a voice I hardly recognize, I ask, "What the hell are you doing here?"

"Is this not Doctenn?"

His joke doesn't alter my shocked expression.

"My flat won't be ready until tomorrow afternoon, and I was wondering if you wouldn't mind letting me stay the night?"

The tiniest fraction of hope hitches my breath.

"Perhaps crash on your couch?"

There's no reluctance to spring to my feet, race across the room, and yank him downwards by his shirt. My lips capture with such ferocity it slightly knocks Kellan a step backward. His hands fall to my hips where they lock in a clear declaration that this is where he belongs.

***This is where we both belong.* Together.**

When I pull back, he teasingly inquires, "Is that a yes? Your answer was unclear."

The amused smile on my face stretches from ear to ear.

"Did you say couch?" Merrick interjects at the same time my hands slide down the front of Kellan's shirt. "Why wouldn't you sleep in her bed?"

Kellan's blue gaze lingers in my brown. "She's quite the bed hog."

"That's true," Jovi needlessly agrees.

"Why do you know that?" Her boyfriend immediately investigates.

"Drunk girls like to cuddle. *Duh.*"

"*Duh*," Kellan mimics prior to playfully adding more to his explanation. "Plus, Brie snores. It makes it almost impossible to sleep beside her."

"You fart."

A crimson color threatens his cheeks, but to my surprise, he simply laughs. "Never had a woman say that before."

"Doesn't mean it isn't true."

His smile softens as does mine. "May we speak in private?"

Linking our hands, I lead us towards my bedroom, giving Jovi one final glance to see her barely able to contain her joy.

All of a sudden, there's another knock at the door, and Merrick announces, "That better be the pizza guy and not another British dude."

"*Doctenn!*" Kellan shouts in return before I shut the door with both hands.

I keep my grip on the handle behind my back, still in disbelief that this isn't some weird delusion. When our eyes connect again, I can feel my heart clawing back up my throat, the very place it was wedged this morning during our goodbye. "*You're staying?*"

Kellan slips his hands into his navy-blue suit pants pockets while nodding. "Yes."

"Why?"

"At any given time, there are several things I dread about returning to Fayeweather – dinners, operas, tea to list just a few examples – but I realized this morning, the thing I would dread *the most* is being *thousands of kilometers from you*."

A sweet sigh escapes.

You too?

"Brie, I'm fortunate enough to have a job I can do from literally anywhere in the world that has a Wi-Fi connection; however, there is only one place in the entire world that contains that *and* the woman I'm *absolutely* mad about." He takes a bold step towards me. "And I am absolutely mad about you. I honestly have been from the moment we met and only grown more so that way each day we've been together. So, with that said, I don't think we should say goodbye if we don't have to."

Finally, I release my death grip on the doorknob and approach closer. "What if things don't work out?"

"What happens if they do?"

"What happens when you grow bored of this place?"

"What happens if I don't?"

"I'm serious, Kellan. You're used to living in fancy places and doing things that require you to wear the nine-hundred-dollar suit you're sporting. Not slumming it in an apartment and eating at hole-in-the-wall burger joints."

"Thousand."

"What?"

"The suit. It's nine-*thousand*."

I let my jaw drop again. "Ohmygod, what is wrong with you?! Who flies home in a nine-thousand-dollar suit?!"

"It's the only one that was clean!"

Disbelief shakes my head.

As much as I want him to stay – and it's actually a shit ton more than I originally thought – he **needs** *to go home. He needs to be in a comfortable setting. He needs…He needs to find someone who fits in with* **his life,** *not force him to fit into* **theirs.**

"And a suit at the end of the day is just a suit. And a burger is just a burger. And where you lie your head at night is just another place you rest on your journey. What truly matters is the *person* you have those adventures with."

His point drops my defensive shoulders.

"That person you want to wake up to every morning."

Melting in place is mindlessly done.

"That person who announces in a room full of her mates that her boyfriend farts in his sleep."

I giggle at the victory of embarrassing him.

Yes. I am purposely ignoring the boyfriend's remark.

"We've spent the last week compromising, and I'm rather confident that we can continue to."

My smile brightens for just a brief moment because insecurity prevails promptly. "What happens when you get bored *with me*?"

Kellan's face hardens in seriousness. "*Not. Possible.*"

Of course, it's possible! I'm the first woman he hasn't treated like she's got an expiration date on her ass. I'll only be the new and interesting thing for so long. Then what? Then we suffer this goodbye thing permanently? Then I have to wonder about him loathing my name rather than just remembering it? Then the struggle to move forward, to move on past this one incredible week becomes a lifetime battle to forget how amazing we were together?

"Stop over thinking this," he commands at the same time his hands slink down my lower back to cup my ass. "We'll figure it out as we go. What works and what doesn't. Isn't that what dating is all about?"

Damn it! He doesn't get to be witty, romantic, and logical.

I let my smile return on a playful, "So they tell me. I haven't done in a while."

"At least you've done it." Snickers are exchanged prior to him asking, "Are we on the same page now, love?"

He's immediately given an enthusiastic nod.

"*Perfect.*" His expression becomes devious. "Get naked."

Ah. How he restores balance.

When I lift my eyebrows in defiance, he grips my ass a little tighter, stealing a small, closed-lip moan from me. "I've spent the entire day looking at flats-"

"Apartments."

"*Flats*," he argues on a squeeze, "as well as furnishings for them. I've spent the last hour alone looking at beds and mattresses and sheets with thoughts of you being naked on them taunting me the entire time. So, for the love of your country and mine, *get naked*."

His hardened cock gives me a light tap of encouragement through his slacks. With a flirtatious smirk, I command, "*Manners*."

Kellan immediately groans prior to imploring, "*Please, get naked, love.*"

I step back out of his touch, let my bottom lip slip between my teeth, and slowly remove my yoga shorts. The mixture of arousal and relief on his face rushes through my system causing an identical effect.

My biggest fear between us was being just another nameless face to him, but now I'm worried about what happens when he becomes the face of my broken heart. What? Of course, this is going to end in heartbreak. Sorry. This isn't a fairytale. Every girl is not secretly a princess waiting for the right pair of shoes to change her life. There's a whole list of women the prince meets and chases before those stories begin. I guess I'm gonna end up on Kellan's list of conquests one way or another, right? Might as well enjoy it while I can.

CHAPTER FOURTEEN

Kellan

"It's been six weeks. Surely, you'll be returning home any day now," my brother insists.

I turn around from where the sun is finally beginning to touch the tips of the Highland downtown skyline.

It has been six weeks, and to say that they have been the best six weeks I've ever experienced would be the understatement of a lifetime. Not only have they been filled with weekends of endless sex, but I've come to appreciate the other benefits of staying in one place such as driving a car, a comfortable couch, and homecooked meals. While Brie is a dreadful cook – she was not exaggerating –, her mother is quite exquisite. We enjoy dinner with her parents Sunday evenings typically after exhausting all our efforts to work up an appetite for something other than one another. Considering this is the first time I've had an actual girlfriend, it's the first time I've met a woman's parents for that particular reason as opposed to political and social ones. They're both delightful and absolutely adore me. That last little tidbit drives Brie slightly mad. It also helps me practically get away with the bread in their company. What? You don't understand that idiom? It means getting away with anything. Murder? Well, that's a bit grim, don't you think?

Seeing the look of concern on Kristopher's face from the other end of the computer screen causes me to smirk. He's sitting at the desk in the downstairs library, the very same room he was chewing me out in for not "growing up" exactly one day before I met the woman who reminded me of why he was wrong as well as right.

We're not ever going to admit that last line. Pretend I never even thought it.

"Oh...," I casually lean back in my patio chair, "is my poor big brother having separation anxiety?"

Kristopher rolls his eyes. "If by separation anxiety you mean the need to share the spotlight with my very rowdy, usually very abrasive baby brother then yes. You have barely made more than a light splash in these past few weeks. Your sudden lack of needing attention has shifted the focus to scrutinizing every, single, detail of my marriage."

"Good thing it's a great marriage."

"*It is*," he forcefully reassures, "however, Soph has been accused of being pregnant three times in the past month. She's so stressed about the bullshit that she will no longer eat in public."

The sun lands on the pool water across from me, relocating my attention with it.

Having a balcony connected to your bedroom is one thing, yet having a balcony with a private heated pool attached and an outside breakfast nook area directly beside it is another. Do you know how incredible it is to have a morning workout in the pool and then enjoy breakfast naked immediately afterward? Do you know how amazing it is this is even possible? Another one of the beautiful benefits of playing coy where the media is concerned. They haven't the faintest idea where I really am.

"*Kellan.*"

I shift my focus back to him once more.

"In our entire lives, you have *never* been this silent about…well, truthfully about *anything*."

"I'm not silent. I'm just not shouting it from the rooftops."

"Like I said. *Silent.*"

"If I'm not shouting, I'm silent?"

"If you're not shouting, you've either had your tongue removed or are bound and gagged."

"Language, Kristopher."

"*Kellan.*"

"Look, has it ever occurred to you that perhaps the reason I'm not shouting or screaming or parading this relationship around is because I'm not quite ready to have it potentially ruined by the media?"

"No."

His quick answer forces me to scowl.

"You love the attention!" Kris throws a hand in the air. "You love the praise. You love the negative reinforcement of your wild behavior. You've been steadily on a war path to let no one forget the Kenningston name since Mum died." He readjusts himself in his seat and leans forward. "You don't just stop being who you've always been because some woman let you see her naked for an extended period of time."

My eyes suddenly catch a glimpse of the topic of our discussion moving in my direction. Unable to resist watching her movements, I let my head fall to the side as I admire the curves that I would give up the Kenningston name for without question. The smoothness of her coffee-colored complexion. The lightness in her steps because burdens seem non-existent when we're together.

"None of that has changed," I mutter, attention still plastered on the minx that is approaching the doorway. "Just because the world has a harder time documenting my fun doesn't mean I'm not having any."

Brie leans her naked frame against the wall right on the other side of the sliding door.

"Believe me."

By the way, fun fact! Anyone who owns a penthouse walks around naked knowing no one else can catch a glimpse. Well, probably *can't catch a glimpse. It's a risk always worth taking.*

Desperate to have her in my lap rather than continue to hear my brother complain, I prepare to end the conversation when she shakes her head slowly and makes a hand motion to continue talking.

I glance back in his direction and grunt, "Change the subject."

"But-"

"*Now.*"

His eyebrows lift in question only to receive a stern expression in return. Sensing the reasoning why, he says, "Brunch was rather uneventful."

The choice of topic hardens my expression. Before I have a chance to inform him how I don't care who is potentially sleeping with who to keep the so-called peace between worlds, Brie's movements begin again except this time in an unexpected fashion. She slowly drags one finger down her chest taking my stare helplessly with it.

"There was one particular moment you might find hysterical."

Her finger slips between her thighs and sinks into the depths that I claimed as only my own. I prepare to command her to stop when she winks, drops her bottom jaw, and releases a silent moan.

She's purposely fucking with me while I'm on a call with my brother. I'm clearly dating a sexual terrorist.

"Are you even listening?" Kristopher huffs when he notices I'm not.

Brie's salacious movements cease as she lifts her eyebrows to encourage me to continue the conversation.

"Yes," I lie and readjust the computer screen to make it less obvious he's become a prop in a sexual game. "You were rambling on about Sir Conan Ledger and deviled eggs and his poorly glued on toupee."

Both people now pleased, they each return to their very different tasks. Kristopher resumes his story while I pretend to stare on with complete dedication to our conversation. The fact he is unaware of what is happening on the other side of the screen stiffens my already hard cock to the point of pain. I fold my hands in front of me to block any possible proof my attention is elsewhere. Brie begins to increase the speed of her motions, shamelessly shoving her fingers in deeper, soaking them in stickiness that I want covering my tongue rather than her palm. The back of her head hits the wall on a silent cry of my name that causes my dick to weep pre-cum in the same fashion. My eyes, which are struggling to keep their attention split three ways, primarily oscillate between the expression on her face and the actions of her hand.

"Hysterical, yes?"

I offer Kris a forced chuckle alongside an absentminded nod.

Brie winks, bites her bottom lip, and rocks her hand faster, an orgasm clearly on the horizon.

For fucks sake, this conversation with him has to end soon because the moment she comes – and I mean the very bloody moment she comes – I'm going to take her and show her why orgasms from me are always better. And that's something I don't think my brother wants to witness.

"Speaking of unhappy royalty, Father has a request of you."

Of all the things capable of killing the hard-on I'm sporting he offers the one with the highest possibility. My brother is a world-class cock block. From an early age, I swear! He's the reason I had to start masturbating only at nighttime when we were home. Intrusive bastard.

Brie's legs lightly buckle, and the sight grabs a throat growl from me. "*Not interested.*"

"Please," Kristopher begins to beg, "You're already in the states."

"No."

Her jaw begins to shake stealing my sanity in the process.

"It's just a one-night event."

"No."

"*Kellan*," his voice rises commanding my full attention.

Rather than look completely at him, I gesture my hand to assure him I'm listening.

Which I'm not. Not to him. Not to the birds. Not to cars honking faintly down below. No. The only things I'm actually listening to are the muted moans escaping my girlfriend's parted lips.

"Look, it's a few weeks away in Camelottlin or *Camelot* as it's better known. Plenty of time to mentally prepare having to do the family a bloody favor."

Her free hand suddenly combs through her hair, yanking it as she teeters on the edge of ecstasy.

Fuck, I want to be the one to push her over.

"It's a fundraiser to help feed those starving in third world nations. It's being hosted by Victoria Chasizer, the Marlesqueer born actress who has the huge hard-on for hosting Doctenn friendly events in the states. You know the one who is always trying to fuse our countries together. Anyway, it'll mainly be filled with celebrities and other money-hungry bastards desperate to show they care about something other than themselves."

"Father can't be bothered to help fight the increasing homeless child population in his own country but has no problem throwing cash at a fundraiser that's nothing more than a publicity stunt?" My irritation begins to outrank my arousal. "*Bloody hypocrite.*"

"Please, consider going."

"No."

"It would do well for one of us to be seen there."

"I'm sure it would."

"Plus, if *you* attend *that*, he'll *probably* let you out of the spring banquet this year for having fulfilled a different social obligation."

Temptation tickles itself along my vocal cords.

"Besides, they have a silent auction, and you'll be allowed to bid on expensive things in his name for a good cause."

I prepare to snap once more when the moment I've been waiting for finally arrives. Brie's beautiful chest starts to heave profusely while she recites my name in audibly restrained repetition. Her cries claw their way through me convincing the hard-on that was beginning to waver to stay for the long haul.

With all my attention now on my bleary-eyed love, I mumble, "Yes, I'll consider it. I have to go now, Kristopher." My brother's voice starts some sort of retort, but it's cut off by me ending the call and closing my laptop. "Did you enjoy torturing me?"

Brie gives me a wide, far from innocent grin. "Did you enjoy being tortured?"

"Not as much as I would've enjoyed you letting me be the one to get you off," I sigh before adding, "but perhaps we can rearrange that now."

She shakes her head as she slowly saunters over to me.

I instantly frown. "What do you mean no?"

"I mean," her voice fills with heat, "let's even the score a bit."

With a sultry smirk, she lowers herself to her knees in front of me and glides her hand over my gym shorts.

A blow job on the balcony? What bloke could ever say no to that?

After rearranging my chair to allow her better access, Brie tugs my bottoms off and discards them carelessly over her shoulder. The instant my cock is free, her tongue snakes out to lick away the weeping drops her sexy show created. A sharp hiss of satisfaction is followed by a long deep sigh of relief as I watch my dick disappear into her eager mouth. Thoughtlessly, my head falls backward, and I gently wind my fingers through her thick, wavy locks for leverage. Brie immediately hums her approval of the reaction she conjured, which only makes my dick swell more against her cheeks. Her tongue relentlessly shifts between polishing my cock like it's a goddamn royal gem and heedlessly sucking like it's the only thing she intends to have for breakfast. Her abrupt change in tactics receives another happy, heavy sigh of gratification. She guides my dick deeper down her throat, and it clamps around the savage invasion. My fingers impulsively hold her head in place, obsessed with the way the new action is making me delectably dizzy. My hips continuously roll to feed her sexual starvation that's seen in every bob until there's a tightening at the base of my bollocks. At that moment, Brie's fingers cut into my bare thighs at the same time I anchor her mouth in place, unsure of who's more desperate for a drop to not be spilled. I lazily drag my head back around to watch her swallow the last bit of her reward for flawless execution and breathlessly groan my content.

Trust me when I say her skills are absolutely flawless. I've had...Well, it's best not to ask a gentleman just how many blowjobs he's had in his life, but regardless of the high number – and it is high – she is by far the best. Head of the class, if you will. Oh...Don't be a poor sport. That was clever this time since it was being delivered as a compliment as opposed to a way to ruffle her feathers.

Brie leans back onto her heels. "Scores tied. Now, the real fun begins…"

I release a small chortle and wet my lips in anticipation.

The fun began six weeks ago when I was dragged to a terrible art showing only to meet a larger-than-life struggling art student. The impressive part is that it hasn't let up once. It's mindboggling to me that I can have so much endless fun with one person. And not just doing the things I personally enjoy like catching The Robbery, a classic play, at the Mulane Theater – here in downtown – but the things I never saw myself involved in like dart competitions on Taco Tuesday. Or trying to truly understand her best mate's strange Van Gogh obsession. Or owning one of those coffeemaker things with the little cups to make a quick bit of tea. Oh, and then there are the more sentimental things I adore like the way she studies in my office while I go over reports or conference calls for the company. I love how even when we're apart, we're still together. There's more fun in "ordinary" and compromising than anyone lets on. Use this morning's evening of the scores as another example. Now, if you'll pardon me, I have to put more points on the headboard.

CHAPTER FIFTEEN

I anxiously rock on my feet as I try to see around the people in line in front of us.

Kellan lightly chuckles. "You can't possibly be *that* excited."

"*I can.*" Frustrated with my fruitless efforts, I finally give up and return to waiting. "*And I am.*"

His hand slides onto my waist at the same time he smugly states besides my ear, "How about instead of this, we do something *else* that makes you this excited, love?"

Temptation instantly runs rampant.

I have never had this much sex in my entire life. I've also never been this insatiable before. In two months, I went from basically ready to devote my body to a convent to barely being able to walk across campus some days. Complaining? Absolutely not! What woman in her right mind would ever bitch about having a guy exhaust every effort he has every time in bed? Kellan's reputation is ironclad, and his cockiness is well deserved, but let's

not mention that to him. And by that, I mean* never *mention that to him.

Wiggling out of his grasp, I shake my head. "No. We can do that *after*."

He groans and lets his head dramatically fall backward like a brat beginning a tantrum.

"Hey, I squeezed myself into that backless cocktail dress you bought me to eat a bug and part of Bambi's mother for you earlier this week. The *least* you can do is indulge my love of art for half an hour."

Kellan laughs as his head lowers for our eyes to meet. "It was a *snail*. Not a bug."

"Snails are bugs."

"Snails are not bugs. They're in a completely different species class."

"In America, they're bugs."

Yes, they are!

"They're not bugs in America or any other country for that matter."

"Whatever," I mumble and fold my arms across my chest. "Regardless, if they're a bug-"

"Which, again, they are *not*-"

"I ate one for you with snot sauce drizzled on top of it-"

"*Pesto*-"

"And didn't puke all over your ten-thousand-dollar suit."

"Seven."

His correction receives a glower. "Enduring your food warfare comes at a cost."

"I thought that was already paid in the back of the limo," he begins with a smirk. "And then again in the elevator, and once more in the doorway of the penthouse."

He insisted! We were celebrating our two-month anniversary, which should've been done during the weekend, but he had to fly back to Fayeweather for a family gathering in remembrance of his mother's birthday. According to him, instead of thinking about the day she died every year, they made a habit of celebrating the day the world was blessed with her presence. Kellan explained how it's the one time of year no other obligations matter. After eating her favorite pasta dinner with their father, he and his brother load up with a shit ton of alcohol and disappear to the private cabin in the woods. It's just the two of them, and they spend the time getting drunk while reminiscing about her, growing up, and her untimely death. He wouldn't tell me much more about what goes on, but it wasn't hard to gather that it was intended to be a secret. A brotherly bond never to be broken.

"Nice try," I brush off his attempt to bail, "but we're doing this."

"Yes, but must we do this?"

"Yeah."

He rolls his eyes at the same time we approach the counter.

A thin, bearded man greets us. "Hello. Welcome to Balloon Bust. Do you have reservations?"

"You don't think it's *odd* you have to have reservations to throw paint-filled balloons at someone?" Kellan quips under his breath.

I give the man behind the desk my name before quietly snapping back, "You don't think it's *odd* to wear the price of a new car to the movies?"

My reference to his wardrobe gets a humph. "I enjoy expensive clothing."

Looking up sweetly as the man swipes my card, I coo, "And I enjoy ruining it."

"Here you are," the man states loudly to grab our attention. I slip the card into the back pocket of my jeans. "You're going to go to the left where you'll find Wendy, your guide and referee, waiting for you."

After we politely thank him, Kellan questions, "Referee? Is this a competition?"

"Against each other," I cheerfully hum. "One you're going to *so* lose."

"Lose?"

"Yeah, as in *not win*. I know the meaning of *that word* is the same in every country."

"Love, you get winded during a popcorn catching session, so there's *absolutely* no way you're going to beat me regardless of the sport."

My body comes to an abrupt halt. "Care to bet on that?"

He cocks an eyebrow of intrigue. "A wager? That might make this more fun."

"Winner picks dinner."

"That's it?"

"And the loser has to serve the winner dessert," his look of boredom only lasts for a split second, "*naked*."

Kellan grins wide. "You know I can't resist you naked."

"Don't worry." I give his chest a condescending pat. "You won't have to."

Okay, yeah, he may be a little...er...fine, **a** lot *more athletic than me – thanks to the ninety minutes he puts in at the gym every day –, but he has no idea what he's getting himself into, and more importantly, I have an advantage. I don't mind being covered in paint. He will. He'll go out of his way to stay protected, trapping him like an animal. I've got a plan. Believe in me! Go Team America!*

"You're rallying American war cries in your head, aren't you?"

I thought these conversations were private.

The two of us finish our path to the employee. Immediately, she bounces with joy in place. "Hello! My name is Wendy! I'll be your guide and ref today! I am so excited, and I hope *you* are excited! Have you ever been to Balloon Bust before?"

"I have," I announce proudly. "But the one in fancy sneakers hasn't."

"They're not *fancy*," Kellan attempts to explain to her. "They're simply *new*."

An impish smile creeps onto my face. "*And white.*"

"So?"

"So, they're probably going to get paint-stained, sir," Wendy kindly explains. "While the white jumpsuits will cover your clothing and the goggles your face. Your shoes and hair will be exposed."

The frown that appears on Kellan's face is priceless. When he glances down to where I'm giggling, he sneers, "Goggles over your goggles? Lucky you."

I adjust my glasses at him with a childish smirk. "That's right, Posh Spice. Be pissy my eyewear gets coverage while the hundred-dollar product in your hair is about to go to waste."

"Should've asked to borrow your hairnet."

"Oh...*Game on*, Prince Jerk Off."

"*Game on*, Lunch Lady."

Wendy tries to dial back her look of horror.

Guess not everyone is as accustomed to our banter as we are.

"If you'll follow me to the lockers, I'll explain the rules and cover the basics before you sign your consent forms." The two of us stay on her heels through the set of double doors where there's a waiting area. To the left, there are several places to sit including a couch, but to the right, there is a wall that's covered in monitors. "This is where you wait if you have selected a particular course that is currently being occupied. Parents are also welcome to wait here if their child is here for a birthday party, or if a child is here for the party, and they do not wish to participate." Her hand gestures to the screens. "These are broken up by the courses they cover, which are labeled above and below."

Kellan steals a glance at the names, but I don't bother. It's not new information to me.

She moves a little further into the room and extends her hand towards the maps pinned on the other side of the screens. "Here are your course options. There are six. They're broken into Beginner,

Intermediate, and Expert. As you can see, in each division there is an easy and difficult choice."

"We want The Kingdom," I state confidently before giving Kellan a glance. "Unless that hits too close to home for you."

He resists the urge to mouth off. "Whatever will make my pretty, pretty princess happy."

I instantly gag and turn back to Wendy. "You can continue."

She nods, spins on her heels, and begins walking again. This time we go through a set of double doors on the right. On this side, we see people being handed their white suits while others are being handed their bags.

"You will be given a white suit as well as goggles to protect your clothing and eyes. Occasionally, paint has dripped through the suits and stained clothing. You will be signing on your waiver that you will not hold Balloon Bust responsible if that happens. Your waiver will also have you acknowledge the risk of possible damage to your eyes or any other exposed body parts. The paint in the balloon is non-toxic; however, if for some reason you swallow an amount, please end the game and report directly to me so that we can handle the situation accordingly. Once you two are dressed, you will each be given a bag of balloons filled with watered-down paint. You will each have separate colors, which will help identify the winning team. The object of the game is to cover the other person completely in paint. Whoever has the least amount of paint on their suit wins!"

"And *you* determine who that is?" Kellan quickly questions.

She enthusiastically nods. "An unbiased third opinion."

"Meaning don't flash her your winning smile to try to score extra points."

To my surprise, he gives me a sweet smirk and declares, "My winning smile is only flashed for you, love. Everyone else is just fortunate to catch a glimpse."

Don't swoon! He's the enemy right now! Though…with that comment, I'm almost tempted to forfeit.

Wendy gushes a faint awe before continuing, "The entire course is roped off in the same colors as your balloons. Do not go past these points. You are welcome to use any part of the course to hide or gain your victory, but you should be aware you are only given twenty minutes to destroy one another and a limited amount of ammunition. You are given two minutes to hide, twenty minutes to battle, and two minutes from the sound of my whistle to report back to me. If for any reason in the middle of the game you have an emergency, there will be a white flag you can wave. In the booth where I will be waiting, there are multiple screens from which I monitor your movements as well as another team member in case I miss something detrimental, such as an injured player. Any questions?"

The two of us shake our heads in unison.

She instructs us to wait a moment and crosses to the counter closest to the doors that will lead to the courses. We watch her grab two clipboards and two pens. Promptly, she returns and offers us the forms. "This re-explains everything I just did and covers negligence as well as poor player conduct."

Having read the forms before, I quickly scribble my name.

Kellan can't help himself from teasing me, "You do know it's *never* a good idea to sign something without reading it first."

"This isn't my first time here, *newb*."

He lets his eyes scan the document. "Just how many times have you played?"

"Why?" I push. "Worried about how much of an advantage I might have?"

He hums, signs his name, and states with a smirk. "No. Wondering how humiliated you're going to feel when you get destroyed by a novice."

My eyes are slightly narrow.

"Humiliated is a word *I know* means the same thing in every country."

His lack of humbleness isn't surprising yet still spurs me to snap. "Game the fuck on, Duke Dilhole."

"Dilhole? Is this 1996? How'd we make it back here?"

"I'll grab your equipment," Wendy meekly interrupts.

The process for getting dressed and equipped isn't long. Thankfully for us, our choice of course isn't currently occupied allowing immediate access. Before we follow our guide, Kellan takes a moment to snap a photo of his shoes, insisting it's to post to his followers, though I'm convinced it's to commemorate the short lifespan of his sneakers. Afterward, Wendy escorts the two of us out to the field but doesn't go through the gate.

"Three sharp whistles and you can begin. Three sharp whistles and it ends. Got it?"

We nod and Wendy slips into the small monitoring booth.

She pushes a button to open the gate, which is when I give Kellan's smug face one last look. "Hope you're ready because I'm gonna tell the whole world Prince Kellan got beat by a girl."

He winks. "Not a bloody chance in hell."

Yup. I'm gonna enjoy watching paint drip down his face so much.

The two of us split ways, and I head left towards one of the far perimeter walls. While at first glance the entire course looks like a Kindergartner sneezed on their over-priced castle-themed playground, the paint area is filled with traps and tricks to use to your advantage.

If you know that they're there.

On my way, I stop, quickly plant the trap I had in mind when I selected the course, and crouch behind the wall, allowing myself to keep an eye on the direction he's most likely going to be coming from.

Three sharp whistles are blared, and my breath stops. As predicted, Kellan begins creeping around the corner of the wooden area, eyes scanning the empty area at a rapid rate. The predatory concentration on his face is equal parts entertaining and exciting. His footsteps continue slowly, face still in my direction until he briefly turns to grab a quick glance of the upper level of the playground. At that moment, I pop up and hurl my balloon across the way, aiming not for him but the ground at his feet.

The balloon shatters splashing paint on his shoes and lower pant legs. "Sonofabitch!"

While he's hunched over inspecting his ruined footwear, I throw another, grateful when it lands on his neck and back. My triumphant giggle is cut short when he quickly retaliates throwing one where he believes I still am. His initial miss only encourages him harder to rush after me tossing numerous balloons at any part of my body he thinks he can hit. Barely able to dodge, I sprint back in the direction he came and up the very stairs, he thought I was originally hiding at the top of.

Hearing Kellan's steps slowly approach where I've crawled makes me smirk as I prepare to play out my first idea.

"You made a big mistake going after my shoes," he scolds, his body now approaching the crawl space I'm in.

Kellan's body rounds the corner to find me waiting in a crab walk position. Immediately, he prepares to throw when I kick my foot out, the balloon I had been balancing smashing against his chest and splashing his goggles.

"Damn it!"

I quickly scurry away, crawl through a tunnel, and head for the back set of stairs. To no surprise, Kellan chases after me. One of his balloons crashes against the pole beside me causing his yellow paint to splash against my shoulder. He sprints after me, running laps around the playground, attempting to cut me off when he can, and successfully nailing me three times with cheap shots; however, he ends up suffering damage in the process. Although it's obvious we are both playing to win, our laughter is out of control to the point of distracting at times. We continue behaving like overgrown children by climbing on the walls, making goofy faces, and missing more often than hitting. Once I'm certain he's down to just one balloon, I rush towards the area where I began the war and pretend to be trapped.

Kellan smirks and toys with his last piece of ammo. "I told you I would beat you."

I slowly move backward until I bump against the wall, hands purposely behind my back. "That's your last balloon."

"Only one I need," he reassures, confidently moving closer. "I smash this one, right…here…," Kellan's free hand roams down the front of my suit. "*I win.* You'll be completely dripping with my paint."

My fingers subtly wrap around my hiding weapons. "Then you better not miss."

"No need to fret." His face leans down to mine. "*I won't.*"

I tilt my head slightly to the side. "Haven't you learned yet that arrogance isn't sexy?"

"Everything I do is sexy, love," he smugly chuckles. "You ready to get wet?"

With an additional premature victorious smirk, he pulls back to throw his final balloon. Swiftly, I duck, lunge forward, each of my hands loaded with a balloon, and smash them at his sides. The unexpected action causes him to lose the grip of his weapon, which splashes our shoes.

"Sorry," I sneer. "Looks like you're the wet one."

His jaw falls, which only makes me burst into giggles. All of a sudden, he reaches out and traps me in his arms before I can get away. I squeak and plead for my freedom while he ignores the request, tickling me in the process.

Luckily for me, three sharp whistle blows become my key to freedom.

I toss my hands in the air. "Yes! I win! America wins!"

Kellan glances down at the white suit that's significantly covered in more paint thanks to my final move and sighs heavily.

"You got beat by a girl," I tease and skip back towards the gate where our ref is waiting.

"You cheated!"

"Strategized!"

The two of us arrive in front of Wendy who is attempting to stifle her snickers.

"He's being a sore loser."

"I am not."

"Would you two like a photograph?" She politely asks.

"Yes!" I exclaim. "Let's commemorate the day the lacrosse player – 'that's better at all sports' – lost to the – 'winded during popcorn battles' – art lover."

He groans yet wraps his arms tightly around me.

Wendy steps back into the booth to take the photo.

Through my smile, I state, "We are *so* framing this photo."

Kellan lets out a laugh, which replaces his staged smile with a genuine one as I hoped. After Wendy gives us a thumbs-up to let us know we're finished, he whispers in my ear, "I can't wait for us to clean up together in the shower…"

That's definitely a better prize than just picking dinner. Looks like I'm gonna win twice this afternoon…or maybe even three times if you know what I mean.

CHAPTER SIXTEEN

Kellan

"Love…" I lean against the door frame of our hotel bedroom as I adjust my watch. "You almost ready?"

"Give me one more minute."

She said that twenty-five minutes ago. I'm not exactly in any hurry to get to this thing, believe me, *but I would hate for our first publicly announced event to include the word* late *in the headline.*

The door to the bathroom opens and my jaw instantly becomes agape at the sight.

Brie slowly saunters into the room effortlessly slaving my attention with every sway of her hips. The thin, floor-length white gown, has a low v neckline, which has her voluptuous chest displayed most enticingly. My eyes reluctantly trace the remainder of the dress that only accents her most flattering curves. As my tongue and cock swell in unison, she casually turns, exposing the hip-high slit on her right side and her beautiful back being covered only by her straightened hair.

Bloody hell, how are we ever supposed to leave now? And why would I ever let anyone else see her like this? Have I completely lost my mind? Do you know where? I'd like to pick it back up and lock her up immediately afterward.

"Well?" Brie pulls her hair to the side of her face where the crystal hair pin is located. "Do I look okay?"

Would it be so wrong to tell her this isn't the only time I hope to see her in a white dress?

"You look..." The sentence seems to drift away while my eyes drink in the impeccable sight once more.

She gives me a nervous yet playful smirk.

"I mean," I clear my throat to try again, "you look...Well, you look..." Helplessly, I steal another long, hard stare, my almost rendered speechlessness now actually complete. My mouth continues to move despite the fact a single word does not escape.

What do you do when there are literally no words for how sexy your girlfriend looks? I mean the hair, the makeup, even her glasses are practically sparkling.

Brie slowly runs a finger down my chest causing me to groan. With a teasing smile, she saucily declares, "I'll take your caveman speak as I look amazing."

My hand slides possessively onto her hip, and the feeling of her bare skin on my fingertips sways all thoughts towards the sexual end of the spectrum. To no surprise, my cock stiffens desperately in my black suit pants. "*Quite the understatement, love.*"

She gives me another mischievous smile. "Did I mention I'm not wearing anything underneath this?"

Mad. This woman lives to drive me mad. She literally wakes up each day to drive me bloody insane.

I stifle a growl and pull her closer. "Is this payback for having you spend the day at the spa? You know most women would appreciate an afternoon of being pampered and treated like a queen."

"*Duchess*," she sassily corrects. "You're not a king. You're a *Duke*."

"*And a prince.*"

"Who – unless your brother dies in a freak beer-chugging accident – is not going to be king."

"And the great country of Doctenn should mourn that fact because I am entirely more fun than my brother."

"I don't doubt that." Brie lightly laughs. "But to answer your question, yes. I *am* punishing you for having me spend the day with strangers rubbing and pulling on me. Do you have any idea how weird it is to have three different people working on you at the same time like you're a-"

"Masterpiece?" My artsy interjection causes her to fight a smile. "Because you *are*, and you deserved the royal treatment for enduring a night of torture with me." I link my free hand with hers. "Are you sure you want to do this? You don't have to. You can spend the evening in this hotel room in that dress, simply waiting for my return. Sort of like a slutty angel I can cover in sin after my night of charitable good fortune."

She shoots me a sarcastic look.

What! It was worth a shot!

As we arrive at the suite door, I stop us from exiting. "In all seriousness, I do understand if you're not ready for this. If you want to wait. If you-"

"Kellan, are you sure it's me you're worried about and not yourself?"

The accusation lifts my eyebrows in surprise.

"Maybe *you're* not ready to announce to the world this way that you have a girlfriend. I mean photos with coffee mugs or candlelight or tickets to a play is entirely different than showing up with her on your arm. Maybe you're ashamed to be seen with-"

My tongue swiftly slips into her mouth smothering the end to that sentence. Brie squeaks in surprise and instinctively reaches out to grasp my jacket for balance. Our mouths melt together in a heavenly combination of hot breaths and hard pushes. Before the situation can spiral out of my control or my point for interrupting can be completely forgotten, I pull back and say, "Never doubt that I view myself as the luckiest man alive to have you on my arm." When I receive a soft smile, I warmly announce, "I'm ready if you are, love."

Brie ushers her hand at the door. "After you, Prince Kellan."

Now you're probably having a moment here, wondering how the hell have we been together for months and the world does not know? It's one of the benefits of no one other than my family knowing exactly where I am. While I've still got thousands of people stalking my social media accounts, I don't post anything that would give them a real hint to my whereabouts or who I've been spending time with. Online, Brie is nothing more than "her" in my posts, not only to protect her anonymity but to preserve the bit of my own ''ve managed to cultivate for once in my life. Don't get me wrong. I may only post photos of objects or selfies, but we take tons of personal couple photos. Brie doesn't post them online out of her own free choice, and I have enjoyed sharing them only with my brother and Soph. I knew we wouldn't be able to hide forever, but it doesn't mean I have to be thrilled to toss the woman I love into the limelight and watch it attempt to burn her.

The two of us casually stroll into the swarm of hungry photographers surrounding the building's entrance. We take a moment to pause for an obnoxious multitude of flashes before we continue into the fundraiser with Swiss trailing a safe distance behind us.

As soon as we're on the other side of the door, past the host waiting to take our invitations and allow my bodyguard's entrance, Brie sighs, "I think I'm blind."

"Of course, you are love. That's why you wear glasses."

Her jaw is floored split seconds prior to a waiter offering, "Champagne?"

I grab us each a flute and give him a polite nod of gratitude.

When I offer her one, she snips, "You're right. I wear them to see but also to let the world immediately know that I'm smarter than you."

We share a small chuckle and clink our glasses together.

I know I shouldn't be worried about an attitude like hers in a room full of people whose egos could afford to fall a peg or two, but that's precisely what makes me nervous. They're used to being flattered and favored to their faces and criticized behind their backs. A little too much honesty might end in disaster.

Swiss lingers towards the back where several other security details happen to be waiting while the two of us head into the heart of the event. Almost instantly, I'm approached by familiar faces of both men and women and begin casual introductions to Brie. Each conversation closely resembles one another as do their expressions upon meeting her. I expect a degree of shock; however, the abundant amount on several faces has me concerned it's not over the simple fact I'm showcasing a girlfriend for the first time.

Perhaps I'm being paranoid?

The two of us veer towards the right when our path is blocked by a dainty blonde with a bobbed haircut. She immediately coos my name, *"Kellan."*

"Gwen," I greet back, tightening my grip on Brie's hip. "Always a pleasure."

"You as well," she replies before giving the woman attached to me a skeptical glance. "I see you've brought a date."

"Yes, my girlfriend." Pride pumps through my voice and my expression. "Brie Sanders meet Gwen Dickens. She's an award-winning actress in Doctenn."

"Several," her snip is directed at the woman in my arms.

Now is not a good time to wander if that snip is because things didn't end well between us.

They shake at the same time Gwen says, "I don't recognize you; however, I'm still becoming familiar with those on the American screen, so to speak. What films have you been in?"

"I'm not an actress."

"You're not?"

"No, I'm an art student."

The sneer on Gwen's face is unmistakable. "Is that a joke? An American quip I do not understand?"

She slowly shakes her head.

"You're a *student*? Not even a graduate?"

"Soon," Brie politely retorts.

Gwen pins her green eyes back on me. "She's not your normal type in so many ways, Kellan." Her eyes cut Brie an additional glare before adding, "You two don't seem as if you…*match*."

My chance to retort is nonexistent.

"On a different note, how is the program?" Her expression hardens further. "Hopefully my donations are being spent *wisely* and not on something frivolous like a colorful art student's tuition."

Of course, her remarks are cunty because she was one of those women who assumed that because we slept together and she was famous, I'd naturally call, but tell me – and be honest – do you hear an additional hatred Brie's direction for...Hm. How do I put this delicately? For not being fair skinned?

Brie uncomfortably adjusts herself in my arms. "I pay my own tuition."

"Sounds unlikely."

"Your donations," I interject to prevent the conversation from getting more grotesque, "are going to the same place they always do, Gwen."

"Expanding?"

Reluctantly, I reply, "Not at this time."

"But I thought-"

"It is the intention; however, at this moment, it is not our direct focus."

Someone calls her name from over her shoulder. After glancing to see who it is, she turns back around, smiles, and says, "All right then. I hope it becomes your focus once more, perhaps when your judgment is clearer. If you two will excuse me, there's someone I need to speak with."

Gwen sharply turns on her nude heels to head in the direction she was summoned.

The moment she's out of earshot, Brie moves in front of me and questions, "Did you wedge the stick up her ass, or was it there before you tried to put your dick in it?"

Her comment cracks my jaw in surprise.

"And what do you mean you're not expanding? What happened? Just last week you were going on and on about opening shelters in new locations."

I slip my hands into my pockets. "That is what I *want*, but unfortunately, the funds are not permitting it at this time. We are bringing in enough revenue to keep the current shelters open in the ten largest cities in Doctenn and the five we have here in the states, operational. As of right now, we must focus on the changes we can make to those shelters that are open in order to make them more beneficial to the children and youth who rely on them. Right now, our main priorities have to be on keeping the shelters a warm place to stay, them having enough food to eat, and clean, functional facilities to use. Some of the shelters in Doctenn have volunteer doctors and nurses, but that's something I want all of the shelters to eventually have, along with some sort of education. Because pocketbooks aren't currently popping open without constant persuasive dinners or pushy called in favors, I have to ensure every dollar we receive sufficiently makes a difference for those already relying on our program."

To my surprise, Brie steps forward and places a kind hand on my chest. "Have I mentioned how amazing you are?"

"Not in the past hour. I was beginning to wonder if you had forgotten." When a smile starts, I lean down and capture her lips with mine for a brief moment. "What do you say we grab a drink from the bar and check out the silent auction?"

"I say-"

"Kellan!" A woman's voice squeaks behind me.

Bloody hell. Where are the other men at this thing?

I turn to be greeted with a lively grin by a lanky brunette. "Rumor was you would be showing your face this evening."

"And here I am." I wink and slip Brie back into my grip. "Brie Sanders meet Nancy Therlan. She's a writer with the *Tenntinal*." My attention lowers to my girlfriend. "Think your *New York Times*, but for my country."

"Oh! That's-"

"You must be his date." Nancy interrupts at the same time she shoves her hand out to shake.

"*Girlfriend*," she corrects for the first time all evening.

At that moment, Nancy's expression grows in curiosity. "Is that so?"

"Yes," I swiftly concur.

"But she's…Well, she's…" Nancy's eyes give Brie a long look prior to presenting me a pleading one.

I arch my eyebrows in anticipation of a response.

"*Different*," Nancy quietly finishes.

The words "how so" are right on my tongue when she cuts me.

"Do you mind if I ask you a few questions, Kellan. For the article?"

There's a hint of panic in Brie's voice. "What article?"

"The one regarding this evening's functions," I answer before Nancy can. "It's just a puff piece she does to remind the good people in our country that we are giving to those all around the world." My head tilts sarcastically at the journalist. "Though, it's usually packed with more gossip about those who attended rather than the difference they might've made for the evening."

She stifles the desire to sneer. "Questions, Kellan?"

I let out a deep sigh of irritation. "*Three*. And then I'm taking my lovely girlfriend to shop the silent auction for something worthy of a Duchess in the making."

The statement gets an intrigued look from both women.

Was that too forward? What? I'm not planning on asking her today. Perhaps…someday. Perhaps when I'm a little more certain her answer would be yes. Save your breath. There's no need to give me the how long we've known each other speech. If you'd like me to be completely honest with you, there's not a person in my life who knows me better than my brother. Not to mention, I loathe the idea of another man ever – and I do mean ever – worshiping her the way I do. No other caveman shall be taking her back to his place to enjoy the savage sounds she causes a man to make.

I motion a hand at her. "The questions."

Nancy attempts to regain her focus. "Yes…Let's start simple. How long have you two been dating?"

"Months."

A little more than three. I know. Makes the marriage comment seem even more mad, doesn't it?

"Is this the first event you two have attended together?"

"Formal, yes. Informal, no." I answer and glance at Brie. "She attended the annual run I do here in the states."

The recalling of our first night together brings a slightly rosy color to her cheeks.

"You mentioned you plan on bidding on something for her at the auction tables. Do you have something in mind? *Jewelry perhaps?* Maybe something gold, which is most likely her tastes."

See. That there. Was that a dig at African Americans' stereo-typically preferring gold jewelry, or am I yet again reading into her word choice?

"No jewelry tonight, Nancy; however, that doesn't mean it is off the table for the future."

Her lips round themselves in shock.

"I'll probably bid on something fun like the yacht. It'd be quite amusing to sail down the coast of Doctenn with her before hearing my brother complain it can't be parked at the palace."

The interviewer girlishly giggles and tosses me a playful hand. "Oh, Kellan, *stop*."

"You only say that because you can hear his nagging too." Additional chortles escape her prompting me to use the lighter note as one to leave on. "Enjoy the evening, Nancy."

The two of us begin to the right once more, this time with me actively avoiding any remotely familiar face.

My girlfriend quietly inquires, "Kellan, are you really gonna bid on a boat?"

"*Yacht.*"

She lets out an annoyed sigh. "Ugh. Fine. Are you really gonna bid on a rich people boat so we can travel the coast?"

"Why?" I cease our movements and face her. "Does that interest you?"

"I don't know. I've…I've never done anything like that before. I've never even been on a sailboat."

"Yachts are much bigger, love."

"Duh."

"They're also much more luxurious."

"*Again*, duh."

"How about we do that this summer after you graduate?"

"Do what exactly?"

"Sail around my country's edge, lounging by the water, drinking pints, and having sex in the sun. I know you're still uncertain with what you want to do once you've gotten your degree, so perhaps some time to truly relax is what you need to have a clear vision."

The excitement increases at the same time she whispers, "*Maybe*."

I link our fingers together and step closer. "Maybe is enough for me to bid on that yacht."

We lock lips for only a moment before heading to the tables with the items for bid.

The two of us scan the sections one by one, most of the objects offered far from appealing to us. While Brie takes her time closely examining every item along with the current bid, my gaze helplessly wanders around the event. Various sets of eyes try to avert themselves away when caught staring, yet others seem to narrow in disapproval. I do my best to write off the glares as jealousy from women who wish to be in her place; however, it doesn't stop me from observing their quick snickers followed by their swift fingers across the keys of their phones.

Brie sharply gasps and panic instantly ensue. "Are you alright?!"

"There's a private showing at the McAllizter Art Studio!" She joyfully exclaims. "Do you have any idea how amazing it would be to go there, never mind a private viewing?! The McAllizter Art Studio showcases some of the most profound painters of this decade!"

I fold my arms firmly across my chest. "Let me get this correct. I offer you a summer vacation on a yacht, and you would rather spend an afternoon staring at paintings?"

Brie eagerly nods.

"You're serious? You'd rather spend a single afternoon with me in misery making snide remarks about artwork than two or three months of aimless sex and sailing?"

She sweetly drags a hand down my chest. "You had me at making you miserable…"

Her snicker causes me to roll my eyes and reluctantly add my bid to the sheet of paper. Under my breath, I state, "The things we do for love."

After I sign, I look up to see a surprised expression covering her face.

I just realized why thinking about marriage is even madder than it was before. I shouldn't even be considering such a thing when I haven't actually mentioned that I love her out loud…to her conscious face. But I'm siding with Soph on this matter. Just because it hasn't been said, doesn't make it any less true or real.

Brie begins to say something when an older male huffs from beside me.

I turn in his direction prompting him to grumble, "Excuse me. Do you mind if I place a bid?"

"Of course not." Handing him the pen, I casually joke, "Bidding is only fun when someone is willing to compete with you."

The dark-haired man smirks. "True. Though, if we're being honest, I prefer to have at least one thing I can fall back on as knowing it's in the bag if you know what I mean."

Out of natural habit, I slink an arm around Brie's waist and sigh, "Normally, yes, especially since all of this is for a good cause, but my girlfriend has her heart set on this one, so you might want to consider another fallback."

Brie offers me a sweet smile.

The stranger signs his name and bids regardless of my warning. "Your girlfriend's taste is surprising." When he looks up, he gives her a brief look before stating to me, "Surprised someone like her could ever actually take interest in something not endorsed by an overpaid celebrity."

I defensively snap, "I beg your pardon?"

He holds up a hand as if to keep the peace. "I just meant, it's unusual for people like her to have a real interest in the actual arts rather than what a hip-hop mogul might've mentioned."

Do you believe me now?

Equal parts disgusted and infuriated, I bite, "And I think it's unusual for people like you to be let out of your cages among those of us who are actually civilized."

The man doesn't seem to be bothered by the retort. He merely gives me a sympathetic smirk and strolls away as if nothing happened.

Unbelievable.

With horror still plastered on my face, I look at Brie who appears unphased by the entire thing. In a sweet voice, she urges, "Could you please outbid him now? I really, *really* wanna see the only painting the French artist LuTu was willing to display in our country."

Unsure if her nonexistent response to the blatant hatred is a well-executed act or her honest reaction, I simply snatch the pen, scribble my name alongside an outrageous price, and question, "Shall we get a drink?"

Brie hums in contemplation. "Can we get food instead? Maybe something that's not bite-sized? But I do want it on record that I totally approve of how many appetizers here have bacon. I really couldn't get enough of the bacon bread."

"Those were steak and blue cheese bruschetta bites with onion and roasted tomato jam topped with bacon shavings."

"Uh-huh. *Bacon bread.*"

Her playful retort successfully relaxes the tightness tangled throughout my chest. "No more bacon bread for you, love. We can grab an actual bite on the level above."

Once she threads her arm around mine, I lead us towards the stairs, burying my indignation to the best of my ability.

On the upper level, we're seated at a balcony table where we're given a remarkable view of the room. We order another round of drinks, several seafood dishes to share, and exchange travel stories. While mine to most people would be considered more exhilarating, I'm helplessly caught up in every one of her ordinary tales of amusement park disasters.

How many times can one child get lost in a theme park before their parents decide maybe that's not the best place for family adventures?

"I need a bit of clarification here, love. Are you telling me not to let you wander around the city by yourself or not to take you to an amusement park?"

Brie giggles and gives me a small shrug. "Mmm...*probably both*."

The two of us erupt into laughter only to be almost immediately interrupted.

"Kellan," the man says warmly. "Surprised you're here."

"Someone has to spend my family's money," I chuckle and extend my hand for us to shake. Afterward, I introduce, "Brie, meet Ronald Randolph. He's an investment genius who married a bikini model."

"Only reason I attend these things," Ronald responds while shaking Brie's hand. "She gets to give to the needy, and I get to look like I give a damn about more than my sports car collection."

Judge him all you want. He's one of the most honest and blunt individuals I've ever met. It's actually the reason people are drawn to him.

Brie politely laughs prior to him questioning, "And what about you, beautiful? What are you doing in a stiff place like this?"

"Keeping Kellan out of trouble."

"There's an endless job," Ronald chuckles.

"Thankless too"

More laughter falls from him. "What are you two lovebirds bidding on?"

I lean back in my seat. "Why? So, you can snake it from me or remind me what a terrible investment it is?"

"Everything here is a terrible investment," he teasingly scoffs. "That's what they should've named this fundraiser. Hell, on the invitations it should've said in big bold print 'Where Your Money Will Go to Help No One'. These things are an absolute waste of money *and* time. They raise millions of funds, yet it hardly feeds anyone, unlike your program that doesn't promise fake execution to fluff your own pockets."

Brie curiously questions, "Do you donate to Kellan's program?"

"Second biggest donor to Kellan himself."

I can get Ronald bloody Randolph to invest a portion of his cash, but not my own father. Fucked up a tad, don't you agree?

"That's incredible."

Ronald innocently shrugs. "Gotta have something to look good on my taxes."

The two of us smirk in tandem at his remark.

"Do you work for him?" He casually asks my girlfriend. "New secretary, he's showing the ropes? Maybe mixing a little business and pleasure?"

Brie starts to answer when my irritation gets the better of me. "Why do you assume that she's my secretary?"

"I-"

"Why do you assume that she's *help*?"

"I-"

"Why do you assume that she must be beneath in some form?"

"I don't recall saying *beneath you*," Ronald mumbles as he slides his hands into his suit pockets, "but she's not your usual type."

Outrage begins to slowly boil. "*Meaning*?"

"She's not blonde. Not a socialite. Not a celebrity to my knowledge. And she doesn't seem to have any trouble completing a thought without her brain overheating."

"Booze keeps that from happening."

Ronald begins to grin at her comment when I interrupt the action. "Anything *else* makes her not my 'usual type'?"

His head tilts at me in question.

At that moment, Brie nudges me under the table with her, encourages me to stand down.

"Forgive me. That was quite rude." I clear my throat. "I must have had too much champagne."

He gives me an incredulous look yet states, "It's alright. I think I'm gonna go find Emma. See how much money she's successfully spent. The two of you enjoy the rest of your night."

Brie waves sweetly, and I give him a polite nod goodbye.

The moment we're alone she asks, "Are you okay, Kellan?"

Rather than answer immediately, I let my attention roam the room once more. Spotting judgmental eyes in our direction for what feels like the thousandth time prompts me into taking in a harder observation of our surroundings. I scan the room for other people besides Brie who are – from a glance – of different ethnicity. As soon as I realize it seems to be just her, a wave of nausea washes over me to the point it feels like I'm drowning.

How is this possible? A room full of people and she's the only one not sporting the same shade of pigment? I thought diversity was the spice of life! I thought the world had progressed past this particular point!

"Kellan…?"

My eyes land on hers. "I'm ready to leave. Are you?"

She tries not to pout. "What about the auction?"

"I'll arrange for one of the hosts to keep bidding in my name if we get outbid."

Her glowing grin returns. "You really wanna get laid for winning, don't you?"

I struggle to return the smile. "Always."

After swinging by the auction area to assure our win, I lead the two of us promptly out of the event, thankful to be away from the uncomfortable stares and hateful thoughts swirling around us.

In the limo, Brie attempts to make conversation about those we encountered throughout the evening to who she was introduced to. I do my best to engage yet my mind involuntarily wanders to the faces of women who were snickering and texting.

ced*Unless they weren't texting…*ced

I pull out my phone and give my name a quick internet search. The immediate results capture my complete attention as well as return the rage to its rawest state. My eyes scan everything from hateful racial and salacious tweets aimed at Brie without naming her directly to blogs bashing the bold choice of dress and body-shaming her. With every passing cold and callous comment created by the user and the additional ones from their followers, the grip on my device tightens.

The limo comes to an unexpected halt, which is when I finally lift my eyes to Bries. She simply shakes her head, politely bids Swiss good night, and exits the vehicle.

Shit. Did she see them? Is she upset with me for subjecting her to those things?

Our ride up to our room is in unexpected silence. Each time I open my mouth to say something to her, I clamp it shut, terrified I'm only going to make the situation worse.

The moment we're on the other side of our hotel suite door, she makes a bee line for the bedroom forcing me to plea, "*Brie, wait.*"

She spins around and snaps. "For what? For you to ignore me some more? For another weird mood swing? For you to decide whether or not we should attend another one of these together?"

My jaw bobs, the answer to each of those questions surprisingly harder to answer than they should be.

I just...I need a minute to bloody breathe. To think clearly. Perhaps let some of the champagne wear off.

"I'm going to bed," she states with sadness suffocating her tone. "*Alone.*"

"Brie-"

"No," she instantly denies. "Kellan, I didn't do any of this shit tonight *for me*. I did it *for you*. I could care less about fancy dresses, fancy shoes, and weird fancy food. I did all of this because I love you, and I know that we can't hide in my world forever. If we're going to be together then that means I'm going to have to suck myself into a suffocating gown and smile in smug faces that not so secretly are disgusted by me. Being together means we're going to have to face uncomfortable looks at times and backhanded comments. It's just a fact. Not everyone is accepting or understanding."

"Yet they should be! Look at the times for fucks sake!"

She gives me a short shrug. "What *should be* isn't always *what is*. And the truth is, Kellan, I didn't give a shit about what any of them said or did or thought. The only thing that mattered to me was *supporting you*. But obviously..." Her voice stumbles, "Obviously, that wasn't the only thing that mattered to you. So, you need to decide if being with me is worth the stares and judgmental remarks. If you can stomach the hatred certain members of society still have. If you love me enough to taint the image the world desires."

Without another word, she disappears around the corner. The sound of a door shutting echoes throughout the suite seconds later.

A frustrated groan grows in the back of my throat, and I squeeze the nape of my neck in hopes of releasing some sort of pressure.

She's completely right. I've never had to deal with this type of animosity before. Prudes for me flashing my private parts. Sure. Women disgusted at the rapid rate I run through them. Of course. Brie herself was initially displeased with that until she realized I was capable of more. But this? Having strangers hate the woman I'm with simply because she was born to a different race? It's ludicrous, and I can't control how furious it makes me.

I make my way to the living room where I flop down on the couch. Loosening my tie, I try to shake away the comments I scrolled past in the car. Instead of disappearing, they amplify the desire to look at more, to pick at the pain like a fresh scab that still needs time to heal. I ditch my shoes, stretch out across the piece of leather furniture, and open my phone. The pages are still pulled up, taunting me instantly. For what feels like hours, I tromp through internet posts, scowling at gossip sites and grousing at unflattering photos captured to purposely destroy her image.

When I finally reach the point that I can barely breathe anymore, I dial the only number I can think of.

It only rings once before he answers, "You're calling in the middle of breakfast and it's crepes. This better be important."

The sound of my brother's voice brings me unexpected comfort.

My lack of retort, however, receives immediate concern, "Kellan…is everything alright?"

No words leave my lips.

"Are you injured?"

Physically no.

"Do I need to ring a medic?"

"No." The slow shake of my head is followed by further clarification. "No, physically I'm fine. Mentally…" I blow out a harsh breath. "I'm a bloody idiot."

"Is this new to you?" He teases with a chuckle. "Is it a scary feeling, baby brother?" When there's no jab back, he returns to worrying, "Oh, you're serious. Why are you a bloody idiot? What did you do?"

Silence settles momentarily between us. Shutting my eyes, I attempt to answer, "I did the one thing I knew better than to do."

"Please, tell me you kept your pants on."

The corner of my lip tugs upward. "I took Brie with me to the fundraiser."

"And?"

"Then I spent most the evening being livid over their remarks and unfriendly glances." Another exasperated breath escapes. "And to top it all off, I then searched the internet to read the hateful dribble they had to say in regards to her."

Kris gasps. "You didn't."

"I did."

He tries to hide his obvious amusement. "You must really love this girl."

"I most certainly do."

"Normally, you couldn't give a rat's arse about what one of those trolls has to say, yet from the tone in your voice it's apparent that you're seething."

"To say the least."

"Is it because you assumed she was just so amazing that the rest of the world would have to love her? You know, sort of like you assume they feel about you?"

"No." I pinch the bridge of my nose. "No, I'm…I'm upset because it wasn't about her as a *person*. It wasn't because she was rude or classless or even bloody American – and we all know how people in our country can be about Americans. It was the mere simple fact she was being judged by the color of her skin. She was being judged and hated for something out of her control! It was because-"

"You couldn't protect her from it," Kris finishes for me.

The ache in my chest deepens as I drop my hand. "*Yes.*"

"You're not upset because people are arseholes. You're upset because you can't shelter her from it. Because you love her so much that the idea of anyone hurting her drives you mad. Because you would rather endure all the pain being thrust in her direction than ever have something or someone threatens her smile."

I nod despite the fact he can't see me.

"It's the same thing I went through the first time Soph and I attended an event. It was the first time she stopped being just mine. The first time I had to share our love with the world and deal with the repercussions of being in the public eye. The fact of the matter is, baby brother, being watched is a part of who you are whether you wish it was or not. And with that comes a very frightening inability to shield your heart once the world sees it."

My voice shakes. "How did you do it? Bloody hell, how do you keep doing it?"

"I remember that everyone is allowed their own opinion, and I'm equally allowed not to care." There's a short pause in which I swear he smiles. "Soph is more than just the future queen of this country. She's the queen of my heart and for her, I'd endure anything."

A small groan of disgust seeps out. "You sound like a bloody chick flick."

Even if it's true and also how I feel that doesn't make it less feminine.

"I pour my heart out to you, and that's how you respond?"

"You spilled your purse. You might want to put your tampons back in before Soph sees."

"You are the *worst* brother in the history of brothers, you know that, yes?"

"You have no concrete way to prove that."

"I don't feel I need one."

"Thanks, Kris." For the first time in hours, I smile. "*For everything.*"

His response barely begins before Sophia squeals. "Eeeeeekkkk! Look at how adorable they are together!"

Oh no.

There's a ruffling sound followed by me being put on speaker phone. "Yes. *Absolutely adorable.*"

"Oh, shut up," I grunt.

"You're smiling," Soph coos from what I can only assume is beside him. "Like actually smiling. He's smiling at an event, Kris! Like *actually smiling*, not the fake bullshit smile you both share, the one that's equal parts creepy and transparent."

My brother quietly disagrees. "It's not creepy."

"*Very creepy,* but this...This is a real smile! You look so happy, Kellan!"

Brie's beautiful face floats back into my brain causing me to thoughtlessly retort, "She makes me happy. The happiest I've ever been."

"Now who sounds like a chick flick?" Kris teases before whining, "*Ou.*"

I snicker over his pain prior to teasingly coo, "Enjoy your breakfast, big brother."

"Enjoy your couch."

"How did you-"

"Because if you responded the way you said you did and the way I'm imagining, there's no possible way she'd let you sleep beside her tonight."

Makes you wonder how bad he messed up with Soph their first outing, doesn't it?

"Trust me. It's for the best. Give her space to breathe. Collect your apology. And return to her in the morning with your tail tucked neatly between your legs." The mirth in his tone actually spreads to me. "It'll be fine. Try to get some sleep. You're an even more insufferable pain in the ass when you haven't slept."

"God, I miss the days where I could wear dresses with that much cleavage," she sighs in the background.

"No one should be seeing your cleavage but me," my brother defensively announces.

"Night, Kristopher."

"Night, Kellan," they say in unison.

I end the call and toss the phone onto the coffee table.

I hope my brother's right. I hope Brie's still willing to make this work when she wakes up. I hope that while I've been in here basking in the mental brutality of my own choices that she hasn't talked herself out of being with me. **Again.** *Out of…loving me. It's quite exciting that she really does love me. That it's not just an idea I assume from her actions. No. She said it out loud. She confirmed it. She announced it without second-guessing. Damn it! She said it and I couldn't even stop being a self-righteous dick long enough to say it back. Why is it the hole I've managed to swan dive into keeps getting deeper and deeper? Be honest with me. Do you think things are truly finished between us?*

CHAPTER SEVENTEEN

There's a soft knock at the bedroom door. I grab my glasses, roll over onto my back, and prepare to grant him entrance when I abruptly stop.

Not sure I'm awake enough for the possible, "we should end this now" conversation. Then again, I'm not sure I'd ever been awake enough for that. What? Of course, I'm expecting it. I basically bullied him into an ultimatum last night. Choose me or the limelight. It's not exactly how I meant for it to come out. I was just trying to tell him learn to deal with racism and prejudices but that's like commanding a brand-new baby bird to fly. That kinda change takes time. Adjustment.

The knocking repeats and Kellan calmly announces, "I need to change before we head to the art studio. May I please come in?"

"Yeah," I answer and lift myself up to a sitting position.

He opens the door to reveal a disheveled vision I've never seen before.

Of course, we've had our fair share of actual disagreements, but they all ended basically the same way. One of us decided to head to our respective home only to then be stopped by the other, argument resolved, and makeup sex to some variation to conclude it. This is actually the first time we've even slept apart since our first night together. Should I be worried that it won't be our last?

Kellan cautiously enters the room. "I received a call late last night confirming our winning bid. We're allowed a private showing of the studio anytime from ten to four. It's their normal business hours for Sunday."

"I can go alone if you want."

My suggestion sinks his entire demeanor. His shoulders plummet while the rest of his body struggles not to buckle.

"I mean…I don't have to. I just…um…I just know how much you hate art stuff. Figured maybe there was something else you'd rather see in the city before we go."

Kellan starts to retort yet quickly clamps his jaw shut. After a long exhale, he states, "I want us *together*. Wherever that is."

The possible double-sided answer lowers my eyebrows in confusion.

Well, what do you think he meant?

"I ordered us breakfast if you would like to eat while I grab a shower."

I attempt to lighten the mood. "Are there berries smothering it?"

Kellan lets go of a small smile. "There are berries on the *side* and plenty of bacon to keep my favorite All-American girl cheerful."

With that, he strolls into the en-suite bathroom and shuts the door. Once I hear the shower start, I hop out of bed and hustle to the kitchen portion of the hotel room. On the bar counter, there is a buffet of options to suit both of us. I smile at his thoughtfulness as I reach for a plate. I stack it with pancakes, bacon, eggs, and strawberries on the side before I relocate to the table where I enjoy watching the last half of *Legally Blonde*.

You know every Spring they play this movie a ridiculous amount. Not that I watch it every time it comes on. Just occasionally. Oh…Don't give me that look! You know it's funny! And more importantly, you know the message matters.

By the time Kellan comes out completely changed, the credits are beginning to roll. We exchange a few casual words about the breakfast choices before I disappear the way he came to shower as well. A little after ten, we're both changed, luggage packed, and strolling side by side to the McAllizter Art Studio. The crisp wind hits my bare legs instantly making me regret not putting tights on underneath my jean skirt.

The temperature implied a warm day. Forgive me for not bothering to read how cold the wind was predicted to be.

Kellan opens the door to the studio, and I rush inside to enjoy the blasting heat.

"We're closed today," a woman says from an unseen location.

My eyes do a quick scan of the room for the voice yet come up completely empty.

The voice instantly repeats, "We are closed today for a private showing. Bruno, please, show them out."

The security guard who was patiently waiting for his cue motions his hand towards the door while the other lingers at his side.

"We *are* the private showing," Kellan announces firmly. "Kellan Kenningston. I bid on the afternoon yesterday during a silent auction."

Suddenly there's a clicking sound that reminds me of heels. "Kellan!" Our eyes shift up to the second level where a stunning blonde woman in a sultry black dress is standing. "I didn't recognize you on the monitor!" Her hands curl around the railing. "You look even more amazing than the last time I saw you."

Under my breath, I snip, "Is there any one woman on the planet you haven't slept with?"

He clears his throat and says back, "Why thank you, Candy. You look quite stunning as well. I see marrying a yoga instructor has a multitude of benefits."

Candy giggles and shakes her head. "I did not marry her because she was a yoga instructor. It just made working out easier."

Okay…My mistake.

Kellan smugly smirks at me. "Candy and I met through her wife who is an avid donor to The Collin Murphy Foundation. It's the one who hosted the run I attended earlier this year. Her wife, Mandy, had a younger sibling who died of acute lymphocytic leukemia when she was a teenager, which led to her decision to want to give to the foundation. I met Mandy who is actually from Rortaverian, a coastal city in Doctenn, during a triathlon for the foundation."

I attempt to un-wedge the foot down my throat. "Oh…"

He hums victoriously and returns his attention to her. "So, are there specific instructions for our private showing? Things we can and cannot touch."

"You are *never* allowed to touch the artwork unless you've purchased it."

"Are the paintings available for purchase?"

His question grabs my attention, yet he doesn't look in my direction.

No way do I leave here with a one of kind…anything. Do you have any idea how much these paintings go for? I barely belong sharing the same air space with them. I definitely don't belong having one to hang in my bedroom. Well, of course, it would be for me. Kellan is allergic to the actual artwork. The walls of his penthouse are primarily bare except for the signed lacrosse poster from his favorite team, which hangs over his bar, and the few photos of us we've had framed. You don't think he'd buy one of these paintings as a "remember me" break-up present, do you? That's not…That's not something normal people do when they end a relationship. They don't give the other person a parting gift. Then again, this is Kellan. Very little about him or this relationship is normal.

"They are!" Candy warmly answers. "If you find one that you wish to take with you, you can summon me down, and we can discuss a price. Other than that, the studio is yours to enjoy. No photography. No videos. Something I'm sure you can appreciate, Kellan."

After last night, that makes two of us. I don't think I've ever had my picture taken so many times in one night. I've also never been trending before. Can't say I enjoyed it. Having an audience of strangers judge me on my looks and ridicule me over them felt like being back in high school but on a much larger, much more vicious scale. Jovi's panicked texts over the whole thing didn't exactly help, either.

"Because the private showing is *you*, Kellan, I will have the cameras shut off with the exception of the exits. There's a thin red line that looks like tape in front of the displays, which is actually an alarm trigger. It will sound if you are too close. At that point, please be aware, Bruno will be forced to verify you haven't compromised the art and escort you out. If you have any questions, feel free to hit one of the intercom buttons, and it'll promptly grab my attention."

"Thank you," Kellan says kindly.

"Yes, thank you!" I exclaim, over-eager to see artists I've spent years following.

Candy heads back into her office while we make our way straight down the hall, past the welcoming area. On the other side is the first set of paintings positioned on a bright red wall. Each of the creations seems to come to life with the assistance of the accented background.

Making sure to keep behind the line, I longingly stare at the masterpieces secretly sad that I'll never create anything remotely worth being in a place like this.

Best case scenario? I graduate and get to run a place like this. You know, if I ever have the desire to do that. Worst case scenario? I end up working at a craft store selling overly priced paint to parents who have enrolled their teenagers in advanced art classes. Either way, being showcased in a well-renowned gallery isn't happening.

"That looks like a porcupine with a party hat," Kellan jokes from beside me. "And not a good party hat, either."

I roll my eyes at the comment.

"Sorry," he sheepishly mutters. "It's just…I've seen thousands of paintings and not one of them has ever looked like something worth spending a fortune on."

"We discussed this when we first met," I sweetly remind him as we move along to another wall where a single painting is displayed. "You'll eventually run into a piece of art that screams at you so loud you won't be able to ignore it. That'll move you in ways you didn't even know possible." My head tilts at the abstract piece. "I just hope I'm around to see it."

Realizing my confession, I quickly move further into the building, this time heading for the right corner in hopes of gaining my composure before he catches up. The section is dimmed darker than the other half of the room presenting the paintings in their ideal lighting, and I take advantage of that along with the bench positioned directly across from them.

Seconds after I'm seated, Kellan slides down beside me in silence.

Unable to take the tension any longer, I quietly snap, "Did you bring me here as some sort of unusual way to say goodbye? To say you don't wanna do this anymore? Am I here to pick out a consolation prize for losing you?"

Kellan doesn't respond, and the compression in my chest I battled all night returns.

*Wow...okay. So **this** is over.*

"I hate art," he begins slowly, "and yet I've been to more galleries and showings and art stores in the past three months than I ever thought imaginable. I hate art yet one of my favorite things is listening to you ramble on about what you're studying when you get home from class."

A smile threatens my face.

"I hate art yet each passing day part of me hates it a little less simply because you love it a little more."

My head wants to turn, but I refuse.

"Simply because it brings you so much pure unadulterated joy. Because it brings passion and purpose to your life. The only thing I find myself truly wanting anymore, Brie, is *your happiness* as if it were my own." Unable to resist any longer, I allow our eyes to meet. "It's why I handled last night's moments so poorly. I couldn't stand the idea for one minute that you were hurt by their words or angered by their actions. I...I was upset because, for the first time since we started dating, I felt your happiness would be in actual jeopardy. The notion that it was, and that there wasn't anything I could do to protect it drove me to a level of madness I've never experienced before. My brother says it's what happens when you love someone."

My mouth slowly creaks open.

"And I do love you, Brie. I don't care about what anyone thinks or says or does as long as I know you're all right. That you'll be all right. And if for some reason you're not, I want to be the one who helps make it all right." His hand gently grazes my cheek. "*Always*."

Kellan doesn't bother waiting for a response before softly smashing his lips to mine. The moment our tongues reunite, a sigh of relief slips free from both of us. My arms wrap around his neck as I allow his apology to transform into a deep declaration of so much more than a simple I love you.

I've been in love before, and it's never felt anything like this. I've never had anyone who makes me feel so naturally beautiful inside and out. Someone who is willing to sacrifice himself or his own happiness for the sake of my own. I've never met anyone else I was willing to do the same for. Someone I was willing to be ridiculed or unfairly judged for simply standing beside them. I've never met anyone I was this willing to fight with and for. Between you and me? I hope whatever we have, lasts a lifetime. I hope that I was wrong before. I hope this prince someday turns me into his princess.

CHAPTER EIGHTEEN

"Ugh, what is that?" The red-headed teen gags.

Politely, I answer, "It's cauliflower macaroni and cheese."

She gags again before sneering at me. "What was wrong with *regular* mac and cheese?"

Despite the nasty attitude that came with the question, I'm totally with her on that one. I mean I get it. They're all for healthy eats and blah blah blah but come on. It's mac and cheese! It's meant to be cheesy and creamy and terrible for you.

I force another polite smile. "This is the choice approved by the school. Would you like a scoop?"

The teen skips the decision to answer me and returns to talking to her friend who is texting beside her.

"It's the last week of school in shithole, can't you serve better food?" A guy in a letterman's jacket questions as he glances at his selections.

"It's the last week of school, can't you be a better person?" is right on the tip of my tongue; however, through gritted teeth, I professionally repeat, "This is what was approved by the school."

"School sucks so the food sucks. Makes sense," the guy chuckles with the support of his two friends behind him.

Last Monday of the school year and almost every person who has come through the line is making sure I appreciate that fact. For the past three hours, it has been an endless parade of youth complaining about the lunch choices. Never mind the fact we have no say in what they're served and usually very little say in when it's served. They don't give a shit that it is completely out of our hands. They just blame us as if our secret mission in life is to make them miserable. Newsflash. If it was? I personally wouldn't be secretive about it.

The last wave of students file out of our serving area and Bernice closes the garage-style door behind them.

"Ungrateful sons of bitches," she mumbles, locking it to insure they don't attempt to return. "If I wasn't trying to help put my youngest through college, I swear I'd go back to working at Toni's Ice Cream Parlor."

I hit her with a smile. "I'm sure he appreciates it."

"Mmm…He can appreciate it a little better by picking a damn major." Bernice makes her way to my side of the station. "Don't you finally graduate this week?"

"Hopefully. I took all my finals last week, and I meet with my professor tomorrow to discuss my finished portfolio. If everything goes smooth, I will finally walk across the stage in two weeks."

"You excited?"

I scrape the leftover pasta into the trashcan she's wheeled over. "Relieved."

"I bet," she hums, following my action with the bowl of salad left over. "Have you decided what you wanna do? Applied for jobs anywhere?"

Sheepishly, I shake my head.

Not a fucking clue. Unlike Jovi who has already made her way into the art industry, I have never worked for anyone in the business other than a required internship last year. To be honest, after talking to Candy a few weeks ago, I'm not sure if the gallery life is for me. Sure, the idea of being surrounded by promising pillars in the industry would be exciting, but at the same time, I think I'd begin to feel inadequate like I did at the Treme showing. I think if I were a talent scout the same feelings would occur. Graduating and having no clue what you're going to do sucks, just for the record. At the end of this week, I don't even have a day-to-

day job anymore. Hm. That reminds me. Post-graduation I may not have an apartment anymore, either. Adulting sucks.

After Bernice and I clear out our food stations, help wash dishes, and prep for the morning, we're able to leave a little earlier than expected. Within the first three minutes in my car, my cell begins to ring.

I don't hesitate to hit the speaker phone button. "Hello."

"Thought you'd still be at work," my dad says with a hint of surprise in his tone. "Everything okay?"

"Yup. Just off a little early."

"Headed home?"

"Yeah." As quickly as the word leaves, I correct, "Well…to Kellan's."

Which is practically home. We spend most nights at his place even when we've spent the day at mine. It's been working out for the best. I spend the night at Kellan's, Merrick spends the night at our place, and we all hang out most days somewhere in the middle. Maybe that's why I'm not panicking more over having to leave the apartment. I've basically already moved out.

"Speaking of, I was calling to see if you had any special requests for your party."

Pulling into the far lane, I question, "What party?"

"Your graduation party!"

The confusion completely remains.

"Kellan told us not to worry about taking you to dinner after your graduation because he had already booked a place for your party. I thought the least we could do was bring something like a cake or cupcakes or some sort of dessert. I tried calling him, but there was no answer, so I figured I would ask the graduate herself."

Awe settles into my system.

A surprise party?! Ugh. Does he have to keep getting sweeter?

"Chocolate with chocolate frosting."

"That's my girl."

"And be thankful he didn't answer. He would've said some sort of cheesecake with berries or pineapple or some other bizarre topping, and I would've had to smash it in his face."

The two of us laugh. "Glad I called then."

"It's for the best." I accelerate onto the highway. "Is it just you, mom, and Candice coming?"

"He told us we could invite whoever we wanted to celebrate in your success," Dad sings like a jay bird. "Unfortunately, I've already had to cut your mother's list down three times. I figure at this rate that by next week it'll look more reasonable. With the way she was just adding names left and right you'd think you two were getting married."

The idea makes me smile.

What?! Ohmygod, yes. Fine. It's crossed my mind! I know! I know! It's way too fast and way too soon but…

Too much silence passes, which spurs my father to ask, "Brie, you two aren't-"

"No," I deny quickly this time. "We haven't even discussed living together let alone marriage." To my surprise, there's a huge exhale. "You can relax, Dad. Your little girl isn't about to walk down the aisle anytime soon."

"Good."

"I thought you loved Kellan."

"I do," he assures, "and I wouldn't mind the two of you living happily ever after someday. Key word is *someday*. Not today."

My father's protectiveness makes me grin wildly.

Daddy's little girl. He says that now, but something tells me someday will never happen in his head. I don't think he'll ever be ready to give me up.

"Alright dad, I'm here. Gonna head up." I pull into the private parking space reserved for me. "Was there anything else you needed?"

"No, enjoy your evening."

"I love you, Dad."

"Love you, too."

The call ends, and I slowly shake my head.

A party? He's throwing me a party? I thought my mother sending out a million graduation announcements was more than enough. Why is he insisting on making this day such a huge deal?

It's not like it's impressive. It's taken me ten years to get a bachelor's degree thanks to paying for this shit out of pocket, and I still have no idea what I'm going to do with it.

I grab my bag as well as my portfolio case and take the elevator connected to his building. Once I've reached his floor, I swipe my card to allow me access to the level, quickly walk down the hall, and use my card again to enter his penthouse.

The moment I enter, I hear Kellan's voice rush to end a call. "I appreciate you calling to let me know the results."

The entire place looks like something you'd see in a movie, right? A perfectly staged over-priced movie. For the most part, I don't mind the lack of color. The dark grays and the whites create an expected crisp modern vibe, but they also make it impossible to hide any sort of spill. Hey, it's not like I'm Fred Sanford or something. It's just that sometimes getting a midnight snack while half sex stoned can get a little messy.

There's a short pause followed by, "Mmm, you as well."

Veering to the left where his small open kitchen is located, I carefully place the bags in the bar seat, and ask, "Was that a phone call about my surprise party?"

"No, it was my physician calling with my latest lab results. Apparently, I'm completely clean." He wipes his hands with the dish towel before tossing it over his white t-shirt. "And it's not a surprise if you know, love."

I helplessly smile. "Dad let the cat out of the bag."

Kellan immediately frowns.

"It's not his fault! He thought I knew!"

"Why would you know? It wouldn't be a surprise then."

"I think he thought it was just a party."

"What exactly did he call for?"

"To ask me about the cake."

"I can handle the cake," he huffs, planting his hands on the counter.

"I don't trust you with cake."

"You don't trust me with cake?"

"Cheesecake is not cake."

"It's in the bloody name!"

"*See.*"

Kellan rolls his eyes. "Your parents don't need to bring anything. I've got it all covered."

"Well, they're bringing the good cake, so just accept it."

"The good cake? Does that mean you won't eat whatever cake I ordered?"

I bob my head with a playful expression. "Depends."

"On?"

"Does your cake include fruit substance of any kind?"

"No."

"Then maybe." He rolls his eyes again while I lightly laugh. "You do know that you don't have to throw me a party, right? I'm just doing something a normal person would've done like four to six years ago."

His expression softens. "It's an accomplishment no matter how long it takes to finish, love. Enjoy it. You've earned it."

I try to smile.

I know I have. I've put in the work to finish and the work to pay to finish. I guess part of me is still in disbelief it's happening.

My head nods towards the stove behind him. "Whatcha cookin' good lookin'?"

"Currently, a tomato cream sauce from scratch."

Impressed, I fold my arms across my chest. "Scratch? Like, cut the tomatoes yourself kinda scratch?"

"Indeed."

"Have you had to use the fire extinguisher?"

"That only happened twice!"

Cooking is definitely something neither of us is good at. However, he is more adamant about changing that than me. Kinda hope he never conquers it. Not sure I need him adding to the reasons he's already practically perfect.

"Wanna try it?" Kellan cautiously asks.

"Have you tried it yet?"

He slowly shakes his head.

"Let me get this straight. You wanna poison me to save yourself?"

"It's not poison."

"Then you try it."

"No."

"You are trying to kill me. Seems like there are easier ways to break up than a murder, suicide situation."

"Fine. We'll do it together."

"Like a suicide pact?"

His head tilts at me in an annoyed fashion.

Giggling, I make my way around to him and watch as he dips the wooden spoon into the pot. When he pulls it out, he gives it a long, slow blow before offering it. At the same time, we lean forward and slurp the taste in tandem. To my surprise, it tastes fantastic.

"Holy shit," I whisper. "*You made that?*"

"*Right?*" He whispers back, his own disbelief prevalent. "Now, let's hope the rest of the meal tastes equally as delicious."

"Need me to do anything?"

"Set the table?"

I nod and make my way to the black round table that's closer to the front door. Normally, it's only home to the set of roses he buys me each week, but today it's completely covered in paperwork along with his computer.

Before touching anything, I ask, "Is there a certain way you want me to gather this stuff?"

"No, just try to keep it neatly stacked if possible."

I helplessly prod, "What is all of this anyway?"

"Most of it is just expansion ideas for the current program; however, a couple of those files contain the plans for the orphanage."

Curiosity causes me to toss my head over my shoulder. "You're actually ready to open it?"

"No," Kellan quickly answers, "but in case the day ever arrives, it'll be nice to have everything in order."

The hint of sadness in his tone tugs sharply in my chest.

You know, I have no clue what I wanna do with my life or where I wanna go or see, but Kellan knows exactly what he wants, who he wants to help, and can't make that happen. I think the only thing worse than not having a dream is having a dream that seems impossible to ever come true.

Once I've cleared the table of his work items, I reset it with dishes, silverware, and wine. Kellan relocates the spinach salad, fresh-baked bread, and the pasta dish he spent the afternoon working on. Our conversation unfolds as freely as it always does. We take turns recounting parts of our day, and he, of course, has to include the portion of swimming laps after lunch, simply to watch the color in my face brighten in excitement at the thought of him naked.

You've seen him that way. If he wasn't a prince or a duke, I'd say he should be an underwear model. They might have to cover up that lucky ace tattoo on his ass that he got on a dare, but I'm sure they do that sort of thing all the time.

Our meal begins to wind down, and Kellan leans back in his seat with his wine glass. "You nervous about meeting with your professor tomorrow?"

I do my best to hide the insecurity over the situation. "Not as nervous as I could be."

His head tilts at me in question.

"I'm not a complete and total wreck. Doubt I'll sleep well tonight, but it could be worse."

A sly smirk slides on his face. "I can help with that sleep thing. I have a number of proven methods that make it impossible for you to do anything else afterward."

I squeeze my anxious thighs together, refusing to let him see the desire his words always cause. "You mean like lecturing me for hours about lacrosse?"

He gives me a brief glare before he asks, "Have you given any more thought to what you want to do after graduation? I know we've discussed how you'll be taking off a couple of months to search for viable options, but that's usually where you change the subject."

"Like I want to now…" I mutter to myself.

"Brie, you don't have to decide exactly where your life is going to go right this minute. I'm just curious as to where you *want* it to go? You don't seem to want to paint professionally, and the idea of working in a gallery like Jovi seems to cause your face to wrinkle."

I scrunch my nose at the fact he's noticed that. "I don't paint or draw for profit. I do it to help convey the things my brain has trouble expressing."

Do you have an outlet like that? Does everyone?

"Art restoration? Perhaps an art administrator? Organizing events like the one we met at?"

"Maybe?" A shrug escapes. "I don't know. I like the idea of connecting with those in the community, bringing them bits of the industry they would've never been exposed to otherwise. Sometimes I toy with the idea of finding a way for youth to get better acquainted with artists other than the basics. Show them art is so much more than just pencil or paint on canvas. Maybe if you would've had a better art teacher when you were younger you wouldn't hate art so much as an adult."

"Unlikely," he denies with a crooked smirk. "However, your optimism is admirable." After I roll my eyes, Kellan puts down his glass and asks, "Do you mind if I see the final piece of your portfolio? You've shown me all the others-"

"Which you made fun of in your typical Kellan way," I mock his body language and accent.

He shakes his head. "And I will make fun of your horrific acting skills next if you don't distract me with something else like your final piece."

"Fine, but…you have to promise me you'll take all those snide remarks you're known for and shove them so deep down no one is going to find them without a colonoscopy."

Kellan winces, has another sip of his wine, and stands with discomfort on his face.

My imagery a little too much? Good.

The two of us leave the table and relocate to the bar area by the kitchen where I left my bag. During the process of removing the hefty object from its case, I explain, "When I began to build this, my art professor explained it was the easiest thing I would do in my time as an art student, yet it would feel like the most difficult. His requirement was simple. You were to track where you began and where you ended during your time in the program. Essentially you would be adding pieces, semester by semester that expressed who you were at that particular moment in time. What you were going through. What mattered most. He also explained how most students fail this simple task, inevitably postponing their future." With it now open on the bar counter, I carefully move towards the last page, and Kellan appears over my shoulder. "I don't know if you remember the first piece-"

"It was an abstract painting. A weird mesh of muted colors. No idea what it was supposed to be or represent. I just remember thinking it looked like a sad take on the classic Pac-Man board."

I press my lips firmly together to stop from biting his head off.

Did he really just refer to my painting as an 80s arcade game?

We finally land on the page, and I can feel my entire body tense. "My final piece is actually a pastel drawing."

Together we study the picture of the single blue eye. I proudly stare at the lines I studied for months while he slept, while he ate, while he yelled at sports on the couch beside me. I committed every detail to memory until it felt as if I could draw them with my eyes sewn shut. I studied the different hues of his eye in various lighting, in various situations, and then spent hours mixing colors in an attempt to capture it.

At one point I'm fairly certain that I was reciting color compounding in my sleep.

It takes longer than anticipated for Kellan to speak. "That's...That's *my eye*."

"You're quick," I tease, still staring at the drawing, too terrified to face him.

"The final piece of your portfolio…is…*me*." Despite my reluctance, he shifts my body to allow our eyes to meet. "Explain it." When I don't start talking, he sweetly adds, *"Please."*

A deep sigh seeps free. "This is where I am in life. The colors are bold and bright and deep because for the first time I can remember that's how I feel. You have this way of making all of those things pop out of me. When you're around I stand a little taller. Feel a little smarter. Hell, believe I'm more…beautiful than I ever could've imagined. I chose your eye because they're a metaphor for the place I've finally reached. In this particular shade, they're accepting of an unfamiliar situation and eager to understand their changing surroundings. I chose you as the subject of my final piece because in a way…I guess I feel like you're bridging the gap between the end of my days as a run of the mill art student and whatever the next step in my life is going to be."

Did that sound okay? God, I hope so. It's more or less the speech I plan to give my professor if he requires it.

To my surprise, Kellan's mouth is agape.

Feeling beyond exposed and painfully vulnerable, I playfully state, "You can pick your jaw up off the floor, narcissist. I highly doubt I'm the first person to ever make some sort of portrait of you."

There's no hesitation in his response. "You're the only one who matters to me."

Before I can shy away, Kellan's lips descend mine with so much ferocity that I stumble backward into the empty bar stool. Rather than sweep me away with his typical dominating demands, he slowly rolls his tongue around mine conveying something unexpected. Something softer. Sweeter. More sentimental. One hand anchors itself to my cheek while the other wraps around me to draw me closer. With every gentle press, he reciprocates his own surrender of self, allowing me to be the judge and jury in the one aspect of his life he's never shared with anyone else.

His mouth falls from mine to whisper, "I'm going to show you how much you matter, love."

Incapable of a well thought out reply, I simply shut my eyes when his mouth returns to my skin. The heat of his tongue blazes a trail down my neck that has me panting in anticipation for what's to come. Kellan sends his hands on a mission to undress me while his mouth unhurriedly devotes itself to praising each exposed portion. My body eagerly pushes itself towards him, anxious for more than the teasing tastes of pleasure being presented. Once my clothes have been banished from the situation, he lifts me up to sit on the edge of the bar stool and tugs one of my nipples between his teeth, toying with it mercilessly before repeating the action on the other. Despite my whine and pleads to lower his efforts, he laps at the hardened points while my pussy aches in envy. His fingertips take turns assisting in his torturous efforts by lightly grazing the wet lips between my hips and smearing the discovered treat onto my nipples for his tongue to lap up. Each time a wet streak is slathered, I whimper in objection to such a filthy act, yet each time it's washed away, I call out his name in a request to repeat the dirty deed. Just as my body begins to tremble in desperation, his mouth latches onto my pussy tightly, trapping my clit against his tongue's tireless efforts to have the teetering orgasm tear ruthlessly through me. Kellan savagely sucks while my shaky fingers strain for leverage in his hair. Every twirl, every thrust, every brush elicits an earth-shattering cry that makes me thankful he doesn't have close neighbors. His wet muscle pendulates its merciless maneuvers between dominating my pussy from front to back and spinning around the sensitive, stiff nub known for making me arch my back. Suddenly, my breath becomes shallow, and my bottom lip slides between teeth in preparation for the inevitable. Knowing this warning sign, my boyfriend devours me harder and faster and even more devotedly until the quivering in my legs, which are over his shoulders, spreads to my entire body. My orgasm erupts, and his mouth locks in place as if he's swallowed the key to my pussy's freedom and has no problem spending the remainder of his life right where he is. The moment my mind threatens to stop spinning from the overwhelming orgasmic high, Kellan slowly allows the tip of his tongue to dip back inside for seconds.

At this rate, I can't imagine I'll have any trouble sleeping. If a night filled with endless orgasms doesn't knock me out then nothing will. More importantly, regardless of my sleep situation later, Kellan's relentless efforts to prove his love still get him an A plus in the boyfriend department. He's definitely on the "Girlfriend's List" if catch my metaphor.

CHAPTER NINETEEN

Kellan

"You're serious? You're actually going to ask her?"

I turn my attention away from Brie, who has her head thrown back in laughter at something her sister has said. "Tonight. When we get home."

Hugh puts down his pint. "What if she says no?"

God, I'm praying she doesn't say no.

"Then she says no." I casually shrug. "It doesn't change how I feel about her."

He arches his eyebrows in an impressed nature. "Wow. That's really mature of you. Gotta admit I'm amazed Brie managed to make you grow up. I thought for sure you'd never shake your Peter Pan syndrome."

With a cocky smirk, I deny, "I wouldn't say I've grown up quite yet. Just last night we had an ice cream party."

"Seriously?"

"Yeah. Though in all fairness, it did contain a different type of nuts than you're probably imagining."

Hugh groans and I chuckle profusely.

It gave an entirely new meaning to chocolate, vanilla swirl.

"Speaking of desserts, it's time we serve them." I summon one of the waitresses helping with the party to let her know we're ready for the next portion. She quickly nods and scurries away while I make my way over to where my girlfriend is mingling with her family.

Watching her walk across the stage a few hours ago was surreal. I'd never been so proud of an individual in my entire life. Perhaps it was because I knew exactly what she had endured these past few months. Stayed up late helping her study ancient methods of sculpting. Spending hours on a Saturday in the art store after spending hours replenishing my wardrobe. Whatever the reason, seeing her stroll across it swelled my chest with so much happiness, I could barely breathe. Had her sister not nudged me to start clapping I would've completely missed the opportunity to join in the applause.

My arm slides around her waist. "Hate to interrupt, love, but it is time for dessert."

Brie beams up at me. "The cake my dad bought, right?"

"Yes, the one your father brought. However, in case anyone doesn't like chocolate-"

"Who doesn't like chocolate?!"

"Those people exist," I insist with a smirk.

"Have you ever actually met them?"

"*Yes.*"

"Lies."

"For those people who don't like chocolate or are not *in the mood* for chocolate, I've got carrot cake and a few other treats."

Brie instantly gags. "Carrot cake? That's not even cake! That's like vegetable bread."

"Who hates carrot cake?!"

She immediately raises her hand, and I swat it down.

"You have terrible taste in food sometimes."

"You have terrible taste in food *most* of the time."

"You two are perfect for each other," her sister, Candice sighs. "You're equally stubborn."

The party members begin to gather at the table on the opposite side of The Silver Tap Pub where the servers are setting up cake alongside other desserts. While the place is filled with an array of people ranging from her cousins to her friends who weren't graduating today, we wind up at a table consisting of those she's closest to.

With my arm loosely draped around the back of her chair, I enjoy embarrassing art mishaps from her youth told in tandem by her parents. She squirms. She blushes. She disagrees yet never insists they stop exposing her past to me. She allows me the opportunity to accept her as a whole and not just the parts she's proud of. With every passing story, the desire to ask her the question I've been holding onto for weeks increases.

She has to say yes. I know I told Hugh I'd be fine if she didn't, but I lied. I'll be devastated if she says no.

After a playful topic change to favorite foods, which Hugh and Dana join us for, I dismiss myself to pay for the meal, tip the waitresses, and load her graduation gifts into the back of the SUV with the help of my best friend and Swiss. Brie meets me outside just as we finish up to let me know people are starting to leave. We spend the next thirty minutes letting people coo over her accomplishment and thanking them for joining us. By the time we've managed to make it home ourselves and unload the presents into the apartment, she's an exhausted mess of smiles and giggles.

Her body bounces onto the edge of the king-sized bed in my penthouse on a pleased sigh. "Thank you again for the party, Kellan. It was *amazing*."

I remain standing while she kicks off her heels. "Almost as amazing as my gift."

"You mean the La Dega painting above our bed?"

Yes, I caved and bought her one of the pieces of art when we had that private tour. I wanted the bloody thing to hang in her apartment, so I didn't have to stare at it constantly, but the fact is we spend almost every night here making it a much more logical place. I don't have feelings for it one way or another, but she was over the moon to have it. And the entire evening devoted to sex that night further reiterated that.

"No, that was just something I bought for you to have."

"But you said-"

"I said what I needed to say in order for you not to be angry I was purchasing it."

She gives me a small glare. "You lied."

"I...*fibbed.*"

"Semantics."

It's impossible not to snicker at the reference to our earlier days.

"So, what I'm hearing is...you got me another gift?"

"It's your graduation, love, of course I got you another gift." A deep exhale escapes at the same time I remove the small box from my pants pocket. My voice tries to hide its tremor. "I...I hope you like it."

Brie silently stares at the small velvet box extended her direction. Her eyes lift, revealing their bewilderment. She gives me one hard look before taking the offering. Nervously, I watch as she tugs at the ribbon and slowly opens it. "It's a locket."

Yes. Just a locket. Relax. As much as I wanted that to be an engagement ring, I know I should probably wait until we at least reach the six-month mark. That's only a couple weeks away, might I add.

Brie carefully removes the white gold heart shaped necklace. I continue to admire her while she examines it, noticing the B on the front for her and the K on the back for me.

It's got a cursive engraving made out of tiny diamonds. Soph helped me decide which one. Thank God she did. I realized that day I knew absolutely nothing about women's jewelry. Shocking, isn't it? I can easily pick out an outfit that would put some of the best stylists to shame yet couldn't last an hour surrounded by seas of diamond encrusted broaches. Not one of my finer moments.

When she finally opens it to the picture, I state, "I lost that day."

She giggles at the photo and then up at me. "You lost to *a girl*."

"I did." My face tries to hide its lingering insecurity. "I lost *to you*, but I never want to *lose you*." The puzzled look returns, and I continue. "My lease is up in a couple of weeks. I plan to renew it regardless of your answer, so that you have a home, and I have a place in the states for when I have opportunities to return, but I'm needed back in Fayeweather. I've got family obligations I can't break and a few business meetings to attend with potential investors for the program." Just as her face begins to fall, I announce, "I want you to come with me. I want you to meet my overbearing brother and sassy sister-in-law. I want you to see the country that I grew up in. See why it's better than yours."

Brie hits me with a stern expression.

"Fine. You're right. It's *almost* better than yours. After all, the states have you."

She flashes me a sweet smile.

"I understand if you say no, but please, truly consider it. We could travel along the coast like we talked about. You could check out the galleries there. Perhaps find somewhere you want to work. At the very least, you could enjoy your first real summer. One filled with a vacation and sunshine and reveries." The moment I see longing beginning to blossom, I finish, "If you say yes, if you come home with me, if you let me introduce you to the rest of my world, money is no object of your concern. Whatever you want, wherever we go, is yours and would be your *true* graduation gift."

Stillness spreads in the room rapidly, taking my breath prison in the process. For what feels like an eternity, she doesn't move, nor does she speak. The silence reaches deafening levels, and I quickly realize I have my answer.

I attempt to swallow my sadness. "It's alright, love, if you say no. Nothing will change between us. *I swear.* It'll take more than a few weeks of distance to tear me away from you."

"Could we come back to visit if I got too homesick?"

Her question sparks hope. "*Of course.*"

Another lull of quietness occurs before she says, "Then yes."

Disbelief darts down my throat. "Yes?" She nods slowly, and I question once more. "As in *actually* yes?"

"Is there a different kinda yes?" The snark in her tone frees the remaining anxiety. "Now, could you come over here and snap this thing on already? I wanna see how it looks!"

With a playful smirk, I state, "Don't be pushy. It's your graduation day not your birthday."

She sasses back as she extends the jewelry for me. "I'm sorry, do you want me to come fly across the world to be with you?"

"Not even halfway around the world," I correct, lowering myself to the bed space beside her. "And it's too late now. You've agreed. No turning back."

She giggles at the same time I clasp the necklace around her neck. Brie angles her face to allow our lips to esuriently mesh. Overwhelmed with appreciation for the sacrifice she will be making by leaving everything she knows behind to join me in my required endeavors, my mouth romantically ravishes hers while we fall backwards onto the bed. Our tongues take turns teasing one another while her fingers greedily grope my lower abs underneath my white dress shirt. Her hands begin to paw at my pants in unison with her whimpers until my own hunger becomes too much to bear. In a swift motion, I undo my belt and allow her warm grasp to graze my boxer brief-covered crotch. A deep groan sticks to the back of my throat, forcing me to accelerate the speed of my own undressing. As soon as I'm done, I yank up her lavender sundress and quickly discard the delicate fabric standing between me and the only thing capable of making her verbal agreement to go back with me even sweeter.

Unable to wait any longer, my cock guides itself to gormandize on the most delectable treat known to man. Another harsh growl is grabbed as my dick attempts to savor every single smothering sensation. The way Brie's pussy fits so snug around my shaft, there's no denying that she belongs to me. That I belong to her. That together is the only way we should ever be. My hips fervidly buck, completely callous to the idea of dragging this memorable moment long into the night. Brie's nails bite into my biceps while her bottom lip slips between her teeth, silently begging for more. Nonverbally crying for me to dive deep. *Pound harder.* Her own hips harshly rock upward causing me to frantically thrust in order to meet her blow for blow. The two of us tumble into what feels like a ceaseless cycle of passionate pumps met with sharp back bowing from her brazen body.

With the faintest warning, her orgasm shatters forcing her lips to fumble from mine on cock-swelling scream, "*Ohmygod! Kellan!*"

Brie's pussy wildly pulsates, and the pleasing pressure from her throbbing muscles shuts my eyes. Overpowered by the endless convulsing around my bare cock, I completely surrender and allow her body to milk me dry. Scorching surge after surge knocks into the ones pouring from her while her mouth turns my name into an invocation only she has the right to say.

Through our shared inability to breathe, I somehow manage to whisper, "*I love you.*"

Her mouth struggles to return the words, but they don't have to.

She never has to utter them again for me to know how she feels. There's something unspoken between us that has nestled itself past my heart and into the lining of my soul. This woman isn't just any woman. She's the only woman for me, and there's not a damn thing in this entire world that could ever change that.

CHAPTER TWENTY

Brie

Kellan stretches out on the plush couch beside me with one arm tucked under his head and his feet in my lap. "Comfortable?"

I give the interior of the plane another glance.

It's basically a living room in the sky. We're lounging on a long white leather couch with black pillows and a coffee table in front of us where a throw blanket is folded. On the other side there's a set of matching recliners, each with a pillow and blanket stacked neatly on them. Towards the back of the plane is another leather couch currently being occupied by a drowsy flight attendant. Sandwiching that solo piece of furniture are two closed doors. One is the restroom facilities while the other is the kitchen. Yeah. That's right. He not only has his own plane with a damn living room, but one that includes a kitchen to fulfill his snobby food whims.

Still tense despite the fact we've been in the air for an hour, I question, "Is this the plane you always fly in? Like the one your family owns?"

"Jet."

"What?"

"It's a *jet* not a plane."

"Oh, good, the coffee, latte conversation but on a grander scale."

My boyfriend lightly chortles prior to informing, "What I fly in really depends on what's available when I'm ready to leave and whose schedule might need the one with the sleep accommodations."

"Meaning…?"

"The jet with the bed."

"Of course, the other one has a bed," I mutter to myself in annoyed astonishment. "And you just…jet off whenever you feel like it to…*wherever* you feel like it?"

He casually shrugs. "Most of the time."

"What about the rest of your family?"

"Kristopher and Soph hardly ever leave the country, so they typically use the smaller one that has only one couch-"

"Smaller one?! Your family has three planes?!"

"*Jets.*"

I instantly swat at his leg.

"*Ou!*"

We all know that didn't hurt.

"Do not make me reprimand you for striking royalty."

"You are a royal…a royal pain in the ass."

"I am that, *too*." His expression remains playful as he explains, "Yes, we have three jets that vary in size and purpose. Typically, I fly to the states, so I take this one. My father on the other hand is often required to fulfill numerous social responsibilities for weeks at a time – almost like a popstar tour – making the one with the bed a more reasonable choice."

"And these social responsibilities…is that all he does for a living?"

Kellan's face unexpectedly hardens. "Now? Yes. When my mother was alive? No. She cared about more than outdated traditions and frivolous spending."

"You wanna hate on your father for frivolous spending? This from the guy who is wearing a three-thousand-dollar suit?"

He glares. "I have expensive taste, that doesn't make me frivolous."

"That's like the *definition* of frivolous!"

"No, enjoying the benefits of a tailor fitted suit and a pair of Banini oxfords is one thing, buying the Duke of Lostengrenge a golf course for a wedding present is frivolous. That's the type of spending you do to remind others they are beneath you. That's the type of spending you do when you're purchasing your good deeds rather than actually practicing them. Once upon a time, he lived alongside a woman whose sole purpose in life was to make a real difference. To actually enrich and treasure lives others had cast aside. I may not throw every penny I have into making sure the entire world is fed, but there isn't a day that passes, that I'm not trying to do more to help others who are simply too young to help themselves."

The tenderness mixed with blind infuriation in his speech shuts my lips tightly.

I know almost nothing about his father. His brother, his brother's wife, his mother – rest her soul – are all open topics. In fact, we talk so much about them some days it feels like I've spent the same amount of time with them as he has my family. While I've video chatted with Kristopher and Soph during a few of his calls and seen old photos of his mother that were posted online, his father is more like a fairytale than anything else in his life. He's the king always behind a shut door. The king who seemingly appears only when he has to attend a wedding or yell at a prince for causing too much trouble. That's basically the extent of what I knew about him until this moment.

"Think we can swing by the space you want to build your orphanage?"

His face softens. "How do you know I have a space picked out?"

"Because you've been dreaming about opening it for two years. Of course, you have a space picked out."

He lets a full-fledged smile develop. "It's this quaint little area right outside of the city. It'd be a perfect place to allow them a field for sports, plus the housing area to be completely separate from the sleeping quarters."

"Is that a yes you'll show me?"

"I'll consider it," he teases with a wink. "That is if you do something for me."

"Like?"

His eyebrows salaciously wiggle.

"No way! We're not alone."

"Come on," he encourages, mirth dripping from his tone. "Betty's practically already asleep, and as long as we're quiet we won't be caught." Kellan wets his lips slowly. "Don't you want to join the mile-high club?"

I give him a sarcastic stare. "Aren't you already a member?"

"Not on this jet."

My expression doesn't change.

"Truth! I've had sex on planes and jets but never the family one."

Excitement sparks, which causes me to smirk. "So…it'd be like your first time?"

"*On this particular jet*, yes."

"So…you're like a family jet virgin?" I snicker.

"Why do I have the inkling you just want to call me a virgin?"

"That means we're basically virgins together."

"Stop saying the word virgin."

"Shouldn't we wait?" I fake concern. "Shouldn't we get to know each other in the sky a little better, first?"

He lifts himself onto his elbows with a huff. "I am *far* from a virgin and given how hard you came this morning in the shower with me bullocks deep inside you, it's safe to say, neither are you. Now, grab that blanket and climb on top of me."

I giggle, follow his instructions, and cover the lower half of our bodies in the process.

The moment I'm properly positioned, a small thought hits me. "Is this why you demanded I wear a loose dress to fly in? So that you could screw me in the air?"

Kellan cocks a grin. "I'm clever."

"You're arrogant."

His hand creeps up the back of my thighs to push me against his stiff cock. *"I'm hard."*

Extremely. Is it normal for a guy to be this fired up at the blink of an eye?

Rather than continue the conversation, Kellan uses his other hand to tug me to his parted lips. Upon impact, I whimper, first from the force and then from the satisfaction of having our tongues in a lascivious link. A low growl seeps out in an objection of my attempt to take control of the kiss, yet he allows me. The unexpected surrender from his mouth is promptly explained by his hand palming my bare ass cheek. I attempt to pull back to free my stifled moans, but he anchors me to him, swallowing the lecherous sounds like a fiend. The combination of friction from his grinding hips and exerted control of my wriggling body, intensifies the ache in my pussy to the point I'm panting between brief breaks in kissing. Now pleased that he's transformed my body from wanting to needing, he relinquishes his grip on the back of my neck. In a swift, shameless execution, the two of us part just enough to dispose of lower restrictions and fuse together in a muted, carnal cry. My figure blankets his once more except this time my face is buried in the crook of his neck. Both of his hands greedily guide me by the ass to a slow, titillating rock. I abandon all care or concern with being heard and breathlessly sing his name during each voracious plunge.

His whispering only causes me to get wetter. *"You want to get caught, love?"*

My pussy answers without my consent.

Kellan's fingers grip harder while his dick dives deeper. While he harshly heaves again and again muttering to himself as much as me, *"Bloody hell, I can never get enough of you."*

The slick, tensing muscles ceaselessly beg to be stretched and taken and forced into submission. My boyfriend's neck naturally strains from the increase of my pussy's squeezing. I lightly drag my tongue along the displayed area in a long, languorous lick. The simple action shifts his movements from forcefully controlled to ferociously chaotic. He clamps his hands firmly on my hips and barbarically bounces my body back into his cock's every thrust. Before we know it, the two of us are propelled over the edge of ecstasy, gasping in a glorious tandem as our orgasms crash into one another. Our mouths gravitate together not only to muffle our moans but to overdose on one another. To suffocate in the lustful euphoria that we've fallen into.

When our bodies finally reach a point of satiation, I drag my lips from his and tease "Glad you waited for the right girl?"

Kellan lets out a wide grin crawl onto his face. *"Absolutely."*

We share a chuckle and a chaste kiss before collapsing together again.

I don't know if you're a member of this club or not, but I will say join it if you can. And by if you can, I mean as long as it doesn't get you kicked off a plane or banned from an airline.

Thankfully, the remainder of our flight is filled with a long-overdue nap.

For the past two weeks, it's been nonstop prepping for this trip. We spent the first few days moving the rest of my stuff from my old apartment to the penthouse, which went quicker than expected. However, once all my things were there, arguing over decorating and sharing space turned brutal. It became more than apparent he had never had to share his living area before. After all, that was settled, the days were spent searching for my passport – that I got four years ago when I thought I'd be able to go with friends to Mexico for Labor Day weekend – and struggling to pack. I mean, how the hell does anyone pack for an unknown amount of time for a trip to an unknown country? Exactly. Despite Kellan's insistence on just buying me an entirely new wardrobe, Jovi helped guide me the best she could between breaking down into tears over losing another best friend. There was no convincing her that I would be back before she knew it. I get the feeling I'm not the first friend who's told her that.

Once we've safely landed and our bags have been tucked into the trunk of a black Rolls Royce, Kellan makes my first introduction.

"Brie this is Vincent, my security detail. Vincent, meet Brie. An extension of me."

Was that sweet or possessive? Sweetly possessive?

The large, tall dark-haired man extends his hand for me to shake. He doesn't say a word as we do or even once we're finished. Vincent gives me a firm nod and turns his sunglass-covered face to his employer. "Home, sir?"

Kellan gives me a brief glance before answering, "The scenic route."

He nods his understanding and opens the car door for us. I try to hold in my awe at the sight of the inside of the vehicle.

There's a major difference between being in a limo and being in something like a Rolls. This screams high class to the point my ears are bleeding. The deep tinted windows. The embroidered deep gray leather bench seats. The pulled down tray with two glass flutes and a bottle of champagne chilling. Why do I feel like the plane was just the teeny tiny tip of the paintbrush?

As we pull away from the area, Kellan politely offers me a drink. After quickly denying him, I divert my attention outside the glass, enthralled by the gorgeous greenery. While pouring himself a glass, he begins to explain how the royal airstrip is right on the outskirts of Fayeweather and how we'll be taking the country roads, so that I can see the true beauty of his country. I admire the rolling hills, the quaint villas on acres of property, and the way the city itself creates a striking contrast in the background. For what feels like hours, we drive through empty streets and discuss how breathtaking the sight is.

"Slow down," Kellan abruptly announces as the city life appears in the near distance. "Make a right here."

Vincent obeys and turns onto an unpaved road.

About three minutes down it, he commands, "Stop here." The car glides to a smooth halt and Kellan leans over to let down my window. "Right there."

I give him a questionable glance.

"Right there is where I want to build Hannah's Hope."

After surveying the huge unoccupied space, I turn completely around and ask, "You named it? When did you name it?"

"It's always had a name," he tries to brush off.

"But this is the first time I've ever heard you use it. Come to think about it, even your program is only referred to by its acronym, MINOH."

Kellan lifts the glass to his lips.

"Hannah? Who's Hannah?"

I watch as his eyes gloomily gloss over. He attempts to answer yet seems unable.

"Hannah was the queen, Miss Brie," Vincent speaks firmly for him.

A small gasp escapes.

It takes a moment before Kellan finds the strength to explain. "Hannah Olivia Kenningston had one giant hope I have spent most of my adult life keeping alive. She wanted a world where children could be cared for. It did not matter to her if they were sick or homeless, rich or poor, she wanted to be able to help provide for them, to give them the foundation to become better people than perhaps they had ever imagined possible. When she died of breast cancer, Kristopher turned his efforts towards fighting that battle, and I sought to finish the one she started. I went to school to better understand why people become the people they do, to get a better understanding of the true effects of one's upbringing from social status to the simple exposure of a book at an early age. I convinced myself that if I could understand her vision, it would be easier to complete. But in the process of it all, my own was born, and so was the idea of a string of orphanages around the world. A safe haven for those without parents. A safe alternative to help drain the clogged foster care systems and provide better health, education, and love to those who need it. To take the structure of an elite boarding school and provide it to those the world is so quick to disregard before they've even had a chance to start. Both MINOH, which stands for Minors in Need of Hope, and Hannah's Hope are named directly after the woman who refused to ever believe in hopelessness."

What…What do I even say to that? God, just when I thought I knew everything about him, he still manages to find a way to surprise me.

"To the palace," his voice whispers in what sounds like pain.

I roll up the window and curl my body into his. The moment I do, he wraps his arms around me and I quietly state, "Thank you for sharing that with me."

Kellan plants a soft kiss on my forehead prior to replying, "Thank you for letting me."

Neither of us says another word the remainder of the car ride. I shift in his arms to get a glimpse of the highways that lead to the heart of the city, but the view is short lived. We take another road resembling the ones from our countryside tour except about ten minutes later, tall gray stone buildings begin to appear. Before I know it, we turn to the right and head down a guarded driveway with several soldiers on each side. I quickly sit up straight, anxious to see anything and everything I can.

Holy shit. I'm really about to see an actual royal palace! Ohmygosh, which Disney song do you wanna sing right now? Come on! I know you wanna sing one!

At the first gate, Vincent swipes his keycard, granting us instant access; however, at the next iron gate are two armed guards on the outside right below security cameras and another one waiting in a booth. The man steps out and strolls over to inspect the inside of the vehicle.

He approves Vincent but lifts his eyebrows at the sight of me. In a cautious voice, he greets, "Good evening, Prince Kellan."

"Evening David," Kellan says warmly in return.

"I wasn't aware you would be returning with a guest, sir."

He leans forward with a wicked grin. "It's kind of a surprise."

David tries not to stare. "Indeed, it will be, sir."

Because Kellan never brings home guests or something else?

"Relax, David. Take a picture like you would any other guest and upload it."

He hesitates. "Upload it to the private database for…*personal family guests*, sir?"

"Yes."

"Not tourists, sir?"

"No."

"Are you sure, sir?"

"Positive."

David nods and steps away, which is when I ask, "Take my picture?"

"Documentation upon visiting. The cameras capture images, but this is just an additional part of security. They take your face, and it goes in a secure file. When you return, with or without me present, they'll take another picture and check it against the database. Those in the small, private personal guest files are permitted after a phone call of approval from the person they are visiting. Those in the other file are not permitted unless the palace is open for a public event in which they will need to provide proof they were invited to the grounds. Then there's obviously the employee database, which are given coded passes with their photos attached. The code grants them access to *only* the parts they are permitted to be in. There's security spread throughout the property that scans them to reassure employees aren't wandering where they have no business. And then are those who work for vendors and delivery companies; however, they are not allowed access past this part of the gate. Employees from the inside have to come and escort whatever needs to be escorted in alongside a member of security."

There's a light tapping on the window and Kellan rolls it down.

I nervously smile, extremely grateful it only takes a second with his device. Afterward, he gives us both a polite nod, disappears back in the booth, and opens the iron gates for us. As we're driven past the guards, they stand at full attention and salute.

Another wave of anxiety rolls through me, but Kellan playfully attempts to battle it away, "They get paid to do that."

I roll my eyes at the comment though he succeeds in getting me to let go of the breath I don't remember holding.

Now on the other side of the gate I'm exposed to more buildings in the same gray rock that was on the outside except they appear to all be connected. We continue veering to the left to take the track around the courtyard, which has a stone fountain surrounded by blooming red roses.

"This stretch of the palace is where we host an array of events in our name. Some private for those with equally pointless titles and some for the selected portions of the public. This entire area is fitted to hold overnight guests, banquets, and weddings," Kellan quickly explains. "Then over there," he scoots his finger over a smidgen, "is where private, custom projects are conducted. Art pieces. Elaborate wardrobe creations. Private one on one concerts. It's a much smaller designated area yet still has accommodation for those who might be staying for the night. Now, over there," his gesturing moves to the approaching area right where the track curves, "is more or less the area for those who serve at the palace. Security guards, maids, cooks, really anyone who spends the majority of their life here as opposed to anywhere else. They live in this area, and there is also a private tutoring area for those who have children. While they're not required to live on the grounds, it does make their lives quite easier." He motions his hand past the stretch of building between the curves. "That tower and the one at the opposite end are security. There are several safety measures set in place to ensure the safety of the royal family if there was ever a threat and each area tower has a separate purpose not only in that but in day-to-day security as well. The path over there between those buildings leads to parking for employees, several gardens, and Kris' personal dwelling that was built for him and Soph to live in when they needed space outside the palace walls. There are additional security structures back there as well. There is also a back entrance though it is guarded the same way the front entrance is. It's just an easier access point for Kris' home." The vehicle finally comes to a complete stop. "That direction is where our personal vehicles are parked as well as the ones, we use for travel like this. In the area above it is where our security details are allowed to congregate and relax between outings. They have separate living quarters than the rest of security, which are also in that building."

All of a sudden, Vincent opens my car door and extends his hand to help me out.

The moment Kellan is standing beside me, he states, "And this is the entrance for the stretch of the palace occupied by my father, Kristopher, Soph, occasionally myself, and now you."

I feel my lungs constrict in apprehension again.

Yeah…I don't think I can do this.

His fingers slip with mine at the same time he sweetly promises, "You'll be fine, love. You have my word."

After an additional moment of hesitation, a long deep breath, and an encouraging kiss to the back of my hand, Kellan leads me through the entryway and into the palace.

Immediately, he's greeted warmly by maids who scurry past him to collect our things.

My jaw drops at the stunning interior that is cloaked in black, red, white, and gold. Everything from the rugs covering the marble floors to the drapery protecting the windows seems to have the same color scheme as their flag. Kellan leads me around the grand staircase that appears to go on for days and towards the back area of the palace. I observe as much as I can along the way, passing statues, painted family portraits, and enough intricate chandeliers I begin to wonder if maybe they just own a company who makes them.

Would make sense, right? And quick question, who in their right mind would want to spend their entire life dusting those things?

Finally, we cross what I am hoping is at least half of the castle and arrive at a set of double doors with a maid waiting on the outside.

"Prince Kellan." She curtsies. "Miss." With a nod she opens the door for us, and my eyes widen at the room on the other side.

There's a long oval table, covered with a black tablecloth, surrounded by black chairs with dark red cushioning. The table itself has red roses in vases and appears to be set for twenty.

Good god, I hope there won't be that many of us for dinner.

On the wall to the right, there is a fireplace with a family portrait of what appears to feature Kellan as a boy while on the wall to the left and the wall directly in front of me are windows with heavy black curtains pulled open.

Suddenly, a brunette woman I recognize slips into the room from behind one of the sections I just assumed was a wall.

Okay…um…they have secret passageways, too? Am I in an old Sherlock Holmes movie?! Yeah! Yeah! I know. That dude was British not Doctenn. Geez. You sound like Kellan.

"Kellan!" The woman exclaims joyfully rushing towards him.

"Soph!" He warmly retorts, letting my hand go to hug his sister-in-law.

When she pulls back, she gives me a sweet smile. "You look overwhelmed. I'm hoping that's because all of this is a lot to take in and not because of something this asshole said before you arrived."

"*Pardon me*," Kellan playfully objects. "I am not an arsehole."

We pin him with similar sarcastic expression.

"Fine, but not *all* of the time."

I thoughtlessly giggle, and she diverts her attention back to me. "It is a pleasure to finally meet you in person."

"You too!" I excitedly agree. "And…if it's okay to say, you're even more beautiful in person than you are over the computer." My eyes drink in her thin, 5'7 frame that's being displayed perfectly in high neck red romper along with her dark highlighted hair and striking crystal blue eyes. "Not sure I should stand so close to you in pictures. I'd most likely look like a troll."

Sophia tosses back her head in laughter before cooing, "Oh, heavens, you are sweet enough to give me a toothache."

"Is that why mine constantly hurt?" Kellan winks.

I blush, yet she slugs him in the arm. "*Behave.*"

"This is me behaving."

"Try harder. This is her first meeting of all of us in person. You'll be lucky if she doesn't run from this palace screaming by the time dinner is done."

Her warning flares my eyes again.

Immediately seeing my fright, she reaches for my hand and gives it a comforting squeeze. "I didn't mean that to sound as bad as it did. I simply meant that you've only seen a smidgen of the Kenningston brothers' antics over the computer. In person, they are *so. Much. Worse.*"

"That can't be possible."

"Oh, sweetheart, it *can,* and it *is.*"

I offer her another amused smile at the same time Kellan asks, "Speaking of those known for ruining a good time, where are my brother and father?"

Sophia's grip on me falls away as she turns completely to him. "They're wrapping up a meeting."

"The kind where they compare terrible tennis scores or tyrant tantrums?"

She rolls her eyes. "They're discussing the annual summer brunch."

"Oh…" My boyfriend's face tightens. "And I supposed Kris is pushing again for more funding to open an additional branch of research?"

"Actually, he's pushing for your program."

I peer up at him with excitement. "That's great, isn't it? That would help you expand like you want."

Kellan hesitates before looking down at me. "It would be amazing if my father ever actually took the proposal with him to present."

"Doesn't this give you a chance?"

"Highly unlikely," he mutters.

"Don't be such a downer," Soph fusses, slugging him again. "Kris has been adamant about getting your father to give the program more attention. He didn't go in with a separate proposal this time. He wants all of your father's focus there."

"Why?" Kellan tilts his head in suspicion. "Why the sudden change of heart?"

She pushes her painted lips together in a sealed action.

"For the past four years, Kris has given every effort to his cause and not mine. Why the sudden change? Why care now? Why give a shit what happens to children whose parents have died? Why-" His voice abruptly halts. "Bloody hell, you two are trying to get pregnant!"

My mouth drops with hers.

"*Bloody hell!*"

"Shut. Up." She swiftly snips. "It is not common knowledge yet, and if you tell Kris I told you, I will turn your collection of Markay suits into lining for Old Red's bed. Do I make myself clear?"

Kellan tries to hide his smirk.

"Who's Old Red?"

"The family dog," they answer in unison.

Because…why wouldn't they have a family dog?

All of a sudden, the door we entered through opens again and Kristopher strolls in.

Damn they do look like twins! Seriously! The only major difference I see right now aside from his slightly bigger forehead is his choice in clothing. He's wearing dark jeans and a polo. Getting Kellan to put on jeans or anything that didn't just stroll off a runaway is like trying to have your wisdom teeth removed without being numbed or put to sleep first.

"States finally kicked you out I see," his brother teases with a chuckle at the same time he embraces him.

Kellan gives him a hard pat on the back and steps away. "More like I got wind that your sanity was almost fully intact again. We both know I can't have that."

"You are the reason I'm graying so early."

"You mean *balding*."

Horror appears on his brother's face, and I instantly nudge Kellan sharply in the ribs. "*Be nice.*"

Kris lowers his attention my direction. "You must be the lovely woman responsible for my brother's leash." When I giggle, he takes my hand and plants a kiss on the back of it. "It is quite an honor to meet you in person."

"You as well," I barely coo before Kellan is removing my hand.

"That's enough," he defensively snaps. "Stop slobbering on my girlfriend. Did you forget your wife is watching?"

Soph shoots me a look and shrugs. "Take him. I'll get more sleep at night in the bed alone."

Kristopher's jaw drops again while Kellan lets out a hearty laugh.

"You deserve a medal for putting up with him," Kris whispers at me.

My boyfriend swiftly changes the subject, "How did the meeting go?"

Kris's response is cut off by the door opening once more.

This time an older man approximately their same height and build with similar striking blonde features enters. Like Kellan he is dressed in an expensive suit except he's wearing a red tie and a blinding diamond studded watch.

Uh...What am I supposed to say?! Is hi, hello I'm the woman dating your son really enough? Should I bow or shake his hand or kiss his ring or something? Why didn't we go over these formalities sooner?!

The man gives a curt nod. "Kellan."

He reciprocates the action. "Father."

His attention turns to me, and I see an unmistakable flash of consternation in his eyes. "And you must be Brie Sanders, the woman my son attended the Chasizer fundraiser with a couple of months ago."

In a meek tone, I reply, "Yes, sir."

"Don't call him sir," Kellan grumbles under his breath.

"She was being respectful," the man corrects and gives his son a stern stare. "Something you've forgotten how to be." Afterward, he lifts my hand to place a gentle kiss on the back of it. "It's a pleasure to meet you, Brie Sanders. My name is Kenneth. You may call me that."

Okay, so, the hand kissing, not a flirty thing, but a way they introduce themselves. Sweet in a throw your jacket over the puddle so I can cross it kinda way.

I try to keep my voice steady. "It's an honor to meet you, Kenneth."

He gives me a small smile and ushers his hand at the table. "Shall we all sit? I'm sure Elliot is ready to serve us his favorite dish to make."

"Elliot?" Kellan questions as he leads me to a seat at the middle of the table. "What happened to Andrew?"

"His wife had her baby a couple of weeks ago," Soph swoons, though she quickly attempts to hide it. "There were a few complications, so they had to stay at the hospital longer than expected. They should be home in the next day or two."

Once he's pushed me in, he sits down beside me while his brother and his wife sit in the seats across from us. However, Kenneth positions himself at the head of the table closest to the windows. The evening light from them adds an unnecessary boost to his aura of nobility.

Honestly, not sure I will ever be able to wrap my mind around having dinner with the king of a country. I know Kellan likes to downplay the entire thing like it doesn't mean shit, but look at this place! He can't tell me his titles are just titles anymore!

Five servants stroll in, each carrying a covered dish. The moment it is placed in front of me, he removes the lid, and exposes a green mess I'm not thrilled to eat.

Kellan leans over to whisper near my ear, "Try everything presented tonight, and if you truly can't stomach it, I'll have them make you a bacon cheeseburger with extra pickles."

I offer him a smile of gratitude.

The conversation proceeds as I do my best to muscle through what Soph announced as summer wedge salad.

Why they felt the need to put strawberries and sunflower seeds in it is a mystery to me. Those aren't salad ingredients! And while I don't mind avocado, I do when I mistake it for a cucumber. Oh, and don't even get me started about the "light dressing" on this thing. Light in this country means nonexistent.

Somehow the topic travels back around to me and Kenneth states, "I assume this is the first time you've been to Doctenn."

I place my fork down in surrender. Turning to face him, I politely reply, "Yes, sir. It's actually the first time I've ever been out of my own country."

He lifts his wine with a scrutinizing stare. "Not a big traveler?"

"Not really," I sheepishly answer. "Pretty much lived in the same place my entire life."

"Small-town girl? Interesting."

"Are you gonna ask if she's livin' in a lonely world next?" Kellan sings the lyric in a teasing manner. "Perhaps mention a train?"

The joke lifts just enough tension from my chest to snicker. His eyes find mine, and I shake my head.

"What? Surprised I know an American classic?"

"Surprised you still think you can sing."

Kris loudly barks, "Ha!"

"Oh, what are you ha-ing at? You sound like a bag of dying cats when you're crooning," Soph snickers, and it spreads to the rest of us. "However, now that we're on the subject of music, we are attending the Shoreline Symphony tomorrow, if you two are interested in joining us."

"What is that?" I ask as our plates are removed and replaced with the next course.

"There's a theater close to the coastline where the world-renowned symphony got its start. They occasionally play classic pieces, but originally, and typically, they play music that sounds like or reminds people of the ocean," Kris explains. "It's all rather laid back and very soothing."

"You should go," their father insists. "Make better headlines for this family than we've been seeing lately. Perhaps ones around your brotherly relationship as opposed to the others the media has been relentlessly focused on."

Kellan's mouth drops in question, but Kris clears his throat and shakes his head to stop him from pushing.

"Brie," Kenneth calls to me.

"Yes, sir?"

"What is it you do for a living?"

The question shifts me uncomfortably in my seat, and my attention away from the mushroom risotto. "Um…at this time? Nothing. I just graduated from The University of Ashwin a couple of weeks ago."

"What was your major?" Soph sweetly asks.

"Art."

Her giggles are followed by a headshake. "The thing Kellan hates the most next to poetry?"

"Both are utterly useless," my boyfriend gripes. "At least being dragged through art showings typically results in getting my girlfriend naked."

A deep crimson color fills my cheeks just as his father asks, "And what have you decided you want to do with your degree? Which career path will you be taking when you choose to become employed again?"

The burning of my face increases. "Not exactly sure."

There's a hum of what I can only imagine is disapproval.

Before the anxiety has the chance to spread further, Soph informs with a comforting smile, "That's alright. I had no idea what I wanted to do after college, either."

"Yes, but you were young and not nearing thirty like I imagine Brie is."

Getting the feeling he doesn't approve of me.

"She keeps Kellan from burning down the other side of the world and from playing strip poker with actresses in front of open windows. That should count for something," Kris attempts to lighten the situation.

The praise from his brother almost tugs my lips upward.

Thankfully, Soph moves the topic towards a fire that broke out in a different part of their country and their efforts to help those in need because of it. The conversation picks up speed and focus in various directions, allowing me to sit quietly and poke at the hunk of mush.

Not too long afterward, our dishes are being replaced again, yet this time I smirk at the familiar sight.

This one is something I am more than familiar with. It's one of Kellan's favorites and one that grew on me, not to mention my parents who he spoiled with at the occasional white tablecloth meal. You know, he made a huge effort to be a part of my family. To understand them and include them in our lives. Even though

his world scares the shit out of me, I hope he knows I plan to make the same strides for him.

"Steak au poivre," Kellan smugly states. "Now, this is my kind of welcome back."

"You mean home," Kris attempts to correct.

He tilts his head at his brother. "Do I?"

"Of course, you do," his father argues loudly. "This is your home, whether you choose to call it that or not."

The animosity I felt earlier begins to rise again.

My boyfriend lifts his utensils and snips, "Home would imply a place where your father is supportive of your ideas yet mine rejects them every chance he gets. Why is that?"

Kenneth folds his hands in his lap. "The dinner table in mixed company is *not* the right place for this discussion, Kellan."

"Neither is your office. Or your bedroom. Or the kitchen. Or the car. Or the jet. Or the golf course or anywhere else for that matter." He shoves a bite in his mouth. "So as far as I'm concerned, here is as perfect as elsewhere."

"*Kellan*," Kris implores quietly.

"No," he denies his brother, "I could tell by the look on your face earlier when I asked that our father had once again said no. I want to know his reasoning this time. In the beginning, I had no idea what I was doing or how to run a company. Then, I hadn't properly put together a proposal. Next, it wasn't the right timing. Lastly, Kris's cause was deemed more valuable than mine. So, tell me, Father. What is the excuse this time?"

My eyes helplessly drag themselves away from the hunk of meat I have been slowly cutting to his father whose entire body appears to be strained.

"There are already foster care programs-"

"They don't work!" Kellan snaps harshly. "Obviously, they don't work or there wouldn't be so many children homeless and helpless!"

Calmly, Kenneth continues, "There are foster care programs in various places in many countries. A string of orphanages like you've presented would be dismissed as already being in place. The program you already have in motion on the other hand would be viewed as undermining these programs that are sponsored by their country's tax revenues. And because your program is small and not large enough to make the charitable donations beneficial – socially or financially – it would be a waste of time and an embarrassment to present it at any of the annual brunches."

The harsh words chosen directed at Kellan cause his locked jaw to begin to throb. Instinctively, I reach my hand over to connect with his. As soon as my touch lands on his skin, the hostility begins to drain, and his chest stops heaving. Our eyes meet, and we exchange an unspoken moment of warmth despite the heavy sigh from the end of the table.

Getting the feeling being welcomed by his father is going to be much more difficult than I was afraid of. If this is how he treats his own son, what he thinks of his own flesh and blood, I doubt I even stand a chance. You heard those snide remarks earlier. Why is there a knot in the pit of my stomach telling me this isn't even a glimmer of what's ahead?

CHAPTER TWENTY-ONE

Kellan

Brie giggles and barely pushes at my shoulder. "Stop. We can't just stay in bed all day."

I give the side of her neck another slow swipe before moving my efforts to the other side. "And that's where you're wrong, love." My tongue whirls around her favorite spot right beside her collarbone until she's whimpering and writhing for more. At that point, I pull back and give her a naughty smirk. "Since all other Kenningston's are away, that leaves me as head of the household, and it means I make the rules."

She playfully rolls her eyes. "*It does not.*"

"*It does so,*" I impishly disagree, "and for arguing with the prince you will be punished." My lips lower to her nipple, which I swiftly tug with my teeth.

Brie begins to whimper again when there's a heavy knock at the door. "Prince Kellan."

I release the hardened nub from my clutches. "What!"

"The door, sir."

My girlfriend giggles and gives me an actual nudge to get out of bed.

On a heavy groan, I grab the fallen sheet from the floor, wrap it around me, and jog across the room to the door. I unlock it and crack it open just enough to gripe, "This better be important because I haven't finished my breakfast yet, and I am on verge of *starving* to death."

There's a giggle from behind me that's followed by the sound of a pillow hitting the ground.

I glance at Brie over my shoulder who is still in the canopy bed. "You throw like a girl."

"You look like one in your wedding gown right now. Are you sure it's not *Princess Kellan*?"

"Doubling the punishment," I growl and turn back around to Mathew, a member of the household servants. "What is it? What do you need?"

"Your father has summoned you to his office."

Ugh. That means he's returned early. Just when I thought we were catching a break.

"He says to inform you it's urgent."

Which means it's not, he just doesn't feel like waiting. And people think I'm impatient.

"Fine. I'll be there in a moment."

Mathew doesn't move.

My eyebrows furrow. "He told you to escort me, yes?"

"Yes, sir."

"Back for a few hours, and he's already ruining my bloody day." I shut the door, turn, and make my way back to the dresser on the far wall. "Alright, love, apparently, I have to be reprimanded by my father for a few minutes."

With genuine concern, she shifts her body completely up. "For what?"

"Don't know nor do I care." Grabbing a pair of silk pajama bottoms, I state, "You wait for me right there."

Her face doesn't change.

"I'm serious. I do not care what I'm in trouble for now. All I care about is you," I saunter slowly her direction, "waiting *right here* in this bed for me. I meant what I said earlier. I have no intention of us leaving it today." When she starts to smile, I press my lips briefly to hers. "I'll be back shortly. Try not to miss me."

"I won't." Brie sassily grins at the same time she slips back underneath the covers.

Just as I leave the room, she turns the television on, the sound of a morning talk show immediately blaring.

Believe it or not this is practically the only time she's had to watch it. Since we arrived six days ago, it has been endless obligations and sightseeing. We've attended the symphony, helped judge a surfing competition, and had lunch as well as dinner with my brother and Soph before they left with my father for the annual summer brunch. Other than that, my time during the day has been divided between meetings with my company about the status of our program and wandering around museums, both art and historical, along with the property. That part doesn't bother me because I've turned it into a game of "where can I have a romp with my girlfriend" bingo. No matter what the place is…I'm a winner.

Mathew opens my father'' office door and waves his hand for me to enter.

The bright sun is illuminating the enormous space, highlighting the red accents on the furniture like that's its only job. To my surprise, the fire is crackling, and he's seated on the couch across from it as opposed to his long oak desk on the other side of the room.

Once Mathew shuts the door behind me, Father frowns. "You didn't feel the need to put on decent attire?"

I glance down at the only article of clothing I'm wearing. "You should feel flattered I put on anything at all. This conversation is interrupting something important."

Father reaches for his glass on the small table beside him. "You should sit."

Drinking before ten in the morning and wanting me to sit are two things that never bode well.

I deny his request. "I'll stand."

"Kellan, you should sit."

"No, because when I sit, you feel compelled to drag on your lectures past the point of annoyance. If I stand, you typically cut straight to the point, and we can both carry on with what truly matters in our lives."

He has a sip and shakes his head. "You've always been this way."

Unsure of what he is implying, I merely fold my arms across my chest.

"Always. Since you were three years old, you've always been defy first, smile in your face after. I'll never forget how you pooped in your pants during your great grandmother's 90th birthday celebration on *purpose*, simply because you knew if you did you wouldn't be forced to sit for the portrait."

I only vaguely remember that, so I am uncertain if that should count for a good example of my headstrong nature.

There's a heavy sigh followed with, "You've always done what you want, Kellan, regardless of what the rest of the world had to say."

My eyebrows arch. "Point?"

He briefly glances away to the fire before back at me. "This time, you have to stop."

"Stop what?"

"Dating her."

Confusion invades my reaction. "What?! Why?!"

My father swallows whatever emotion is clogging his vocal cords. "Because it is what's best."

"Why is that what's best?"

"Because she's...*different*."

Disbelief darts down the back of my throat. "And that's a problem?"

He hesitates, yet eventually, nods.

"And by different are you referring to the fact she's a *full-blooded* American or the fact she's *African American*?" Father doesn't answer and rage rips through me like a hurricane on a warpath. "You are bloody kidding me!"

"It's not as simple as you're thinking, Kellan."

"To bloody hell it's not!"

"This isn't just about you."

"This is absolutely about me!"

"This is about *this family*. It is my responsibility to do everything in my power to honor the Kenningston name, and that means not only understanding the way the world works but *abiding* by it. Brie is *different*, and while you may appreciate *her differences*, others do not. It's my job as not only King but as the head of the Kenningston family to protect our name and reputation-"

"Our reputation?! Our reputation isn't at stake! Being with Brie hasn't negatively affected that! If anything, I behave better *because of her*!"

"This is *not* just about you."

"You mean this is about *you*."

"I mean this is about the headlines being made where we're being accused of disregarding so-called 'valued traditions'. This is about the endless media coverage over an apparent race war drawn in the sand and where we stand on it. This is about the fact we spent *six hours* at a brunch where we were laughed at, taunted, and partially ignored because my son has a 'different' girlfriend. Social expectations aside for the circles we move through, the financial investments we could lose because other people are not accepting of your 'different choice' in a lover could be catastrophic." He places his glass down and folds his hands in his lap. "And I *cannot* and *will not* let the happen."

Disorientation continues to seep into my soul.

This is not really happening. This* can't *be really happening. This isn't real. This is…this a terrible stress-induced nightmare I am going to wakeup from any second.

"This fling has to end, and it needs to end now."

My arms constrict tighter as my voice grows gruff, "And if I say no?"

"Please, do not force my hand."

"*And if. I. Say. No?*"

"*Kellan-*"

"What?" I challenge. "What could you possibly do? Exile her from this country?"

"That's a start."

"That's bloody ridiculous!"

"It is either that or you from our family."

"Father-"

"I cannot have this family lose the respect it has spent *generations* cultivating. We have more than just ourselves to consider with our actions. And you are selfish, Kellan. You have always been selfish. You will most likely always be selfish, but this time, *this one time*, I'm imploring you to consider how this looks to your country. To our fellow associates. To other royal families we have been companions with for decades. We can't just throw all that away because you are hellbent on proving your unwavering ability to defy authority. You may enjoy being under the false veil that leaves you to be believe things like race and ethnicity do not matter to the world anymore; however, you, my son, can't continue to be so bloody blind."

I attempt to collect a breath through burning lungs but am stopped by a broken voice. "I hate to interrupt…"

No…No. No. No. Please, tell me she didn't hear any of that.

"You don't believe in knocking?" My father snaps, his own voice shaky. "Is that not a custom in your country?"

"I um…*I did*," Brie whispers holding back what sounds like a sob. "Repeatedly, actually. You must not have heard me."

"And it couldn't have waited?" He snips again, which forces my face his direction.

"For you to go off in another bigoted tantrum, I imagine *not*." I turn my attention back to my girlfriend's solemn face. "Is something wrong, love?"

"Yes," she answers voice still uneven. "I um…I need to go home."

"You don't," I sigh heavily.

"No…I…I um…I really do. Dad had a heart attack and was rushed to the emergency room. He's…He's in surgery."

The dread begins to drown me as I rush towards her.

Rather than allowing me to embrace, she flinches backwards. "I need to go home, Kellan. *Now.*"

"I'll have the jet fueled and waiting." My father rises to his feet. "I'll send someone to collect your things."

"Thank you, sir," Brie whispers before spinning on her heels and dashing out.

I turn and give him a hard look. "This is far from over."

He gives me a slow shake of his head. "I don't think it is."

Without another word, I storm off after my girlfriend, the condition of her father and callousness of mine combining to create an excruciatingly painful purgatory neither of us deserves to dwell in.

The return flight to the states is as agonizingly quiet as the hasty preparation was. Since having interrupted the conversation with the news of her father, Brie hasn't uttered more words than necessary, nor has she allowed for me to make physical contact. In fact, she's not even making *eye* contact. It's as if she's lost in her own thoughts with no intent of inviting me in to understand them. While I'm doing my best to give her space and understand where it is she's coming from, there's a lump of trepidation lodged permanently in the back of my throat.

She's simply emotional about the possibility of losing her father, yes? She's not upset with me. She can't possibly hold me accountable for my father's hatred, can she?

After the captain announces we're clear to deboard, I quickly stand and extend my hand to help her up.

Brie rises on her own causing the lump to swell.

"You should message your mother. See if she needs us to bring her anything on our way to the hospital."

I begin to head for the door when her hand lands on my arm. "*Kellan, wait.*"

When I turn to face her, my relief from her touch is short lived and the dread amplifies.

"The first time we met I never imagined I would see you again. I never thought we'd date or fall in love for that matter. I damn sure never thought I'd end up in *your country*, experiencing the life you spend so much time running away from." She pauses as if collecting her thoughts. "And I understand why you run. Why you act out. Why you're hellbent on enjoying your time rather than wallowing in the misery looming for you thousands of miles away. It's a burden to be who you are. To be told what to say and taught how to say it. Where to go and when to be there. To fulfill expectations regardless of if you agree with them or not. You run because you know someday that you're not going to be able to. *Someday* you're going to have to stop, turn, and face the crowd, not because you want to, but because you were born to. You brush off all the aristocratic shit because you hate that you can't alter that reality. That you rely on them to get the things you want to get done, done. You are *a duke*. A *beloved prince*. You are an image that cannot be altered simply because it's what you want."

Her words cause my mouth to thoughtlessly tremble.

"You are going to change the world, Kellan Kenningston. You're going to give hope to the hopeless just like your mother did. But in order to do that, you need those people your father mentioned. You need your family. And I know you hate your father right now, but you didn't always, and you won't always. Both of you are sitting on pain from losing the woman you both loved most. Your family matters tremendously to you. It's the real reason you attend balls and functions hosted by zillionaires. You don't want to disappoint them because you love them the same way they love you.

You all want what you believe to be right for one another. And I'm not going to be the reason your family loses another member."

My breathing ceases completely. Brie takes my hand, carefully places the locket in it, and folds it shut. Afterward she rises to the tips of her toes to kiss me on the cheek. In a desperate frenzy, I grip the nape of her neck and press my forehead against hers. "*Please.*" I swallow my sob. "*Please, don't do this, Brie.*"

She sniffles away any conflicting decisions. "I have to."

She doesn't! She shouldn't! We should fight this! We should prove him wrong! We should…We should…We…It doesn't matter next, does it? I've already lost her.

"Sir," Swiss's voice states loudly. "Would you like me to load the bags?"

I pull back to allow my tear-filled eyes to meet hers. Still staring into them, determined to detail every centimeter as I answer, "Just hers." My hand loosens its grip, and I take an unwanted step back. "Take her to the hospital where her father is. Give her the same treatment and respect you would if I was in the vehicle." His voice starts to interrupt, and I divert my attention to him. "Don't worry about your fee. My father will be more than thrilled to continue to pay it."

Swiss gives me a nod of understanding and disappears.

Brie grabs her cellphone and wallet before making her way towards the door.

I stifle another sob. "Brie?"

She hesitates yet turns around anyway.

In a voice I barely recognize, I ask, "When I ring, will you answer me like I'd answer you?"

The reference to the only other time I almost lost her sends the lingering tears down her face. She gives me one last somber look. Her lack of a reply is the final pang that causes my body to cave onto the couch. Brie exits the jet, and I shut my eyes in a pathetic attempt to not shed anymore tears.

This can't truly be over…can it?

Wonder what's in store next for Prince Kellan Kenningston, Duke of Rockbridge and Brie Sanders? Find out for now in Royally Duched (Duched Series #2)!

https://amzn.to/3C26Ris

Did you enjoy reading Duched (Duched Series #1)? I would appreciate you leaving a review if you did!

https://amzn.to/31NsB57

OTHER WORKS

Here a links to other stories that were mentioned in this novel.

Ollander Academy (The Substitute) – https://amzn.to/3qtJ20R

Merrick McCoy (The Adrenaline Series) – https://amzn.to/30hYhz3

Yasmine's Yummies (Hike, Hike Baby) – https://amzn.to/3CcPIm5

The Frost Luxury Hotel (Freeform) – https://amzn.to/3HdrRqm

Camelot (Camelot Misfits Series) – https://amzn.to/3HdsaBw

GRATITUDE:

The list of people who assist in this entire process is truly too many to name. So rather than run the risk of forgetting anyone, I want to just say thank you to EVERYONE. Readers, bloggers (new and old), friends, family, reviewers, and street teamers…you make me feel like royalty in a strange way. Thank you for supporting me and allowing me to be the "queen" of the worlds I create to share with you.

Until next time…

FOLLOW ME!!!

Website

https://www.xavierneal.com/

Facebook

https://www.facebook.com/XavierNealAuthorPage

Facebook Group

https://www.facebook.com/groups/1471618443081356

Twitter

@XavierNeal87

Instagram

@authorxavierneal

Pinterest

https://www.pinterest.com/xavierneal/

Bookbub

https://www.bookbub.com/authors/xavier-neal

Goodreads

https://www.goodreads.com/author/show/4990135.Xavier_Neal

New Release Alerts

https://www.xavierneal.com/newsletter

Tik Tok

https://www.tiktok.com/@authorxavierneal

Spotify

http://bit.ly/XNSpotifyProfile

Store Front

http://tee.pub/lic/authorxavierneal

FULL List of My Works

Standalones

Compassion (Military Romance) - https://amzn.to/2FZnxPj

Cinderfella (YA Contemporary) - https://amzn.to/2pBHZff

The Gamble (Romantic Comedy) - https://amzn.to/2uf4ZFw

Freeform (Romantic Comedy) - https://amzn.to/2IPna7W

Part of The List (Contemporary Romance) - https://amzn.to/2udYwuz

Walking Away (Contemporary Ménage Romance) - https://amzn.to/2pAOEGf

Can't Match This (Romantic Comedy) - https://amzn.to/2XapsVw

Hike, Hike Baby (Romantic Comedy) - https://amzn.to/2PNj456

Baewatch (Romantic Comedy) – https://amzn.to/3izNvaG

Sleigh Bride (Holiday Romantic Comedy) - https://amzn.to/2J0Qk8D

Aleatory (Contemporary Age-Gap Romance) - https://amzn.to/3xKJQ2L

Picnic Perfect (Romantic Comedy) - https://amzn.to/2UZdgeN

Senses Series

(Sports Romance/ Romantic Comedy) (Complete Series)

Vital (Prequel Novella)- FREE ON ALL PLATFORMS
https://amzn.to/2ueL5KJ

Blind- https://amzn.to/2GmEMcO

Deaf- https://amzn.to/2IK71Rf

Numb- https://amzn.to/2pAOYVt

Hush- https://amzn.to/2pzV2gS

Savor- https://amzn.to/2HZsVP1

Callous- https://amzn.to/2pAPmTV

Agonize- https://amzn.to/2ILLaZw

Suffocate - https://amzn.to/2GjLU9T

Mollify- https://amzn.to/2GgRJoJ

Blur- https://amzn.to/2pD1rrK

Blear - https://amzn.to/2DQGb6a

Blare- https://amzn.to/33nnqV8

Senses Box Set (Books 1-5) – https://amzn.to/2Gkxruw

Adrenaline Series

(Romance/ Romantic Suspense)

Classic (FREE ON MOST PLATFORMS) -
https://amzn.to/2I0wd4D

Vintage- https://amzn.to/2HXksMw

Masterpiece- https://amzn.to/2G0tWKj

Unmask- https://amzn.to/2Gn2tBK

Error- https://amzn.to/2pBakC6

Iconic- https://amzn.to/2G1Q8Ua

Box Set (Books 1-3) - https://amzn.to/2IP7GRe

Prince of Tease Series

(Romance/ Romantic Comedy)

Prince Arik- https://amzn.to/2pAuhbF

Prince Hunter- https://amzn.to/2IKzuGu

Prince Brock- https://amzn.to/2ufmghN

Prince Chance- https://amzn.to/2LuclMw

Prince Zane- TBA

Hollywood Exchange Series

(Romance/ Romantic Comedy)

Already Written - https://amzn.to/2G0F2ix

Already Secure- TBA

Already Designed (The South Haven Crew #1) - https://amzn.to/2G8A0fP

Already Scripted (The South Haven Crew #2) - TBA

Already Legal (The South Haven Crew #3) - TBA

Already Driven (The South Haven Crew #4) - TBA

Already Cast (The South Haven Crew #5) - TBA

Blue Dream Duet

(Contemporary Romance) (Complete Series)

Blue Dream- https://amzn.to/2G1296E

Purple Haze- https://amzn.to/2ILKUK2

Havoc Series

(Military Romance/ Romantic Suspense) (Complete Series)

Havoc- FREE ON ALL MAJOR PLATFORMS - https://amzn.to/2HYWOyZ

Chaos - https://amzn.to/2ug1Ox5

Insanity- https://amzn.to/2I3eABs

Collapse - https://amzn.to/2G3cAww

Devastate- https://amzn.to/2IO9GcL

Havoc Box Set (Books 1-3) - https://amzn.to/2G17519

The Just Series

(Second Chance Romance)

Just Out of Reach- https://amzn.to/2ubzfBe

Just So Far Away- https://amzn.to/2DR57KM

Private Series

(Romantic Suspense) (Complete Series)

Private - https://amzn.to/2IN7P7R

Public- https://amzn.to/2pAF7it

Personal- https://amzn.to/2vejdHt

Popular (A Private Series Standalone) – TBA *(This novel will be about how J.T. and his wife, Janae got together.)

Duched Series

(Romantic Comedy) (Complete Series)

Duched- https://amzn.to/2G4Xlim

Royally Duched- https://amzn.to/2pAnvDh

Royally Duched Up- https://amzn.to/2G089SP

Duched Deleted (FREE Novella ON ALL PLATOFRMS)- https://amzn.to/2GlOQTy

The Bros Series

(Erotic Romance) (Complete)

The Substitute- https://amzn.to/2ub9CAc

The Hacker- https://amzn.to/2FZFxJr

The Suit- https://amzn.to/2poTcyX

The Chef- https://amzn.to/2Dgi7MR

Must Love Series

(Sweet, Romantic Comedy)

Must Love Hogs- https://amzn.to/2IMmmkg
Must Love Jogs- https://amzn.to/2pBIiqp
Must Love Pogs- https://amzn.to/2ueUUIu
Must Love Logs- https://amzn.to/2IFGrL7
Must Love Flogs- TBA

The Culture Blind Series
(Contemporary Romance)
Redneck Romeo- https://amzn.to/2vYuPhM
Cowboy Casanova- https://amzn.to/2sxwqGT
Horseback Hero- https://amzn.to/2BhT91r
Blue Jean Bachelor- TBA

Camelot Misfits MC Series
(MC Romance/ Romantic Suspense)

King's Return - https://amzn.to/2TTnNCI
King's Conquest - https://amzn.to/2IaYZo8
King's Legacy – https://amzn.to/2YfvY1i
Wiz's Remedy – https://amzn.to/2PMmJDK
Trick's (Currently Untitled) Novel - TBA

Synful Syndicate Series
(Dark Romance)

Unleashed- https://amzn.to/2VVhcfT

Unchained- TBA

The Hockey Gods Series
(Sports Romance/Romantic Comedy)

Can't Block My Love – https://amzn.to/38HYH0z

My Fair Puck Bunny – https://amzn.to/33t2nSw

The Forward Must Cry – https://amzn.to/3ijTfpm

Defenseman No. 9 – https://amzn.to/3sqAgiJ

Taming of The Crew - https://amzn.to/3jo5gwR

Second Generation

Phin's (Currently Untitled Novel) - TBA

The Bennett Duet
(Dark Romance) (Complete)

Dark Ruler – https://amzn.to/397wK5C

Dark Reign – https://amzn.to/2Q1mjJt

Haworth Enterprises

(Romantic Suspense)

Bulletproof: https://amzn.to/3AUxiHk

The Draak Legacy

(Paranormal Romance)

Saving Silver: https://amzn.to/3BqzaXS
Getting Gold: https://amzn.to/2Xj0ZTa

Made in the USA
Columbia, SC
11 January 2022